RED MOUND

B.D. SMITH

Black Rose Writing | Texas

ISBN: 978-1-68513-697-0
LIBRARY OF CONGRESS CONTROL NUMBER: 2025942609
PUBLISHED BY BLACK ROSE WRITING
www.blackrosewriting.com

Printed in the United States of America
Suggested Retail Price (SRP) $21.95

Red Mound is printed in Plantagenet Cherokee

*As a planet-friendly publisher, Black Rose Writing does its best to eliminate unnecessary waste to reduce paper usage and energy costs, while never compromising the reading experience. As a result, the final word count vs. page count may not meet common expectations.

Maps designed by Aleksandra Simonović

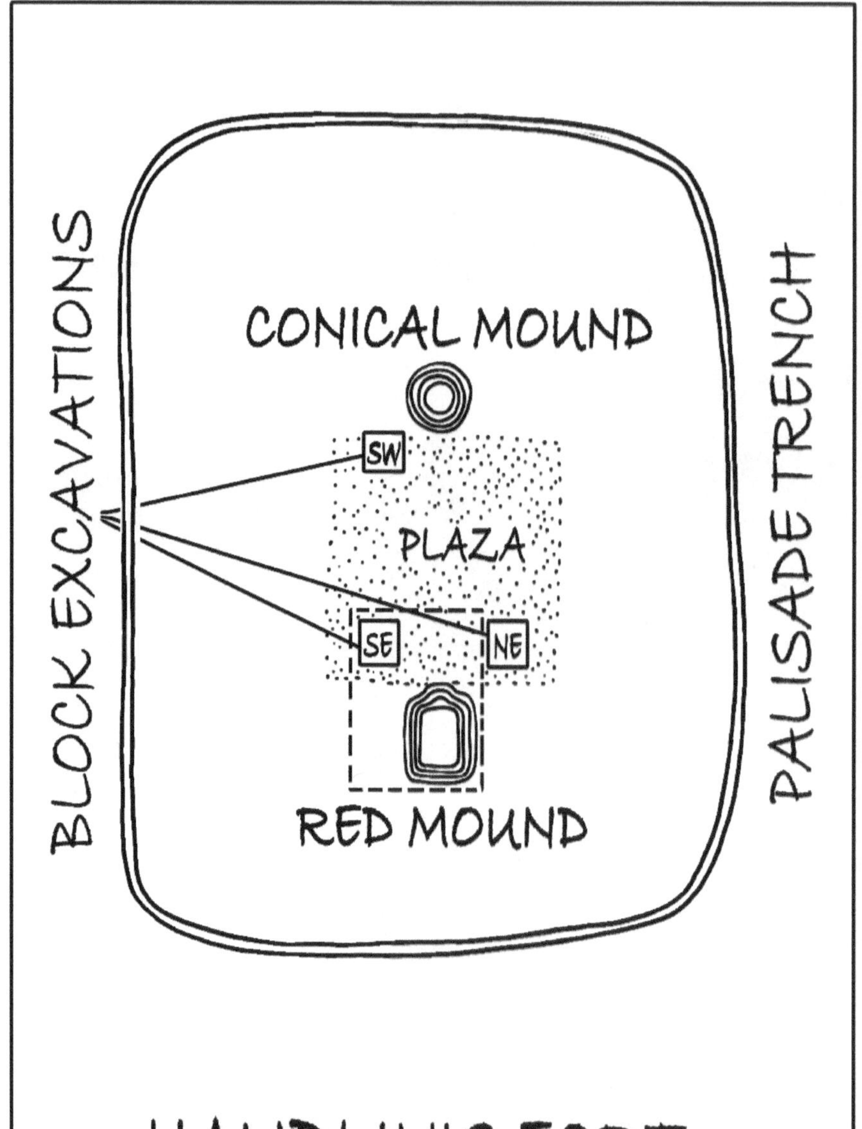

CONICAL MOUND
BLOCK EXCAVATIONS
PALISADE TRENCH
SW
PLAZA
SE
NE
RED MOUND
HAMBLIN'S FORT

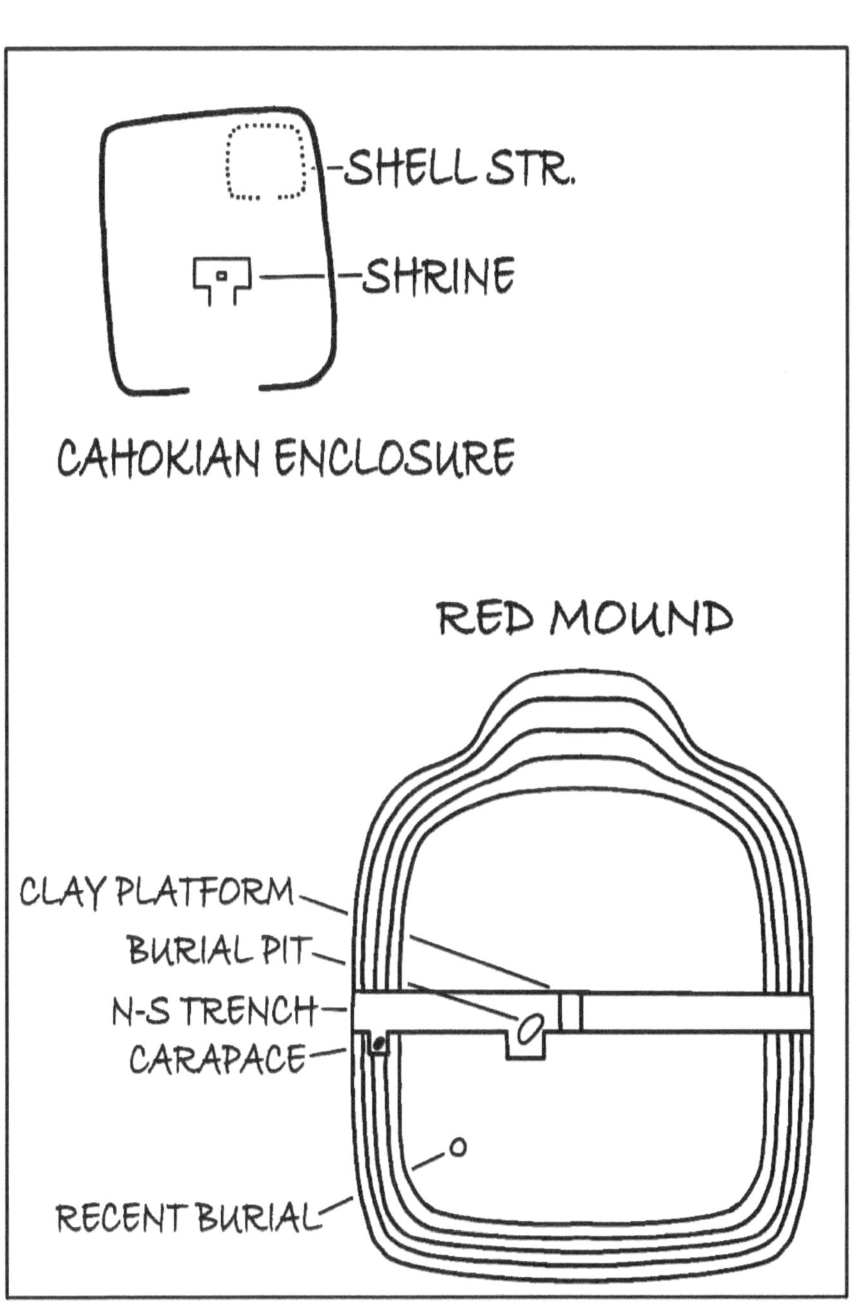

SHELL STR.
SHRINE
CAHOKIAN ENCLOSURE
RED MOUND
CLAY PLATFORM
BURIAL PIT
N-S TRENCH
CARAPACE
RECENT BURIAL

RED
MOUND

PROLOGUE
SACRED KNOWLEDGE

A waning gibbous moon hung over the lower Mississippi Valley, illuminating a bizarre tableau. Four men stood on the summit of a temple mound. They were all facing east, waiting for the sunrise that would end their vigil. Two of the men were naked and shivering in the pre-dawn mist, their shaved heads and shoulders were coated in red ocher. The other two men, standing on either side of them, wore dark, sweat stained deer hide garments.

The four had successfully sealed the temple mound's central chamber around noon the day before. They spent the next twelve hours on additional measures to strengthen the chamber's physical seal, as well as conducting a series of complex rituals meant to keep it secure. These were completed around midnight, and their ritual paraphernalia had now all been desanctified and interred on the mound slope. They were exhausted and anxious for the rising sun to release them. As the first rays of the sun crept across the temple mound summit and reached the four exhausted men, freeing them from their vigil, they silently, somberly retreated down the front of the mound to the adjacent plaza.

A throng of about a hundred people were waiting for them and for the completion of their mound summit rituals. The assembled crowd had until recently inhabited the fortified settlement that contained the mound and the plaza where they now stood. Their village had burned to the ground several months ago and its inhabitants forced to seek shelter with neighboring kin groups.

The displaced villagers would never return and reoccupy this place, but they had been summoned back now for a very specific task. Over the next week or so they would carry thousands of basket-loads of sand from a nearby sand bar location and use it to cap the temple mound with a foot or more of clean white river sand.

Occasionally someone would reach out to touch one of the four men as they moved through the crowd, but for the most part the onlookers averted their gaze. These four men and their sacred knowledge set them apart from ordinary people, and their powers reached across time. Their physical and ritual closing of the central chamber, and the subsequent white sand capping of the mound, was intended to protect the mound and to ensure that the central chamber was never breached, ever. Seven hundred years would pass before the mound and the central chamber eventually would be opened.

1.
SEÑOR ESTÚPIDO

Something seemed off to Josh as he woke up. It was the silence, he realized. The Delta Tau Delta fraternity house, where he had lived his sophomore year, was usually alive with noise and activity in the morning. But it was quiet now except for the sound of the sixties rock song "Wild Thing" that was drifting in the open window from the Deke House next door. Spring semester final exams had ended yesterday and most of Josh's frat brothers had already left, leaving behind the lingering aroma of stale beer and barf. Josh also caught the lingering smell of last night's fire wafting in the window and smiled.

After suffering through his Spanish final exam yesterday afternoon Josh had celebrated the successful fulfillment of his two-year foreign language requirement with a long-anticipated bonfire. He had saved every Spanish textbook and assignment, all the quizzes and bluebook exams he had taken over the last four semesters. Last night he had watched with pleasure as they made a cheerful blaze on the front lawn of the Delt House. Josh had no gift for languages, none, and he never seemed to be able to absorb any aspects of Spanish beyond the very simplest phrases. Somewhere along the line he had picked up the nickname "Señor Estúpido," but had still managed to survive with good enough grades, barely, to now put the foreign language requirement behind him.

None of the other undergraduate curriculum requirements had been a problem for Josh, and after trying some of the hard sciences — he lasted a week before dropping organic chemistry, he found his niche in the soft sciences, the social sciences. He had earned As and Bs in the introductory courses in psychology, geography, and an Asian history course, and had particularly enjoyed an introductory archaeology class the previous fall. The class had met in the archaeology museum, and one afternoon a notice on the museum bulletin board soliciting volunteers for a summer field expedition caught his eye. It sounded cool, he thought, so he signed up. Most of his fraternity brothers were enrolled in pre-law, pre-dentistry, or pre-med programs, and Josh got a kick out of adopting a counter-culture persona in the face of all the nascent establishment careers on display around him. Archaeology went well with his purple bell-bottom corduroys.

He was a little disappointed though, that he wouldn't be going to someplace impressive like Peru or Mexico, or even the Southwest US. The project he had signed up for was in Arkansas — not exactly a faraway exotic destination. But at least he wouldn't have to worry about his lack of Spanish language skills. Two university vans had headed south the previous week with most of the crew. Josh and a handful of others with late finals were to catch a ride south with one of the project's graduate students the day after finals ended.

"Fuck me," Josh blurted out as he checked his watch, realizing he had overslept and that his ride to Arkansas would be taking off from the museum in a half hour, with or without him. His stereo system and Triumph motorcycle, along with most of the rest of his stuff, were already stored for the summer in the basement of the Delt house. After jamming his bedding into an already packed duffle bag, Josh hurried out the front door, past the remains of last night's bonfire, and headed down Geddes Ave to the museum.

It was a beautiful spring day and Josh was both excited about setting out on a new adventure and somewhat trepidatious about spending the summer with a group of strangers. Picking up his pace, he circled a large puddle in the sidewalk that had been freshened overnight by a passing shower. He smiled ruefully as he recognized it as "Charlotte's puddle," so named because his girlfriend, overcome with the joy of life, had suddenly and gleefully jumped into it with both feet one night last fall as they had walked down Geddes to Hill Auditorium for a Beach Boys concert.

Charlotte was effervescent — outgoing and flirty, good looking, great legs, and always up for a good time. She was a self-confident extrovert and wildly popular in her sorority. Josh on the other hand was an introvert. He had an aversion to any sort of large gathering like movies, concerts, or athletic events. He would avoid them whenever possible. If he did end up going to a large crowd event — a football game or a movie, Josh would be anxious at its conclusion to be first out the door. He needed to escape the milling crowd as quickly as he could.

Given how different his personality was from Charlotte's, Josh wasn't that surprised when she broke up with him half-way through the spring semester. To be honest, he was relieved. Now he wouldn't have to accompany her on her busy spring calendar of social events. He wasn't sure how well he would deal with the crew of strangers he would be spending the summer with but figured it was a small group and his social reticence should wane after a week or so.

Josh passed Stockwell Hall on his right, where on Saturday nights during his freshman year he had hurried to get his date safely back before the "closing" hour of midnight. Waiting for traffic to clear, sweating now, he crossed Washtenaw Ave and continued up a long hill to the museum. Guessing they would be leaving from the main entrance, he hurried along the sidewalk on the north side of the building. But when he rounded the corner of the museum and the main entrance came into view, with its mountain lion statues on either side, he could see no sign of his ride. It was said the lions would roar whenever a virgin strolled by, but this morning, as always, they were silent.

"What the fuck," Josh muttered to himself. Checking his watch, which showed it was a little before nine, he heard the bells from the Burton Memorial Tower start to chime the hour. Pissed now, having hustled to the museum only to be apparently left in the lurch, he frantically continued walking along the south side of the museum toward the parking lot and loading dock. He was still a good fifty yards away when he saw what must be his ride — a beat-up Ford station wagon, pulling out of the museum parking lot and turning away from him, heading up to the stoplight at Washtenaw Ave. From there it was a straight shot to route 23 south to Toledo, where they would pick up I-75. Just before the car turned away from him Josh saw the person riding shotgun, a dark-haired woman, look straight at him. She gave him a quick smirk and a little wave before looking away. As the car drove the short distance to the stoplight, Josh realized the woman who had waved knew exactly who he was, and they were deliberately leaving him behind.

"That bitch," he muttered as he broke into a run. Josh had been one of the slowest players on his high school football team, and his duffle bag didn't help. Fortunately, the stoplight had just turned red and Josh was able to catch up with the car. Pounding on the roof of the car and walking up to the passenger side, Josh tried to catch his breath as the woman who had blown him off slowly rolled down the window. "You must be Josh," she said in a calm, measured voice.

Before she could continue, Josh interrupted. "You saw me. You waved at me. You were gonna ditch me."

Looking at Josh with a serious expression, the woman held her hands in front of her, palms up, as if the answer was obvious, and responded in a dispassionate voice. "You were late."

"That's a lie," Josh shot back. "I was here right on time. You didn't even wait till the bells stopped ringing the hour."

"And you're a frat rat. Not really suitable I'm afraid," the woman replied.

At this point the back seat window rolled down and a plumpish teenage boy with a large afro haircut and sporting a tie-dyed T-shirt stuck his head out. Squinting at Josh, the boy grinned as he jumped out of the station wagon, grabbed Josh's duffle, and added it to the other bags in the back. Turning back to Josh, he thrust out his hand for Josh to shake and introduced himself.

"On formal occasions I prefer to be addressed as 'The Teeny Bopper,' but usually people just call me 'Bopper.' And to answer your obvious question, yes, I'm still in high school, but don't worry, I can keep up." Bopper then nodded at the front seat. "That's Tom behind the wheel, and you've already met Dolores."

Ignoring Dolores and giving Bopper a brief nod, Josh walked around the back of the station wagon to the driver's side, eager to get in before they drove off again without him. He was reaching for the door handle when the driver's door flew open, and Josh got his first good look at Tom. He couldn't help but smile and shake the offered hand. In the flesh, Tom was a pretty good match for 'Mr. Natural,' the popular comic book character. Tall and gangly, he sported shoulder-length curly hair brown hair — thinning in front, and a long flowing beard. He had bright blue eyes, a deep tan, and a perpetual somewhat surprised expression. His heavily worn bib overalls were embroidered with a peace sign and his various breast pockets were filled with an array of mechanical pencils. Tom wore a beat-up pair of US Army issue combat boots, and the military theme carried over to his trousers, which were neatly tucked into the top of his olive drab athletic socks, paratrooper style.

"Dig it man," Tom blurted out excitedly, gazing over Josh's shoulder. "Paducah by sundown."

That concluded Mr. Natural's greeting. He bobbed his head a few times before jumping back behind the wheel, moving with an easy grace. Josh had barely gotten in the back seat before the car lurched forward, turned the corner, and they were headed south. Josh noticed right away that the shocks were shot and after every bump in the road the car would bob up and down as if they were in a choppy sea. "Oh great," Josh thought, "ten hours of bouncing with Mr. Natural."

Silence filled the car for a few minutes as Mr. Natural navigated the traffic on Washtenaw Ave, frequently changing lanes and offering occasional unintelligible vocalizations.

Piled up on the rear seat between Josh and Bopper was a messy bunch of USGS fifteen-minute quad maps, notebooks, three ring binders, a small Munsell Soil Colors book, snack food wrappers, an empty Dr. Pepper can, and a half-eaten Moon Pie. Turning sideways in the seat, Bopper looked at Josh over the debris pile separating them and without a preamble started a disjointed and rambling tutorial on what the summer held in store. "I saw you gawkin' at Tom's pants. It looks kinda silly, with them all tucked into his socks like that, doesn't it? Won't seem so silly once we get on the site, though. That's his defense system for chiggers and ticks, and they're all over the place where we'll be digging."

"But why's he tucking them in now? We got chiggers and ticks in the car?" Josh asked.

"No. Not yet. He's just excited to be on the road. And don't worry about his dazed expression and aggressive driving. Tom's a stoner and likes to get a good buzz on for a long drive. He calls it 'wake and bake.' If we're lucky, he won't start talking about the Fabulous Furry Freak Brothers. That could go on for hours."

"He's not bringing any weed in the car, is he?" Josh asked, trying to keep the alarm out of his voice.

"No way, Jose," Bopper answered. "Tom likes to exceed the speed limit, sometimes by quite a bit, so there's no way we would be transporting any pot. And anyway, there's no need. Tom has a solid source for weed in Arkansas — fine Ozark Gold, and it will blow your mind."

"Oh great," Josh thought, "spending the summer with a bunch of stoner hippies in the rural South — what could go wrong?"

Bopper read his expression and laughed before replying. "Hey Josh, don't get freaked, man. Tom's supplier is safe, and most of the crew sticks to beer anyway unless we're all hunkered down in the basement during tornado alerts and people need to chill out."

With a disdainful snort, Josh pushed back. "A safe supplier? There's no such thing. We could have the pigs all over us."

Looking smug, Bopper leaned over the debris pile and said in a low voice. "The pigs won't swarm us Josh. Tom's supplier is the local sheriff. It's all cool man. He's a cool pig."

Stunned into silence, Josh looked out the window for a while before asking Bopper his next question. "Is Tom a grad student on the project?"

"Tom? No, not really. He got an undergrad degree in history from Wayne State and has been teaching seventh grade math over in Ypsitucky for the past few years to avoid the draft. They can't get real teachers over there, so he qualifies for a draft exemption, and it keeps his summers free for archaeology."

"Fuck me," Josh thought, moaning softly to himself, "I think I just joined the circus, and this is the clown car." He half expected Bopper to pull out a Bozo the clown horn to go with his hair and start honking.

2.

THE NUN

Josh was surprised when Tom slowed and made a right turn off Washtenaw Ave onto a quiet tree-lined street by the Tri-Delt house. Seeing Josh's quizzical expression, the Bopper explained their detour. "One more stop. Pickin' up Denny."

"Who's Denny?" Josh asked.

"Oh, you'll see," Bopper replied.

Tom pulled into the driveway of a house halfway down the block, and Josh was surprised again. This was not one of the many houses in town that had been partitioned into multiple student apartments. It was an immaculate craftsman-style home with a manicured lawn and a broad, deeply shadowed front porch.

Josh could see a woman get up from a swing on the front porch and move toward the stairs. As she reached the top of the porch steps and started down, emerging from the shadows into the light, Josh thought she looked familiar, then recognized her from the Archaeology of North America class he had taken the previous fall. This must be Denny. He didn't know her name and hadn't ever talked to her. Josh typically sat in the back of the lecture hall, and being an introvert, he rarely participated in class discussions.

In contrast, Denny sat in the front row and would often stay after class to ask the professor questions. The prof, a famous archaeologist who was also director of the archaeology museum, invariably brushed off the ass-kissers in the front row. But he always seemed to have time for Denny and welcomed her questions. Josh couldn't stand the brown-nosers who chatted up their professors, but Denny was different — good looking, Josh thought, but definitely nerdy, with short black hair — clearly an amateur haircut, maybe self-inflicted, and no makeup. Overalls with baggy shirts and Birkenstocks were her standard daily outfit, which rarely varied. Definitely not sorority material.

Last fall, about halfway through the semester, Josh realized he had made a habit of looking for the girl in overalls each time he went to archaeology class. Her figure was always hidden by the baggy overalls and sweatshirts she invariably wore, but her face, Josh thought, was beautiful — lively dark green eyes, a light scattering of freckles, high cheekbones, and a thousand-watt smile.

While Josh watched from the back seat Tom jumped from the car and gave Denny an exuberant hug, grabbed her suitcase, and then opened the car door for her before throwing her bag in the back. Bopper grabbed all the crap littering the seat between him and Josh and slid over to the hump to make room for her, dumping the junk on Josh's lap and turning sideways to give Denny a quick hug. Looking over Bopper's shoulder as she hugged him, Denny smiled at Josh, her green eyes calmly assessing him. Extracting herself from the Bopper's embrace, she leaned forward in her seat and reached over to shake Josh's hand.

"Hi, Josh. I'm Denny."

Still dazed, Josh was surprised to feel a well-developed set of calluses on her palm as he returned her firm handshake. Bopper had been closely watching Josh for his reaction to Denny and seemed disappointed that he hadn't provided a more entertaining response. Absently scratching his crotch, Bopper turned to Denny.

"How come you know his name?"

"Oh, I have my ways," she replied.

Dolores snorted in the front seat and muttered in a stage whisper. "Brown-noser."

"Hey bitch," Denny shot back. "Still gluing those pottery sherds and huffin the Duco?"

The reply from the front seat was immediate. "Hey Nun, you still fondling your maggoty dead animals?"

Bopper, clearly pleased at the exchange, leaned over to Josh. "Let me provide some context here, frat boy. Dolores and Denny were just referring to each other's areas of expertise. Dolores is the project's ceramic analyst — she's working on her PhD and is in charge of identifying and analyzing all the pottery that's recovered during excavation, and there's a lot of it. Duco cement is the best thing to glue broken pieces of pottery together, hence Denny's reference to it."

"Denny, on the other hand, is our faunal analyst. She's an undergrad phenom and starts grad school in the fall. She runs the project's archaeozoology lab and identifies and analyzes all the animal bones recovered. Since she needs modern animal skeletons for comparison, Denny pays locals to bring her dead animals which, along with the road kills she picks up, she renders down for her faunal collection. She keeps shovels and bags in the crew vehicles, and people aren't too keen about riding with her in case she wants to stop to shovel up something stanky."

Bopper paused, waiting to see if Josh wanted to join in the conversation.

"The Nun?" Josh asked, looking at Denny.

Denny turned serious and replied. "Dolores and some others on the crew call me 'The Nun' because I haven't shown an interest in any of the arrogant, insecure, self-centered, testosterone-charged archaeology grad students in the museum or on the crew, and they can't grasp why I'm not chafing at the bit to jump into bed with any of them. And Dolores's claim I'm a brown-noser? No way. I've wanted to be an archaeologist since I was a kid and I think of lots of questions during lectures. The profs are the ones with the answers, so I sit in the front row with the brown-nosers and after class, I ask my questions. I also ambush elusive profs in the halls of the museum with questions, go to museum get-togethers, and hang out at coffee time in the North American Range for chitty-chat. But I'm used to the nasty comments from Dolores and the others. They're just playing at grad student small group politics. It's kinda irritating, really. But I figure I just gotta keep on truckin. Dogs bark, but the caravan moves on."

Except for Dolores, who stared stonily out the front window, a companionable silence filled the car following Denny's soliloquy. They were making good progress down I-75 toward Toledo, with Tom grooving to some inner melody and staying a safe nine miles over the speed limit. Once they crossed into Ohio, beyond the reach of the despised Michigan State Police, he would jack the speed up another few notches.

Sandwiched on the hump between Denny and Josh, Bopper soon got bored with the silence and started peppering Josh with questions about why he signed up for the field crew. Bopper soon realized Josh didn't have much of a clue about what they would be doing.

"Jesus, frat rat, you don't know shit. Didn't you even read the 'Hamblin's Fort' handbook you got when you signed up for the field crew?"

"Handbook? I never got a handbook," replied Señor Estúpido.

"No?" Bopper replied, tapping Dolores on the shoulder. "Hey Dolores. Didn't you guys give frat rat a handbook?

"Musta slipped my mind," Dolores replied with a smile, keeping her eyes on the road ahead.

"Well then," Bopper said, "Let's just get my copy out and we can give Josh here a tutorial on the way down." Bopper loved to run his mouth. Holding up a dog-eared maize and blue hued booklet he had pulled from his pack, he waved it at Josh.

"We got hours in the car Josh, and you clearly don't know jack about what you got yourself into here, so how bout I go through the basics with you. I'm not gonna read it to you word for word — it's pretty boring. I can hit the high points and you can fill in the details when you get a copy of your very own." Bopper opened the booklet and started scanning the text, paraphrasing for Josh as he read.

"Okay, page one. The site. We're diggin at a place called 'Hamblin's Fort.' It's a fortified Native American settlement that we think was occupied for a short period of time — maybe a hundred years or so, at around A.D. 1300. They grew corn and a bunch of other crops, harvested wild plants, hunted deer and other animals, and fished."

Bopper's cliff's notes rendition of the project handbook was interrupted at this point when the station wagon swerved abruptly into the right lane to avoid a slow-moving truck. After a few choice words for the truck, Tom apologized, and Bopper flipped a few pages in the handbook and carried on.

"Okay, next we got the bigger picture. Let's lump Hamblin's Fort in with similar groups in a larger category — Mississippian societies. There were lots of villages like Hamblin's Fort scattered along the river valleys if the Southeast after about A.D. 1,000, and right up to European contact. Archaeologists lump them all under the general label of "Mississippian" societies, but there were lots of regional differences."

"Now, young Josh, let's take a look at what Hamblin's Fort is like up close and personal. The site's named for Marcus Hamblin, the farmer who owned the land back in the late 1800s. They called it a fort back then cause you could still see the fortification ditch. It was pretty fuckin hard to miss — maybe five feet deep and around six hundred yards long, surrounding an area of maybe five acres. You can still see the ditch today, but what's long gone is the palisade wall that went with it — thousands of posts, just inside the ditch. Last summer we dug a bunch of trenches exposing cross-sections of both the palisade ditch and some of the palisade post holes."

Tom interrupted Bopper's rendition of the handbook at this point with a long rambling recounting of one of last summer's mishaps, when a side wall of one of their cross-section trenches had collapsed. When Tom finished his story, Denny and Dolores resumed their sparring, this time arguing over who had caused last summer's cave-in. As he listened to the two women trade barbs, Josh began to think that maybe this was normal for them. Neither one seemed particularly upset by their exchange, and they both actually appeared to relish trying to out-insult the other.

"Where was I?" Bopper interjected, clearly irritated by the interruption. "Oh yeah, big wooden fortifications. Let's go inside this protecting palisade and check out the community plan. First comes the plaza — a centrally located open area. Then ya got two earthen mounds facing each other across this central plaza. On the east side ya got a flat-topped square mound or 'temple mound', and on the west side there's a round conical mound. Each mound is about two stories or twenty feet tall. Both mounds were constructed with thousands of basket-loads of dirt — a pretty impressive communal labor project, as was the construction of the palisade wall. These Mississippians moved a lotta dirt."

Tom interrupted again, complaining about the lack so far of any excavations into either of the two mounds. He was eager to see what they would yield and how much damage had been done by curious locals over the years as they pursued any number of different myths about what might be buried in the mounds — Spanish gold maybe, or seven-foot giants.

Waiting patiently as Tom wound down, Teeny Bopper flipped more pages in the handbook before taking up his narration. "Now we're getting to the important stuff. The research plan — what we're gonna do this summer. It's gonna be big. Last year was our first year here, and we didn't get a lot of actual digging done. We had to first find and fix up a crew house — the 'Hamblin Mansion.' Then we got out the old alidade and plane table and made a detailed map of the site's major features — the fortification ditch, plaza, temple mound, and conical mound. With the time we had left after all that was done, we dug two house structures just inside the north fortification wall."

"Okay," Bopper continued, flipping forward several pages. "The plan this year is to focus on two other areas of the site. Last year's excavation gave us a good look at what houses just inside the palisade were like — small, boring, with central hearths, burned wall posts, and pottery with typical design motifs. Now we want to dig two house clusters located just off the main plaza, at its southeast and northeast corners, not too far from the base of the temple mound. It's a logical place to look for houses where the big shots lived — high-status residential areas. Once we see what those areas look like, then Dolores is going to start a sampling program to collect ceramics from all across the site. She's hoping to identify different family or kinship groupings based on differences in ceramic design elements."

"Plus, we're going to trench down the side of the temple mound to look for evidence of feasting," added Denny.

"The fuck we are," blurted Dolores. "Your stupid idea is not part of the excavation plan."

Denny smiled broadly. "You wait, Dolores, it will be. It's a no-brainer. I'm betting that discarded food remains from ceremonies and feasts on the top of the temple mound are still present on the mound slopes. We're going to find amazing evidence of ceremonial food consumption that is vastly different from what we usually find in habitation refuse middens. I betcha we got beaucoup feasting debris right here at the Hamblin site. When I sketch out my plan for Boss Man, he's going to give me the green light."

"Boss Man?" Josh asked. "Sounds like a chain gang."

Tom cackled in the front seat, turning to give Josh a wild glance over his shoulder as he swerved around another slow-moving truck in the left lane. "Don't fuck with the Boss Man. He put you in the box."

Seeing Josh's look of confusion, Bopper waved off Tom's comment. "He's seen the movie 'Cool Hand Luke' about a zillion times and loves to recite long stretches of dialogue to anyone willing to listen. Don't get him started. Boss Man is just our nickname for George Johnson. He's the field director of the project, and his PhD dissertation, if it ever gets finished, is going to be a grand synthesis of what we know about Hamblin's Fort."

Tom and Denny both glanced at Dolores as Bopper referred to the slow progress of Boss Man toward his doctorate. She maintained a stony silence and stared straight ahead through the windshield. Josh would later learn that Dolores was five years into her dissertation research and was under increasing pressure to finish.

"Anyway," Bopper said, looking frantically for something in the maize and blue crew handbook. Finding what he was looking for, he went quiet as he read a few pages. Nodding to himself, he continued.

"Can we get back to my brilliant intro to our research? We's gettin down to the nitty gritty now Josh — digging up houses. Hamblin's Fort has hundreds of houses, or what's left of them — house floors stacked up like pancakes. Folks built their square houses with vertical posts set in trenches and walls of interlaced branches covered with clay. Roofs were thatch — piled up grass. After fifteen or twenty years these houses would be crawling with all kinds of bugs and other vermin and would need to be torn down and replaced. And they were often rebuilt in the same location. As a result, once we remove the plow zone — that's the top foot or so of soil that has been disturbed by the farmer's plow, we come down on a layer cake of houses." Bopper paused here, picked at a pimple on his cheek, and continued.

"Let's say, just as a 'thought experiment' here Josh — archaeologists do a lot of thought experiments, that Hamblin's Fort was occupied for a hundred years. If you figure a twenty-year life span for houses, that's four or five teardown and rebuild cycles, leaving behind a four-tier layer cake of overlapping, crisscrossing wall trenches, house floors, refuse pits and artifact scatters."

Bopper paused at this point, gazing at Josh expectantly as if waiting for an answer to a question he hadn't asked. Josh realized he was expected to make some response to Bopper's tutorial and asked the first question that came into his head.

"Why focus first on the houses, not the mounds?"

Another snort from Dolores, followed by her snide response. "Isn't it obvious, frat boy? The mounds at these Mississippian sites have been a magnet for treasure hunters since the late 1700s, with one fuck of a lot of digging into mounds over the past two centuries. Hundreds of Mississippian mound center settlements existed along river valleys in the Southeast, and almost all of them have had their mounds dug into either by looters or by archaeologists. At the same time, we know fuck all about the daily lives of the people who built the mounds. The lives of everyday people took a back seat to the goodies in the mounds."

"But we're not doing that here. Since so many mounds at other sites have been excavated, we pretty much already know what to expect from the ones here at Hamblin's Fort. The flat-topped mound no doubt supported a large structure that was rebuilt a number of times, often when the mound itself was enlarged. There may have been a central burial chamber for a big shot, or a chief's house, or maybe a mortuary for the display of ancestors, or simply a general structure for ceremonies and rituals. And it will long-since have been looted. The conical mound, on the other hand, is not so easy to interpret. I'm thinkin it was built early in the occupational sequence of the site, might even pre-dating it. Could be early Mississippian or even Late

Woodland — maybe A.D. 800? And it probably had burials and no doubt was also looted long ago."

Dolores continued. "At the same time that excavations on Mississippian sites have mostly been limited to mounds over the past century, analysis of ceramics recovered from these sites has also been limited to a few questions – establishing the function of different vessel shapes for example, or looking for similarity in design elements, shape, and temper between ceramics from different sites to assess degrees of cultural affiliation, along with using changes in ceramics over time to help place sites chronologically."

Dolores paused here for dramatic effect before continuing with a zealot's enthusiasm. "But George Johnson and I are doing something radically new with ceramic analysis, something revolutionary in eastern North American archaeology. Rather than using ceramics to try to place a settlement in time or look for cultural ties with other settlements, we're going to look at the distribution of different design elements on ceramics within Hamblin's Fort and tease out the social organization of the community. We think it's likely that the smaller courtyards off the southeast and northeast corners of the plaza was where high-ranking individuals of different social groups lived, clans perhaps. That's why we want to prioritize the excavation of the habitation areas — we're in search of nothing less than social organization."

Silence filled the car as Dolores glared at Denny, daring her to say anything negative about her research plans. Finally, Bopper filled the void.

"Actually, it might work. Some archaeologists out in the Southwest have found some interesting spatial patterns of ceramic designs at Broken K Pueblo that might reflect different social units. But nobody's tried it in eastern North America."

"I think it could well be a waste of time," offered Denny, "but we might get some interesting variation in subsistence patterns from the different courtyards that might show differences in what elite and everyday folks ate, so it won't be a complete loss."

Having worked all the way through the handbook, Bopper dropped it in Josh's lap as the car settled into a long quiet spell. They stopped for a quick dinner in Paducah, Kentucky, where Tom was quite excited about scoring several Smack Burgers and a side of fries. As they got back in the car, Denny offered to sit the hump, and Bopper agreed with raised eyebrows and a slight smile.

Bopper soon dozed off, his head back, mouth open. Josh kept his voice low as he turned to Denny. "I noticed Dolores and Bopper didn't say anything about subsistence — what plants and animals Mississippians ate. How come? I thought the ecological approach, human's place in the environment, was a big new research area in archaeology."

"Right on, Josh. It is." Denny replied. "And nobody has really looked at Mississippian subsistence economy from the right perspective — it's mostly just been laundry lists of species of plants and animals identified at a site, usually included as appendices in archaeological reports. Old farts think that archaeology is ceramics and lithics, and that plant and animal remains are appendix material. But the times they are a-changin man, and we're right in the middle of the revolt of the appendix people."

Denny continued her impassioned speech as Josh, half listening, was more interested in her dark green eyes and the the spray of freckles across her cheeks.

"A new generation of researchers are looking at plant and animal remains from Mississippian sites and asking new questions about these societies' place in the ecosystem. We want to show how they all fit together in coherent overarching strategies of farming, gathering, and hunting."

Josh nodded. "I bet deer were high on their list."

Surprised, Denny smiled at Josh as she responded. "Right on, dude. Deer are always number one by a long shot."

"That's cool," Josh replied, still in a low voice. "It was a safe guess. I took a wildlife management course last fall and the professor talked a lot about deer. I'm not surprised they were the number one prey species for Mississippians. They're a large meat package and have a high biotic potential, which means they easily bounce back from heavy predation. And since they're browsers — eat leaves, buds, and stuff, any clearance of land for farming would create new edge areas and actually increase their population levels."

Denny looked back with a new appraising expression. "We need to talk more," she whispered. "Maybe you could work with me on the faunal remains from the site."

"I'd like that, Denny. Sign me up."

"Well….," she responded, "let me work on it."

"Sounds good," Josh whispered. "I also have a suggestion about your problem with unwanted advances and being labeled a nun."

Denny showed no reaction, just looked at him.

"It's simple, really. You need a 'beard' — a pretend boyfriend who can fend off unwanted advances on your behalf — just the apparent existence of a boyfriend would be pretty much enough for most situations."

Denny looked away, seeming to think about what he had said, then replied. "This pretend boyfriend — he would accept that it's all for show?"

"That's the challenge, of course, Denny — finding someone willing to do that and who is also believable enough to pull it off."

"Where oh where could I find someone like that?"

"I could do it," Josh said in a low voice, putting on his most sincere expression.

Denny laughed out loud, waking Bopper from his doze.

3.

BLACK DOG

Josh dozed off for a while and woke up as they were crossing the Mississippi River at Memphis. It was pitch black outside and he couldn't see the river. But as he listened to the hum of the tires and watched the rusted metal structure of the bridge flash by in the mist, the air seemed suddenly thicker, and laden with the smell of mud and decay. The weak beams of their headlights didn't penetrate very far, and the car seemed to be slipping into a dark and endless void. Tom's face was dimly illuminated by the dash lights, Bopper was gazing out the side window, and Dolores was snoring, her head back, mouth open. Next to him, Denny was also asleep, warmly snuggled up against him. He was careful not to wake her.

Fifteen minutes into Arkansas they turned south off the Interstate and continued deeper into the darkness. They were on a rural two-lane highway now. It was poorly maintained, lacked a center line, and was partially obscured by a low drifting mist. Their destination was still almost an hour away, and as they continued south in the darkness the landscape seemed monotonous to Josh. It was pool table flat, and the road was bordered on both sides by an unbroken expanse of what Josh guessed to be fields of soybeans and rice. It also suddenly seemed more humid. Bopper would later explain that they had entered the lower alluvial valley of the Mississippi River, where agricultural fields increase localized humidity during the growing season. Since both their crew quarters and Hamblin's Fort were surrounded by vast soybean and rice fields, Bopper excitedly told Josh he could look forward to a summer's humidity comparable to Angkor Wat. Bopper then giggled as he delivered the punch line. "And we ain't got us no air conditioning."

The car suddenly slowed as Tom hit the brakes. Josh glanced at the road ahead, where a large black dog had suddenly appeared, seemingly out of nowhere. It was staring straight at the car, its eyes glowing red in the headlights. Josh expected some sort of outburst from Tom or Bopper, but both were frozen in place as the car came to a stop maybe twenty feet away from the ghostly apparition. The dog, which had a droopy ear and favored its right front leg, took a few steps through the mist, directly toward the car, and then snarled, exposing an impressive set of canines. After a few moments the ghost dog slowly, almost casually, slipped off the road, fading back into the adjacent soybean field. Without a word, Tom put the hammer down and they continued deeper into the darkness. Looking over at Bopper, Josh watched as he leaned forward and whispered something in Tom's ear.

Denny stirred next to Josh, lifting her head from his shoulder. Shifting over on the seat away from him with a look of embarrassment, she called out to Tom. "Why did we just stop?"

Bopper turned to her and with a serious expression answered — "Black Dog."

"That's not the least bit funny, Bopper," Denny replied, anger creeping into her voice.

"I saw it," Josh offered. "A big black dog with a floppy ear and a limp. He was right there in the middle of the road, and he snarled at us."

"That's bullshit Josh," Denny replied. "Bopper put you up to this when I was asleep."

"No, it's true Denny," Tom called back over his shoulder. "It was Black Dog. I saw it too."

"Fuckin Jesus," Denny whispered. "Dolores sure as fuck don't need to hear about this, or anyone else on the crew. We need to keep this quiet."

Tom turned back to driving, and under Denny and Bopper's intense gaze, Josh nodded his assent with a puzzled expression. Before he could say anything, Denny leaned in close enough for Josh to feel her breast pressing up against his shoulder and her breath on his cheek as she spoke. "Don't say anything. Dolores might wake up and hear you. I'll tell you later."

As Denny sat back, Josh sensed a shift in the car — it seemed to be going up a slight slope. Bopper also registered the change and noted the significance of the rise in elevation.

"Feel that? We're on Hamblin's Ridge now. Almost there." They had just driven up onto an old natural levee of the Mississippi River — one of the myriad low sand banks left behind when the river meandered away eastward thousands of years ago. Although seemingly unimpressive, usually rising only five to ten feet above the floodplain, these natural levees were often the only dry land for miles around during the peak of the spring flood season. As a result, they had long been the preferred location for human settlement in the Mississippi Valley for both Native American and early European settlers. Natural levees were also made up of fertile, well drained, easily tilled sandy soils, making them particularly attractive to the maize farmers who had lived at Hamblin's Fort more than eight hundred years ago.

Dolores was awake now and pumped her fist as the crew house came into view, windows blazing with light. It was a large two-story frame house dating to the 1930s — a Sears kit house, now far past its glory days, isolated and anomalous in the middle of unending industrial monocrop fields. As they turned into the driveway and parked next to a decrepit pickup truck, an

International Travelall, a university station wagon, and a VW bug, Josh noticed a beat-up Shasta trailer and a small tent, both illuminated from within, in the side yard of the house.

As soon as the car came to a stop Dolores jumped out and walked quickly toward the house. Tom got out and stretched before walking off toward the small tent, where he lifted the flap, peeked inside, and then entered. Bopper and Josh both went to the back of the car for their bags. Bopper picked up his own duffle bag and handed Josh his duffle along with Denny's bag. Seeing that Josh was holding her bag, Denny turned and walked to the house. Bopper and Josh followed, and as they climbed the front stairs, someone sitting in the dim lighting on the porch smiled at them and offered a greeting. "Looks like the Nun has somebody to carry her bag this summer. I think she got herself a go-to sausage man."

Bopper sniggered at the greeting, but Josh paused at the top step and then walked over and looked down at the man who had spoken. Thin, in his mid-twenties, maybe five foot ten, with wire rim glasses, male pattern baldness, and sporting military style khaki pants and shirt, the man now smiled nervously up at Josh and took a sip from his beer. Looking down, Josh affected his best Detroit bad boy tone of voice and asked. "What did you just call me?"

Shifting in his seat, the man looked up and replied. "Just a joke, man, chill out. We like to kid around with Denny." Josh stared back without saying anything, attempting to hose the thin man with fear before turning away and following Bopper into the house.

Bopper had dropped his bag by the stairs up to the second floor and was slapping hands with a somewhat disheveled looking man amid cries of "Gimmie some skin," and "slip me five." Denny had disappeared upstairs and Dolores was sitting in an overstuffed easy chair in the corner, arms folded, looking cranky. Bopper and the other man then turned to face Josh.

"Fresh meat," the man called out before stepping forward and offering Josh a traditional handshake. "Hey Josh, welcome to the Hamblin Mansion. I'm Zack."

"Who's the guy on the porch?" Josh asked.

"Oh, that's Richard," replied Zack. "Not Rich or Rick or Ricky. He has a master's degree from Harvard and prefers to be called by his full name — Richard."

"He's kind of a douche." Added Zack, looking past Josh toward the front door. "Where's Tom? The sheriff's been lookin for him."

"He's out in the tent with Cecelia," replied Bopper, "probably asking for the thousandth time if he can share her tent. She always says no, he can just visit, but he never stops asking." Bopper paused, glanced around the room, and continued. "I'm betting Wilma and Paula, the grad students in charge of analyzing plant remains and lithics from the site, are out in their trailer - probably playing Mexican Train or one of their stupid board games."

"Or whatever," Zack added, lifting his eyebrows knowingly.

"Where do I sleep?" asked Josh, abruptly.

"Good question," answered Zack. "Boss man and his wife are up in Memphis. Trying to inject a little romance back into a strained relationship is my guess. He said you can sleep any place you want or are welcome." Zack pointed to a folded-up canvas army cot in the corner of the room. "There's your bed, just find a place to put it."

Bopper smiled. "Zack's just fuckin with you Josh. You can share the Sunset Suite with me and Tom if you want. We got the western exposure and look out over the vegetable garden and Croquet Court. Zack and Richard have the Honeybee Suite, on the east side, due to there's a honeybee hive in their wall. Denny and Dolores share the Lilac Suite at the front. Wilma and Paula bunk out in the Shasta and Cecelia sleeps in her tent."

"What about Boss Man?" Josh asked.

"Oh, Boss Man don't bunk with the crew. He and Nancy have a double-wide over in Forrest City," Bopper explained. "They have AC."

"What are my other options?" Josh asked.

Zack and Bopper looked at each other briefly before Bopper replied. "Bunk with us Josh, we don't snore."

Zack elbowed Bopper back a bit before overriding him excitedly and moving toward the stairs. "I got just the situation for you Josh - you don't have to share a space with anyone."

Josh grabbed his duffle bag and followed Zack. When they reached the second floor Zack led them down the hallway past several closed bedroom doors. Reaching the end of the hall, he pulled open a door and started up a flight of narrow stairs in the dark. Josh followed. Bopper stayed behind, frowning after them. At the top of the stairs Zack reached up and turned on a bare bulb hanging down from the ceiling on a long electrical cord. The bulb swayed back and forth, casting shadows across a large attic space that featured steeply pitched ceilings and four dormer windows at the cardinal directions. It was empty except for a neatly made double bed that was situated on the floor in the center of the attic, next to a large brick chimney. The attic windows were screened and open to the night breezes, and it wasn't as hot as Josh had expected.

Josh dropped his duffle bag on the floor as Zack recounted the recent history of the space. "Nobody's been crashing up here since midway through last summer. We had a science reporter here for a few weeks, but she left in kind of a hurry, and nobody's claimed the attic since then."

"Looks good to me," Josh replied, relieved he wouldn't have to deal with any roommates. "Thanks Zack."

Zack looked particularly pleased with his good deed and patted Josh on the shoulder before heading back down the stairs. Josh pulled off the sheet of plastic that covered the bed and sat down, surveying his new crash pad. With a few box fans in the windows, he figured, it should be cool enough to sleep at night, particularly following long days at the site and after a few beers or some weed. But it was way weird, he thought, about the bed still having sheets and a pillow. That science reporter must have been in quite a hurry. Josh lay back on the bed and watched the shadows from the swinging lightbulb move across the rafters. He dozed off for a while, and when he opened his eyes again the lightbulb was still swinging, which was weird.

Josh needed to take a leak and stepped carefully down the steep stairs in search of a bathroom. "Cool," he murmured to himself as he saw the John right at the base of the attic stairway. It was a nasty bathroom, he noticed immediately — messy, with multiple toothpaste tubes and brushes on the sink and shelves and various soaps next to a filthy tub. He wondered if the entire crew used the one bathroom.

All the bedroom doors were still closed, and wandering downstairs, Josh found Bopper watching TV — the Tonight Show, on a large floor model black and white TV. He could hear Zack and Richard talking out on the porch but didn't particularly feel like dealing with anyone, so he opted for a quick shower and a good book in bed. He was pleasantly surprised when there was enough hot water for a good long shower. On the way back up to the attic Josh noticed two unused box fans under the stairs and after carting them up to the attic and positioning them so they provided a good breeze across his mattress, he lay down wearing just his boxer shorts and found where he had left off in Truman Capote's blockbuster *In Cold Blood*. He was about halfway through the book and eager to get back to it. It had been a long day, however, and he was only able to read a few pages before falling asleep. He woke several hours later to the sound of footsteps coming up the attic stairs.

"Hellooo" Denny called out in a stage whisper, peeking above the top of the stairs.

Sniggering when she noticed Josh was just waking up, she then turned mock serious.

"Sorry for laughing. I shouldn't make fun of you needing the light on when you sleep."

"Very funny," Josh replied, reaching for his T-shirt as she walked over and sat down on the foot of the mattress. Watching Josh pull on his T-shirt, Denny liked what she saw. "Nice bod," She thought to herself as she recounted the history of the black dog.

"I promised you an explanation about the black dog," Denny began. "It's all tied up with what happened down here last summer. I'm surprised you didn't hear something about it back on campus."

"Oh great," Josh thought to himself as he shook his head. "I'm the only one who didn't get the memo. Looks like Señor Estúpido has struck again." Josh stayed silent and Denny continued.

"We were having some problems last summer with ditch hounds. Stray dogs. There's a scatter of maybe six rundown mobile homes down the road a mile or so, by the corner store, about halfway between here and Hamblin's Fort. The ditch hounds were mostly from there. They weren't really vicious or anything, just made occasional appearances at the crew house or the site, sniffing around garbage cans or angling for a handout. But Boss Man doesn't like dogs — one bit him as a kid I guess, and he was always bitchin about the strays."

Denny paused, thinking back. "We had a big summer solstice party last year — lotsa beer, brats and burgers on the grill, and an all-day croquet tournament. Boss Man was showing Zack his new handgun, a cheap little 22 Saturday night special, and Zack said it looked like a toy. Boss Man was drunk and took offense, so he shot at a black dog that was nosing around the garbage. Everyone, including Boss Man, was surprised when his shot actually hit the dog. It dropped to the ground, then slowly got up and hobbled off into the soybean field. Some of us searched for it, but there was no trace."

Denny paused again, looking down at her hands, then continued. "Zack and Boss Man laughed when the dog went down. They thought it was hilarious. But just about everyone else was freaked out, and Boss Man's wife Nancy threw a fit — screaming at him, calling him an asshole, and stalking off. I think that's when their marriage really started to hit the skids."

"Fuck Me," Josh thought to himself, smiling grimly. "It just keeps getting better and better. Dropped into the middle of a failing marriage with the husband shooting off handguns when he's upset. No better way to guarantee a fun summer."

"That's how the whole 'Black Dog' story line started," Denny continued. "The crew got over the shooting after a week or so and started joking about the black dog now being responsible for anything that went wrong. He went from being just 'the black dog' to something more. Now he was 'Black Dog.' When the brakes went out on the pickup someone joked that they had seen Black Dog under the truck. When Bopper got his hand caught in the mechanical screen out at the site, Black Dog was seen hurrying away. It was funny for a while, then people began, bit by bit, to get spooked for real. We did see Black Dog around occasionally, so he survived the shooting, but he was now elusive, only ever briefly glimpsed before disappearing. And for the rest of the summer the mishaps kept coming — the beehive in the wall of the Honeybee Suite sprung an opening into the house and everybody got multiple stings, thunderstorms blew our tarps off our excavations, two tornados hit close enough for basement sleeping, local teenagers started driving by the crew house yelling threats."

Denny paused, checking to see if Josh was listening. "Probably the scariest Black Dog thing that happened involved Andrea, the science writer who was here last summer. She arrived a few weeks after the shooting and, like you, decided to sleep up here rather than share a room with anyone. But Andrea was always worried about fire danger and getting trapped in the attic if the house ever caught on fire. She even had an escape rope out one of the windows. And her fear of fire was justified, it turned out."

Smiling in the dim light cast by the attic's bare bulb, which had started swaying again, Denny continued. "It took about a week for Andrea to realize that while archaeology might seem really cool in the abstract, in the field it was mostly just hard, dirty, menial labor and long hot and humid days under a brutal sun. Once she figured that out, it wasn't long before she smoked too much of Tom's weed at one of our Friday night parties and announced she was checking out of this rathole and was looking forward to writing an excoriating expose of the Hamblin's Fort project just as soon as she got back to the real world."

"Later the same night she tripped and fell face first into a bonfire we had built out by the croquet field. It was bad — her hair was on fire, and her clothes. I can still see her screaming, running across the lawn and right into a tree in the darkness. She was medevacked up to Memphis — a helicopter right out in the yard here. She claimed, as they were loading her onto the chopper, and before the painkillers kicked in, that she had been pushed into the fire. But nothing ever came of it. She never wrote her story and we never saw her again."

"Any idea if somebody pushed her?" Josh asked.

"Well, Zack was over by the bonfire when it happened and is the only one who could have. He denied it of course, and nobody actually saw her do the faceplant into the flames."

"Didn't she press any charges?"

"No, but it's not surprising. She was really fried that night on Tom's Ozark Gold, supplied by the county sheriff, and he's the one she would have to file charges with. Not a good idea for anyone."

"Let's see if I got it all," Josh replied. "Courtesy of my new buddy Zack I'm sleeping in the cursed bed of a major burn victim who he may have pushed into a bonfire. The Boss Man shoots at things when he's drunk, and his marriage is failing. And judging from our ghost dog sighting last night, some powerful bad juju courtesy of Black Dog looks to continue through the summer."

Denny offered another of her radiant smiles as she stood and headed for the stairs, calling back over her shoulder. "Yeah, maybe so, but just think — if I get my way, you and I will be digging into that temple mound to look for the faunal evidence of feasting! What could be more exciting than that?"

4.
LITTLE MAN LOSER

Boss man rolled over on the couch where he had spent the night and groaned when he tried to sit up. The previous evening's "date night" trip with his wife Nancy up to Memphis had resulted in a bad hangover, and for some reason his eyes were caked with schmutz. His T-shirt and boxers were almost soaked through with sweat. His mouth felt fuzzy.

Although not even eight in the morning it was already oppressively hot and stuffy in the double-wide they had rented in Forrest City for the summer. Their trailer would absorb heat during the day and never quite cooled off at night. As advertised, it did have an air conditioner, but it was a small window unit located in the bedroom, and Boss Man could hear it roaring away through the locked bedroom door.

The trip to Memphis had not gone well. He realized early in the evening that Nancy was in a particularly nasty mood, and he had responded to her endless recitation of his shortcomings over dinner, as he often did, by sampling a wide range of different beers on tap. Soon after they arrived back at the double-wide Nancy had pushed him out of the bedroom and locked the door, then screamed her final drunken insult several times, delivered in a tipsy singsong — "little man loser, pathetic boozer." It wasn't all that witty, but it rhymed, and she thought it hilarious.

Scratching absently at his crotch, Boss Man got up from the couch and shuffled into the bathroom, took a leak, turned on the shower, and gazed into the mirror as he brushed his teeth. He was short, maybe five eight, and pudgy. Interested more in flea markets and collecting arrowheads as a kid rather than any sort of organized sports or other form of exercise, Boss Man had the semi-slumped pear posture and upper body of a couch potato. Given his very fair skin he was prone to serious sunburns. Shielding his male pattern baldness with a pith helmet reminiscent of the Raj, and always dressed in loose, light-weight khaki long-sleeved shirt and pants when at Hamblin's Fort, he was easily recognizable as 'Boss Man.'

After a quick shower he discovered and removed a tick imbedded at the back of his neck, then pulled on a fresh pair of khaki pants and shirt and took a swipe at what was left of his hair. Then it was sunglasses, keys and wallet, and finally, he snapped on his fanny pack, a recent addition to his wardrobe. When anyone asked, he said he carried first aid stuff and energy bars in the fanny pack, and in fact he did. Nestled in among the band aids and power bars, however, Boss Man also carried a snub nose .38 caliber Smith and Wesson revolver. Next time he came across Black Dog, he was ready.

Nancy and Boss Man had tied the knot during his first year in grad school, and things went pretty well for the first few years, with Nancy taking secretarial jobs to put hubby through his master's degree program. Then came the totally unexpected full-ride PhD fellowship offer from a highly ranked university up north, which Nancy suspected had little to do with Boss Man's scholarly promise and everything to do with the recognized research potential of the Hamblin's Fort site. Her suspicions seemed to prove correct as Boss Man never managed to gain much traction in his doctorate studies and research. His professors didn't warm to him, and his initial attempts at a dissertation proposal had all been rejected.

Neither Boss Man nor Nancy liked the cold winters up north, or the perceived distain of fellow archaeology grad students in the museum who were from more prestigious undergraduate programs. It was an aggressive, catty, infighting group with a strong tendency to badmouth the weakest among them. Based on her extensive job experience, Nancy had been hired as a secretary in the archaeology museum, and as a result she rather quickly managed to get a pretty clear idea of what both students and faculty thought of her husband.

On top of being reminded on a daily basis that Boss Man's place in the doctorate program was on thin ice, Nancy also had started to get an inkling, earlier in the spring, that Boss Man's relationship with Dolores, the doctoral student working on pottery from Hamblin's Fort, had gone far beyond scholarly interaction. Dolores, who was struggling to impress the faculty with the types of questions she could address with analysis of ceramic assemblages from the site, had convinced Boss Man to collaborate with her. They would join in an effort to illuminate the social structure and community organization of Hamblin's Fort by looking at the spatial distribution of different design elements on ceramic vessels recovered from the houses clustered around the smaller residential courtyards. This was cutting edge stuff at the time, and their faculty advisors, particularly Professor Shetler, had enthusiastically endorsed their proposal. Boss Man had started spending much of his time in Dolores's ceramics lab at the museum, and he would sometimes have long phone conversations with her in the evenings.

Nancy was somewhat surprised to realize that she really didn't care that much about Boss Man's apparent ongoing affair with Dolores. Both of them were losers, she decided, and her husband was a fool. She was amused that Boss Man seemed oblivious to the fact that she knew what was going on, and she began entertaining herself by interspersing her Boss Man insults with oblique and seemingly innocent inquiries about Dolores and the progress of their "ceramics reflects social organization" research effort.

In the early years of their marriage Nancy would get up in the morning and cook a full breakfast for them while Boss Man lounged in bed — bacon and eggs, grits, toast, and coffee. That stopped at some point after they moved north, and their usual pattern now that they were back in Arkansas was to stop at a 7-11 for something quick and greasy on the way to the site. Neither Boss Man nor Nancy felt like eating much the morning after their ill-fated dinner date in Memphis, however, and Boss Man settled for a Moon Pie and Dr. Pepper that he picked up at a small convenience store on the way down to Hamblin's Fort from Forrest City. Nancy skipped breakfast.

As he took another bite of the Moon Pie and washed it down with a swig of Dr. Pepper, the sugar rush seemed to boost Boss Man's spirits. As was often the case now, he felt like he was alone in the pickup, with Nancy staring out the window next to him in stony silence behind her sunglasses. But soon he would see Dolores. He smiled to himself, and was feeling almost happy, when Nancy started in on him.

"How is the ceramics research going with Dolores? Are you firming up your hypotheses? You must be eager to get back on top of things."

Boss Man ignored her, stuffing the last chunk of Moon Pie into his mouth as an excuse for not answering. Nancy was used to him ignoring her questions and tried again.

"We haven't seen Black Dog yet this summer. I hope he's OK. I still can't believe you shot a poor defenseless animal. I mean, how shitty is that?"

Looking over at Nancy with a calmness that spooked her, Boss Man replied. "Next time I see that fuckin dog, I'm gonna kill it."

Nancy was about to bark back, but she could see that Boss Man was in a particularly ugly mood this morning and thought better of it. Surprised when she didn't react, Boss Man looked over at her. Nancy sat ramrod straight with her arms folded across her chest. She had always been tightly wound, and could be quick to take offense, but still got along well with most of the crew. She enjoyed the edgy banter and practical jokes that people played on each other and often wished she could live in the crew house, the Hamblin Mansion, rather than the depressing double-wide she shared with Boss Man.

Nancy had been a standout volleyball player in high school, due both to her fierce competitiveness and her height. She towered over Boss Man by a good five inches. Somewhat gangly, almost horsey, and awkward seeming in repose, she was surprisingly graceful and fluid when she was in motion.

Given her resting frown expression, sensitivity to any sort of perceived slight, and penchant for criticizing her husband, Nancy could initially come across as a rather dour person — a prude with tightly pursed lips. But there was another side to Nancy that came out when she was with the crew and took a break from broadcasting how unhappy she was in her marriage. As the Boss Man's wife, she was of course forbidden fruit, and she enjoyed taking advantage of her position by casually flirting, in a variety of ways, with the male members of the crew during the workday. She would often wear braless T-shirts and tight shorts that showed off her long legs, and when sifting soil excavated from Hamblin's Fort through one of their screens, she would consciously sway her ass in a quite sensual way, invariably drawing the attention of crew members other than her husband.

When they had weekend parties at the Hamblin Mansion Nancy would start the evening moodily nursing a beer in the corner. But after knocking back a few brews she'd start dancing with Tom, Mr. Natural, who matched her both in stature and in dancing abandon. They could dance to anything, and the louder and more crazed the music the better, as far as they were concerned. Jimmy Hendrix and heavy metal were always in the mix. Tom would be stoned, of course, and Nancy tipsy, and they would move to the music in the brightly lit living room, sweating in the heat and humidity, and mostly oblivious to what else was happening around them. Local teens would drive by on stifling hot and sticky weekend evenings, slowing to take in the unusual scene — an old farmhouse in the middle of a vast and dark expanse of flat farmland, rocking with noise and featuring Tom and Nancy framed in the brightly lit windows as they gyrated to the music.

When Boss Man and Nancy came up over a slight rise and Hamblin's Fort came into view, they both forgot the mutual hostility that filled the cab of the pickup truck. It was clear that something was wrong. Both of the crew vehicles had already arrived at the site and all the doors of the International Travelall were wide open. The open doors on the Travelall weren't all that unusual — it might simply indicate that Denny had scraped up a roadkill that morning on the drive over to the site and they were airing out the vehicle. What concerned Boss Man was the presence of all of the crew on the top of the temple mound, talking and looking down at the surface of the ground.

Bopper yelled out at them as soon as they got out of the truck. "Pothunters, Boss Man. They did some serious digging up here."

The hole dug in the exact center of the temple mound was irregular in shape, roughly oval, maybe four feet in diameter and about two feet deep.

"Well fuck," Boss Man growled when they had climbed the sloping side of the earthen mound and he saw the size of the hole. "Walthall promised he would make sure nobody would mess with the site while we were working here." Homer Walthall was the farmer who leased the farmland that Hamblin's Fort was located on, and who had taken a sizable "crop damage" payment in exchange for permission to excavate, as well as the promise of no interference from local pothunters.

Boss Man was surprised by the overnight digging and doubted that it was one of the usual suspects. Any experienced pothunter would have known that the temple mound at Hamblin's Fort had likely been dug into many times in the past hundred and fifty years and that any further digging most likely would go unrewarded. He figured this hole was probably dug by someone who had recently watched a treasure hunting show on TV or read a magazine article about Confederate gold buried during the war of northern aggression. Inspired, they had decided to seek their fortune under cover of darkness. His suspicions were strengthened when Bopper told him that several of the crew's soil sifting screens had been broken apart.

Looking down at the pothole, Boss Man was quiet for a moment as the crew waited for his instructions. Looking up, he saw Josh standing next to Zack, and smiling at him, reached out for a handshake.

"You must be Josh, the new guy. Welcome. You're going to have a great summer digging with us, and your first assignment is to fill this hole in while the rest of us get back to stripping off the plow zone from our new excavation area."

Zack and a few others on the crew smiled at Josh getting stuck with a backfill assignment. Josh just nodded with a noncommittal 'just happy to be here' expression. Then Richard, the Harvard guy on the crew, suggested a modification to Boss Man's backfilling order.

"Before Josh starts filling the pothole we should probably first square it up into a 5x5 excavation unit and then clean up and record the side-wall profiles. There might be evidence of pits or other features. And it wouldn't hurt to screen the mound fill they dug up to see if there's something worth recovering — maybe some animal bones for Denny to work with."

Boss Man had barely nodded his agreement to this suggestion when Denny stepped forward and insisted that she work on the pothole with Josh.

"There's a very good probability that there are faunal remains, evidence of feasting, in the dirt pile from the pit and in the walls of the pothole, and the faunal analyst on the project needs to be involved. Shouldn't take us more than a day or two, tops."

Shaking his head in reluctant acknowledgement of her reasoning, Boss Man watched as Denny quickly scurried down the sloping side of the mound to grab trowels, shovels, and the forms she and Josh would need to record the side wall profiles of the excavation unit they would create. They would first cut away at the edges of the oval pothole until it was transformed into a five-foot-by-five-foot excavation unit — a square hole with nicely shaved sides. They would sift the soil they removed as they dug. Then they would draw up the side wall profiles and turn to sifting the soil that last night's diggers had removed from the mound, looking for any artifacts or plant and animal remains that were present.

Denny knew that a 5x5 excavation unit — a "test square" or "phone booth," was a fairly standard way of beginning a larger excavation effort, and she had quickly recognized that this could be her ticket. There was a good chance, she thought, that they could find evidence in this 5x5 that would bolster the argument she was planning on making to subsequently expand the test square into an excavation trench across the top of the mound and then down the mound slope. At the very least this would allow them to record and perhaps date the sequential layers of soil that were added to the mound at intervals during its lifespan, documenting the occupational history of the site — a not insignificant goal. In addition, Denny was confident that an excavation on the mound's flanks would uncover assemblages of animal bones discarded down the side of the mound following feasting ceremonies.

She couldn't wait to start shaving down the sidewalls and floor of their 5x5, looking for something, anything, that would justify extending their excavation on the mound summit. Lots of things could indicate the need for such an extension — evidence of a wall trench marking the presence of a structure of some sort, an unusual hearth or pit feature showing up on the floor of the square or in profile in the side walls, or maybe a cache of ritual items. She knew that any such discovery would have to be compelling since Boss Man would not want any distractions or labor drained away from the main focus of the research at the site — exposing and excavating the house structures at the base of the temple mound that he and Dolores were counting on to be the basis of their dissertations. Denny recognized that her mound trenching plans would be a hard sell, and whatever she found would have to be something big.

Leaving Dolores to direct excavations on the house cluster at the southeast corner of the plaza, Boss Man collected the damaged sifters and piled them in the back of his truck. After stopping by the Vaccaro hardware in Forrest City and picking up the screen and lumber needed to repair the sifters, he planned on spending the rest of the day back at the crew house. He could work on the sifters in the shade of the veranda while listening to a top 40 C&W station. Boss Man started humming a happy tune to himself in anticipation of picking up a sixpack of cold brews on the way to the crew house. The day was shaping up.

Tom caught up with him as he was climbing in the truck. "Hey Boss Man, here's your mail from the university museum. I picked it up the day before we made the trip down."

Boss Man started the truck, cranked up the AC, and started through his mail. One fairly large envelope from the anthropology department caught his eye, and he opened it. Inside there was a brief handwritten note to him, and another envelope addressed to Josh.

He quickly scanned the note and then with a quiet obscenity wadded it up and threw it on the floor of the truck before driving off. He stuffed he envelope addressed to Josh into his back pocket.

5.

COSMOGRAM

Boss Man had granted Denny's request to work with Josh in cleaning up the temple mound pothole. The rest of the crew returned to their unenviable task of stripping the plow zone from the suspected high-status house cluster situated just off the southeast corner of the main plaza, not that far from the base of the temple mound. Once that was well along, part of the crew would be shifted over to start exposing the other house cluster just off the northeast corner of the plaza.

Next to backfilling, stripping plow zone was the worst. With the exception of the two mounds, the top nine inches or so of soil at Hamblin's Fort had been plowed many times over the past century, and this heavily churned layer needed to be removed with shallow shovel skims before the undisturbed deposits below could be investigated. It was brutal work under the hot sun and was accompanied by frequent water breaks and chain-gang inspired chants by those involved.

Like Josh, three of the seven crew assigned to skimming detail — Zack, Bopper, and Cecelia, were there for the field experience but with no real pressure to recover information they needed for their graduate studies. Three others, on the other hand, were under pressure: Dolores, who was watching closely for any ceramic sherds that might show up in the plow zone, along with two other women — Paula and Wilma, who were both pursuing degrees in the graduate program in archaeology. The two women were a couple, and glad to be living out in the trailer, away from the rest of the crew in the Hamblin Mansion.

Paula's plan had been to use the lithics — stone tools and associated flakes and other debris recovered from Hamblin's Fort and other related sites, as the basis for her dissertation. Her dissertation committee was skeptical of the plan, however, and she had asked for one more field season to try to build a stronger case. The problem she faced was simple — Hamblin's Fort was not expected to yield very many stone tools. Like most other sites located in the lower alluvial valley of the Mississippi River, Hamblin's Fort was some distance away from any decent sources of chert, which was the primary raw material for stone tools. Other materials near at hand — cane for hide scraping and cutting, gar scales for arrowheads, and most importantly, deer bone for awls, scrapers, hoes, and a wide range of other tools, were used in place of chert.

Although she hadn't mentioned it to anyone, Paula shared her committee's dim view of the research potential of lithic assemblages from Hamblin's Fort and was planning on changing her dissertation topic to something more promising in the fall. She had asked for an additional field season because she wanted to spend the summer with Wilma — they had been together for more than a year and were a solid, happy couple, prone to wise-cracking and partial to lime jello shots.

In contrast to Paula, Wilma was confident that she could pull together a good data set for her PhD from the Hamblin's Fort plant assemblages and was strongly committed to finishing her dissertation as quickly as possible. Several years older than the other crew members, she was an Army brat and had moved around a lot as a kid. Her dad was physically and emotionally abusive, which had contributed to her quiet demeanor as an adult. Wilma was good at blending into the background and not drawing attention to herself. But her quiet exterior belied an inner determination to not be derailed in her pursuit of a doctorate, and a track record of overcoming a wide range of different life obstacles in her path. While Wilma was slow to anger, it was not a good idea to push her too far.

As soon as the plow zone was stripped and they began to excavate the houses, hearths, storage pits, and other features that they had exposed, she would collect a gallon or more of soil from each of them. Once a sizable number of such samples had been collected, Wilma would start staying back at the crew house in the afternoons to process them. She was trying out a newly developed method for recovering plant fragments that had had been partially burned and accidentally charred and carbonized long ago by the inhabitants of Hamblin's Fort, and as a result were still preserved after more than 800 years.

Wilma had modified a 55-gallon drum by connecting a garden hose at its base and had set it up in the shade of a large oak tree in the side yard of the crew house. Once the drum was filled with water and she had the hose on, bubbling up from below, she would pour one of the soil samples, a bit at a time, into the drum. The sandy soil would sink to the bottom and a wide range of different bits and pieces of carbonized plant matter — acorn and hickory nut fragments, corn kernels, seeds, and bits of charcoal, would float to the surface where it could be skimmed off and placed on newspaper to dry. Once dry, Wilma would place the collected plant material from each feature into paper bags and label them with provenience information. It was easy work, and the heat wasn't so bad in the shade of the oak tree, particularly on those afternoons when there was a breeze. Wilma was counting the days until she could spend quiet afternoons back at the crew house water screening, communing with her archaeobotanical assemblages, and listening to eight track tapes of Joni Mitchell, Paul Simon, and a bunch of other folk-rockers. She would do most of the subsequent sorting and IDs back in the university's archaeobotanical lab, but Wilma was also eager to see what floated up from her 55-gallon drum on warm summer afternoons. Corn was of course the main food crop of Hamblin's Fort, but Wilma thought there was a great deal that wasn't known about other crop plants, as well as the relative importance of agricultural crops compared to wild and managed species. She had lots of questions and was confident of some interesting answers.

Removal of the top eight inches of the plow zone over the 20x20 foot excavation area they were opening up at the southeast corner of the plaza, near the base of the temple mound, went pretty smoothly, and by mid-afternoon they were ready to carefully shovel away the final few inches that still covered the underlying, undisturbed soil layers. Tom was recognized as the maestro of the final skim. He would delicately remove thin slices of the sandy soil with the razor-sharp curved blade of his shovel, watching for the color change from the mottled brown and black of the plow zone to the solid light brown of underlying undisturbed soil. He also claimed to be able to feel the difference between the plow zone soil, loose and unconsolidated, and the more compact undisturbed soil beneath.

Tom was running his mouth as he skimmed, recounting one of his favorite Fabulous Furry Freak Brothers story lines, where Norbert the Nark once again attempts, unsuccessfully, to catch Fat Freddy Freekowtski buying weed. Nobody was really listening to his chatter, but they all stopped their shoveling when Tom seemed to loudly nick something mid-skim. Reaching down, he pulled a large pot sherd from the ground, and had started to brush it off when Dolores rushed over and grabbed it away. Turning her back on the skimmers, she walked off several steps, looking intently at the piece of pottery, before holding it up above her head, prancing in a circle, and repeating what seemed to be nonsense phrases. "Ramey Incised. Cahokia cosmogram. Cosmo-grammy-gram."

Tom dropped his shovel, muttered "No fuckin way," and held his hand out for the piece of pottery Dolores was still waving around as she laughed and continued dancing. Nancy and Richard hurried over and joined the plow zone skimming crew as they passed the sherd around for everyone to admire. Up on the temple mound Denny and Josh looked over, wondering what the ruckus was all about. Denny yelled a query, and with a triumphant whoop, Dolores trotted over to the base of the mound to deliver the bad news in person.

"Hey Denny, check this out, bitch. We found a primo Ramey Incised sherd, first thing. Dam good evidence of a direct connection to Cahokia. Looks like your stupid plan to dig into the side of the mound looking for evidence of feasting ain't gonna happen. All the action this summer is going to be taking place down here."

Denny, in a condescending voice, quickly shot back. "I don't think so sweetie. High status ceramics from Cahokia is a strong argument for more investigation up here on the mound summit, where the elite hung out, not down in the low rent district."

As soon as Dolores turned and started back to where the other crew members were standing, Denny started swearing under her breath and plopped down, dejected, on the pothole dirt pile.

Josh sat down next to her. "Hey Denny, what's that all about. What's Ramey Incised?"

Looking over at him blankly, Denny replied. "It's a ceramic type, Josh, and Dolores is going to jam that Ramey sherd down my throat and make sure everybody is digging down there this summer, on her part of the project, and not up here."

Still looking puzzled, Josh replied. "I still don't get it. Why's it a big deal?"

"That stupid sherd indicates a connection between Hamblin's Fort and Cahokia, which is maybe four hundred miles north of here, in the American Bottom, across the river from St. Louis. Remember our North American Archaeology course last fall?

Cahokia is the largest prehistoric mound center north of Mexico. It was the New York City of its time — way larger and more complex than anything else in the eastern woodlands."

Continuing to look confused, Josh asked again. "I know that. But what's the big deal. It's just a pot sherd."

Putting on her best professorial demeanor, Denny did a deep dive. "Ramey Incised is a very distinctive type of pottery, very rare. It refers to a type of large wide-mouth jar-form vessel having a round base, sharply angled shoulder, and above the shoulder a wide, sloping rim decorated with a variety of incised designs or symbols. It's associated with high status or elite contexts at Cahokia and its satellite sites, where the vessels are most commonly found. They're thought to have been made by specialized artisans and used in major ceremonies and rituals for the distribution of food and medicines to outlying local communities."

Pausing to check that Josh was paying attention, Denny continued. "One popular interpretation of these vessels is that they represent cosmograms — iconographic depictions of the broader cosmos, with the angled shoulder marking the boundary between the upper and lower worlds and the designs on the "upper world" rim area referencing the role of elites and their privileged connection to the cosmos. And when a Ramey sherd is found at a site like ours, hundreds of miles away from Cahokia, it shows that there was a direct and significant connection, and that Hamblin's Fort was involved in their religion and cosmology."

"So what," Josh replied. "How does that hurt your research?"

Giving Josh a "how stupid can you be" look, Denny continued her lecture. "Well, as a pompous ass like Dolores might argue, it 'resets excavation priorities.' She can claim that the Ramey sherd indicates that her house cluster was the location of high-status individuals and activities linked to Cahokia, and well worth extensive investigation involving everyone on the crew, while the temple mound hasn't yielded anything promising, just a pothole. And don't forget Boss Man's involvement in Dolores's ceramic analysis. And to top it all off, remember our archaeology class last fall? The professor teaching it is also the director of the museum and is in overall charge of this project. He excavated at Cahokia for a number of years. He's going to love this." Leaning back on the dirt pile, Denny folded her arms and exclaimed in dismay, "I'm fucked."

After a brief silence, Josh waved his hand in front of Denny to get her attention, and wanting to distract her, to see if he could make her smile, make her laugh, he pointed at last night's pothole dirt pile, right by their feet, where they could both plainly see what had been missed earlier — a back and forth trail of canid paw prints, apparently made by a large dog who had been up on the mound in the early morning hours, checking out what the pot hunters had been doing, maybe scaring them off.

Standing up, Josh offered a pretty good imitation of their archaeology prof from last fall as he launched into a punchy half-time pep talk, complete with waving arms.

"We're going to be digging up here all summer, Denny, cause you got Black Dog in your corner. Think about it. You wouldn't be up here now except for the pothole someone dug up here. And here, right at our feet, we have Black Dog's calling card. We got the proof that Black Dog was behind it. There is some serious juju at work here, Denny. We just gotta stick with the plan. Black Dog's got your back, Denny. Black Dog juju is real. Black dog walks among us."

Denny gave a wistful smile in response, much diminished from one of her dazzlers, and gazed past Josh to where some of the plow zone skimmers were spreading tarps out over the courtyard excavation unit while others were loading shovels into the crew truck. They were clearly closing up shop for the weekend. It wasn't "quitting time" yet, as usually declared by Boss Man, but close enough, on a Friday afternoon, and Dolores was eager to share the cosmogram news with Boss Man. A festive mood was bubbling up down below, while Denny and Josh watched glumly from the mound summit.

Josh looked over at Denny, stood up and grabbed his shovel, and walked over to the pot hole.

"We still got three good hours to work, Denny. Let's screen all this pothole dirt first to see what turns up, then start back on squaring up the hole. I figure that if we work through the weekend maybe we can find something that could bolster your case for further excavation."

Denny looked hard at Josh, seemed to snap out of her funk, and turning, trotted down the side if the mound.

"I'll let them know we're staying on for a while, and to leave one of the vehicles for us."

A triumphant Dolores waved the Ramey sherd out the window as the crew vehicles left, blowing kisses and honking the horn rapid fire. Josh and Denny took turns shoveling dirt from the pot-hunter's dirt pile into the screen and working the sifter. It was dirty work and when they had finished, maybe a half hour later, their sweat had combined with the cloud of dust they had generated to cover them, head to foot, in an impressive layer of grime. They didn't recover anything to strengthen their case for excavating the mound, just a few dozen chert flakes, an equal number of small potsherds from undecorated vessels, and a few animal bone fragments. But things got interesting when they started cutting back and straightening up the sidewalls of the pothole. Only one of them could fit in the hole at a time, so they took turns troweling down the side walls and shoveling the resulting dirt up, while the other would pass it through the sifter and pick out whatever turned up in the screen.

Josh was in the hole, carefully troweling the sandy soil floor, when he encountered what felt like a hard underlying layer. Soon he had exposed a hard reddish clay surface that extended across the entire floor of the pothole. He stopped, sat back on his haunches, and called up to Denny. "Hey Denny, we've come down on a hard clay layer here, and it looks burned." Looking closer at the side walls of the square, he continued. "And check this out, once you cut away the rough sidewalls of the pothole, the mound looks undisturbed. I think we have an intact burned clay feature below undisturbed stratigraphy here."

Denny let go of her shovel, knelt next to the pit, and stuck her head over the edge of the hole. "Jesus Josh, you're right. There's no plow zone. They never got a plow up here, that's for sure, and at least this part of the summit doesn't seem to have seen any pothunting beyond this one hole. Amazing. Hard to believe. A virgin temple mound." Denny sat back on her haunches, paused, and continued. "The other weird thing is that the top two feet or so of mound soil that overlies the burned clay layer isn't your ordinary basket loads of mound fill - it's clean white sand. It looks like the mound has been capped or closed with a white sand layer. This could definitely help our case." Standing up, she reached down to give Josh a hand getting out of the pothole and suggested they call it a day.

When they got back to the crew house the party was well underway. Music blared from the open windows and most of the crew were arrayed along the veranda, watching a hotly contested croquet match and easing into the weekend. Tom was puffing on a fatty and passing it around, and Pabst seemed to be the brew of the day, judging from the dead soldiers lined up on the porch railing. Boss Man was well in the bag by now, having been drinking steadily for a good part of the day. He sat next to Dolores on one of the porch gliders and was trying to tell one of his particularly offensive racist Rastus and Liza jokes. As Josh and Denny came up the porch steps, he broke off to greet them. "Look at you two, all filthy from digging that pothole. What a waste of time. That's now all finished Denny, I want you two down working on the southeast house cluster on Monday with the rest of the crew."

Sitting next to him on the glider, Dolores offered a sweet smile, her hands folded demurely on her lap. She was practically squirming with pleasure. Denny was about to tell Boss Man about the intact stratigraphy and burned clay layer they had discovered, but knowing what a nasty drunk he could be, decided instead to not push their luck, and instead to buy some time.

"Monday it is, Boss Man, but we're gonna keep digging over the weekend — see what we can find. Maybe something will turn up."

Dolores's frown indicated that she had heard Denny announce her plans to work through the weekend, but based on his reply, it wasn't clear Boss Man had fully comprehended what she had said. "You're fuckin right about that Denny. I'm calling the shots here."

Realizing that their plan to work through the weekend had not registered with Boss Man, Denny and Josh hurried into the house. Boss Man and Nancy would be heading up into the Ozarks in the morning to spend the weekend with his clan, giving them the next two days to dig the mound summit.

6.
SPARKLE PLENTY

It was still dark out the next morning when Denny crept up to the top of the attic stairs and woke Josh with a loud whisper. Still groggy with sleep, Josh dressed as Denny enjoyed the show. Following her back down the stairs, he ducked into the bathroom where he took a leak and then quickly brushed his teeth and threw some water on his face. The two then snuck out the front door, leaving the rest of the crew still sound asleep after last night's cosmogram celebration. It was a beautiful morning, with the eastern horizon beginning to brighten, a clear sky, and a slight breeze. On their way out to the site they stopped at the small store at the crossroads by the trailer park for weak coffee and stale donuts, along with a small bag of ice for their water jug. Josh grabbed some jerky sticks and energy bars for snacks they could snarf down as they dug. Their plan was to work straight through till three or so that afternoon, then knock off for the day, avoiding the intense heat of the late afternoon. They rode in companionable silence the rest of the way out to Hamblin's Fort, feeling like they were somehow both playing hooky while also demonstrating a virtuous work ethic. It felt good.

Grabbing shovels and trowels, along with their water jug and snacks, Josh and Denny had started up the side of the temple mound when Denny suddenly stopped, causing Josh to stumble into her and grab her arm for support. He held on as she turned with her finger on her lips and then pointed over toward the conical mound on the west side of the central plaza. Someone was sitting cross-legged at the very top of the mound, facing the rising sun. The seated figure was a radiant, shimmering white, and seemed to float above the mound.

Josh quietly backed down the side of the temple mound and walked closer to the conical mound for a better look. The sitting figure remained still as Josh stared briefly and then turned and climbed back to the temple mound summit where Denny waited. "It's Cecelia. She's totally zoned out. I don't think she even knows we're here."

Denny nodded. "I thought it might be her. She disappears sometimes, usually at night, and won't be in her tent in the mornings when we head out to Hamblin's Fort. We'll often find her waiting for us at the site, having walked over in the dark. Other times she'll show up on foot at some point during the day. Some days she decides to just hang loose and stays back at the crew house all day."

"What's the deal with that?" Josh asked.

"Oh, Cecelia gets to do whatever she wants," Denny replied. "Her dad is a close friend of the museum director and a huge donor. They live just off campus, up Geddes by the arboretum. Cecelia and her dad are really close, particularly since her mom died a few years ago. He completely supports her search of self-discovery. The man dotes on her. She was here last summer and liked it well enough to return."

"What does she do?" Josh asked.

Denny laughed. "Oh, she's not really part of the crew. Cecelia likes to come out to the site and dig with us most days, but she doesn't have to. She doesn't have to do anything. Cecelia just is."

Far from being totally zoned out, as Josh had thought, Cecelia was intensely present, completely involved in the world around her. She could feel the grass caressing her legs, the heat of the rising sun on her face, the buzzing of insects and the distant sound of farm machinery. She had seen Black Dog climb the side of the temple mound in the dim light before dawn, where it slipped down into the open excavation unit, only to appear again a few minutes later and limp off. Later she watched Denny and Josh arrive and could hear the low murmur of their conversation from across the plaza. So far, Denny and Josh had not intruded too far into Cecelia's quiet meditation, and she hoped they would respect her solitude and simply go about their business. Cecelia was in general somewhat detached from the everyday flow of life. Raised rich in Bloomfield Hills, outside Detroit, she had attended the exclusive Kingswood School, then went on to Wellesley College, majoring in dance.

With a lithe and well-toned body, Cecelia was transformed when she moved, and at numerous times during the day when the mood struck her, she would express herself through dance. It was Cecelia's way of communing with the world around her, connecting with life. The crew welcomed these spontaneous outbursts and would pause during their digging to watch her move gracefully across the expanding "skim surface" area at Hamblin's Fort where the plow zone had been stripped, or gather on the veranda back at the crew house to enjoy her cocktail hour croquet court performances.

Cecelia was also into what she called "full body freedom," and would have gone buck naked through life if permitted. This wasn't possible in most situations, of course, but here at the Hamblin Mansion and at the site she had discovered a clothing solution that she could tolerate, while also satisfying minimum standards of decency. Her summer wardrobe consisted of a variety of many layered diaphanous dresses that drifted around her, floating weightlessly on the slightest breeze. Some were more see-through than others, but that was of no import to Cecelia. She didn't see her dances as sexual or provocative, but rather as homage to the beauty to be found around her, to the unseen energy that shapes our lives, to life, to living.

Needless to say, not everyone viewed her dances in the same way that she did, and the site started to attract a few locals who would pull up in their pickup trucks, hoping to catch one of her performances and maybe witness a wardrobe malfunction. Cecelia was particularly popular with the county sheriff, who would stop by the crew house to do a weed deal with Tom and then hang around on the veranda chatting with Cecelia. The sheriff wasn't alone in hoping he could end up in bed with Cecelia, but she made it crystal clear that she wasn't interested in sex or romance with the sheriff or anyone on the crew.

She did tolerate Tom, who last summer had started a campaign of sustained casual courtship. His frequent visits to her tent in the evenings, however, had not proven romantically successful, so far. But somewhat surprisingly they had developed a close friendship and now would often share a joint and talk late into the night about whatever came to mind.

The sheriff's interest in Cecelia provided her some measure of protection from harassment by locals, which was good, given her propensity for walkabouts in the dead of night. The men on the crew also took heed of the sheriff's protective feelings as well as Tom's affection toward Cecelia and adjusted as best they could to the daily proximity of her totally naked body hidden by only a few gossamer layers of fabric.

Cecelia's life had taken a dramatic turn in the spring of her junior year at Wellesley, when she was down in Boston for the weekend with friends and had been talked into going to a lecture on self-enlightenment by some professor named Timothy Leary. Totally captivated by the charismatic Leary, Cecelia soon followed his advice — "Tune in, turn on, drop out," and left Wellesley for Taos, New Mexico and a commune experience that promised magic mushrooms, LSD, and altered consciousness. The commune is where she picked up the name "Sparkle Plenty," after the Dick Tracy character, along with several STDs and a pesky sinus infection. Cecelia left after six months, disillusioned with the drugs and increasingly febrile pontifications from commune leaders. Still looking for answers, she moved on to Chaco Canyon.

During her weeks at Chaco, camping out and wandering the desolate and long abandoned great houses and silent cliffs, Cecelia began to seriously consider the possibility of the existence of spiritual force centers, what later would be popularly labeled as "energy vortexes" — locations where powerful currents of energy were either flowing into or welling upward from mother earth. Around a Chaco campfire on her last night in the canyon, Cecelia toked on a circulating fatty and listened to fellow pilgrims talk about their experiences at other spiritual energy points that had been discovered and colonized by the ancients. Gazing at the burning embers rising up into the night sky, she decided to embark on her own grand tour.

Soon after Chaco, and with the indulgent support of her father, Cecelia embarked on a spirit quest of sorts — visiting a number of the energy vortexes of long-lost civilizations that she thought looked promising — Stone Henge, Machu Picchu, the pyramids at Giza, Angkor Wat, and finally, Cahokia. With the exception of Cahokia, none of these energy vortexes seemed particularly impressive to Cecelia in terms of furthering her spiritual growth and enlightenment. They were overdone, she thought, pandering to tourists, too commercial. In contrast, she thought she felt a strong burst of positive energy flowing up through her when she climbed to the top of Monks Mound at Cahokia, and she later experienced a powerful feeling of loss and sadness as she walked along a small ridge-shaped mound to the south of Monk's Mound, where archaeologists would soon uncover evidence of mass sacrificial burials.

It was something about the earth, she thought, how it had been moved and shaped to form the mounds at Cahokia and similar sites across the eastern woodlands of North America, basket-load by basket-load, that captured, held, and focused the energy flow upward, empowering those who stood on their summit. It made perfect sense, Cecelia concluded, that the next chapter in her continued search for enlightenment should focus on sites similar to Cahokia but less prominent, less exposed, less exploited and weakened. Well aware of her dad's friendship with the director of the archaeology museum at the local university, Cecelia had asked him in the spring last year if there might be any projects planned on archaeological sites that were similar to Cahokia, and if so, could she tag along. Hamblin's Fort was mentioned, and after reading the project grant proposal, she thought it sounded like a perfect fit.

Eager to learn as much as she could before joining the Hamblin's Fort project last year, Cecelia had spent several hectic weeks surveying an eclectic mix of literature on spiritual power sources and self-enlightenment. Browsing in a used bookstore shortly before leaving for the dig she had stumbled upon a copy of the influential book *The Third Eye,* by the Tibetan monk Lobsang Rampa. After absorbing its wisdom, and with the help of her carefully curated stash of dried peyote buttons, which were kept hidden in a Prince Albert tobacco tin buried under her tent, Cecelia had also invested considerable energy last summer toward nurturing her budding ability to discern the size, color, and vibration patterns of the auras generated by her fellow crew members. So far, however, she had not progressed the way she had hoped. After all this time, Cecelia still only rarely thought she could discern auras around people or events, and then only at night in the midst of a mescaline haze.

In contrast, by the end of last summer's initial field season Cecelia was convinced that Hamblin's Fort was the location of a powerful energy vortex. She could sense both a constant general upwelling of energy all across the site, as well as a much stronger, more powerful stream of energy enveloping and flowing upward from the temple mound. They had only excavated two small structures along the palisade wall in the habitation area of the site the previous summer, and Cecelia had been eager to come back for a second season so she could be present if they opened up the temple mound. She had hoped to experience the vortex more fully and more intimately. Now it looked like she might get that chance.

Rising from her silent contemplation of the sunrise, Cecelia descended the side of the conical mound, crossed the plaza, and climbed up to where Denny and Josh were sitting on the backfill dirt pile. Denny was filling out vertical profile forms for their now nicely cleaned up and perfectly square 5x5 excavation unit, and Josh was deep into a Fabulous Furry Freak Brothers comic he had found in the truck during the ride out to the site. They both looked up as she approached them.

Smiling when she saw the red clay feature they had uncovered, Cecelia hopped gracefully down into their 5x5. Staring directly at them with a somewhat crazed expression, she raised the hem of her ankle-length gossamer frock and spread it out around her, covering the opening to the 5x5. It was a strange sight, the top half of her body extending up from the surface of the mound, out of the center of a diaphanous dress that encircled her and shimmered in the morning sun.

"Can you feel it?" Cecelia asked in a dreamy voice, trembling slightly, seemingly in the grip of a powerful electric current, or maybe a psychic break. Denny and Josh both shook their heads, frozen in place.

Moving her hands, palms down, slowly across the folds of her dress, Cecelia asked another question. "My dress looks reddish, don't you think? Not a lot, but some. It's a murky, darkish red aura, faint but clear, flowing up from deep in the red core of the mound and infusing my dress. I'm calling this tumulus 'Red Mound' because of its sinister upwelling aura."

Denny and Josh could only smile and exchange wide-eyed glances as Cecelia climbed out of the 5x5 and without further comment skipped lightly down the sloping side of the mound. She stopped and turned about halfway down, however, and delivered a sober and cryptic warning of sorts.

"You need to keep digging the mound. Open up the vortex. I can help. But be careful. Red is good — it's the color of the root chakra — how our bodies connect to the physical realm around us. It indicates joy of life, embracing physical pleasures, adventures, and experiences. But the murkiness, the darker shade I see here suggests associated risks, and the real likelihood of ongoing frustration and difficulty. Digging into the Red Mound may flood your essence with joy, with worldly pleasure, but the murkiness suggests unknown danger."

"Sign me up for some worldly pleasures," Josh joked as Cecelia walked out of earshot.

All business, Denny replied. "Yeah yeah, blah blah. Let's lay out a line of squares over to the south edge of the mound and then down the side — stake out our claim for Boss Man to see on Monday."

It didn't take them long to measure and stake out a line of squares across the flat summit of the mound. Then it was time to decide how far to push their luck. Boss Man was more than likely going to shut them down on Monday, and while staking out an excavation trench was not a big deal, as it easily could be reversed, expanding their excavation without his express go-ahead was clearly going to piss him off big time.

But so far, their tidying up of the pothole had yielded only a burned clay feature overlain by two feet or so of clean white sand that appeared to cap the mound — probably not enough of to make the case for continuing the excavation of the temple mound. To Josh, the answer to their dilemma was obvious.

"We got nada right now Denny. You may as well fold up your tent and get ready to work for Dolores. Unless we come up with something more, our mound digging is done. We won't ever get down to the root chakra. But if we open up more squares maybe we can make a case for continuing. And if we don't find anything, so what. We won't be any worse off. I really don't care if Boss Man gets bent out of shape."

Picking up one of the shovels, Josh started in on removing the sod from the next square to the south of the one they had just finished profiling. Denny watched him for a bit, then picked up the other shovel and started in on the square next to Josh's along their southward extending trench line. Fueled by beef jerky and energy bars they had, by three o'clock, slowly troweled away the top foot or so of clean white sand from their 5x10 extension of the original 5x5 square. Now they had a 5x15 opening into the mound. So far, they had come up empty again. The light-colored sandy soil was undisturbed by pot hunters but devoid of any artifacts or any features — pits, post holes, or hearths, for example, or artifact concentrations. It appeared to be clean fill brought in from the sandbars of the Mississippi River that had once flowed much closer to the site.

They were about to call it quits for the day when Denny's trowel stroke exposed an area of dark red speckles. Reaching over to poke Josh, she pointed at the freshly uncovered reddish smear on the floor of her square. The original 5x5 hadn't shown any red soil inclusions at this depth, which was a good foot shallower than the burned clay area they had exposed earlier. They knew they were coming down on a feature of some sort — most likely a pit. They probably should have waited for Monday, and Boss Man's oversight, before going any further, but who could blame them for continuing. Denny and Josh both agreed, after a brief but quite serious back and forth, that it was imperative that they fully uncover and assess whatever was there in case it needed to be removed before returning pothunters could potentially make off with its contents. They both might have also recognized, not so deep down, that if Boss Man was present for the discovery, then he could well consider the discovery to be his. But if they uncovered whatever might be there right now, today, then it was their discovery, not his. And after all, he didn't want them digging here in the first place.

It took about a half hour of careful scraping to expose an oval pit feature having a fill of soil that looked a little greasy and was packed with small flakes of red ocher. It was maybe four feet by two and a half feet in size, and mostly contained within their new 5x10 excavation unit, with one end disappearing into a sidewall. Denny guessed that red ocher flakes had been mixed in with the pit fill, an unusual feature for temple mounds, but a pretty common indicator of a ceremonial deposit of some sort, perhaps a burial. Josh was all for pressing ahead with excavation of the pit feature, but Denny decided against further investigation of a temple mound summit ceremonial feature on their own, without a clear green light. Better to just partially backfill their trench, then cover it with a tarp, and let Boss Man know what they had found on Monday. The discovery was still theirs, and with some luck they could avoid any negative backlash for their Saturday exploratory digging.

7.
CHUCK AND LISA

Nancy woke up on that Saturday morning with an impressive hangover from the Cosmogram celebration of the night before. She decided even before getting out of bed that there was no way she was going to spend the weekend in the Ozarks with her husband and his folks. She had overheard Dolores talking with Wilma and Paula at last night's party about maybe spending today visiting the ongoing excavation at the Chucalissa temple mound site in Memphis and then enjoying the live music and nightlife scene downtown. Dancing to live music and getting hammered sounded much better than shelling peas and hearing again from Boss Man's relatives about all the recent trouble the blacks were causing with their escalating demands and demonstrations for civil rights.

Greatly cheered by her decision to blow off the weekend with the in-laws, Nancy showered and threw on a favorite tie-dyed T-shirt and some faded shorts and sandals. When Boss Man saw her outfit, he was not amused. "You can't go to my folk's wearing that."

"Right on, genius. Guess what? I'm not going with you. Drop me off at thecrew house. We're headed up to Memphis to see Chuck and Lisa and hit the music scene."

There was stony silence in the truck on the drive down to the crew house. Nancy made sure to slam the truck's door as she got out. Boss Man responded by shooting gravel across the yard as he popped the clutch and sped off to the Ozarks.

Zack and Richard observed the kerfuffle from the crew house veranda with considerable interest — they always enjoyed the squabbles between Boss Man and Nancy, which seemed to be growing more frequent and more entertaining. Zack cackled and announced in a loud voice. "Oh, my goodness. It looks like trouble in paradise."

Sitting next to Zack, Richard had his Australian outback hat — part of his archaeologist getup, pushed back on his head, and laughed along with Zack at his clever remark. Nancy ignored them as she climbed the porch steps, opened the front door, and went looking for Dolores. She found her sitting at the kitchen table with a cup of coffee, admiring her Ramey cosmogram sherd as she carefully placed it in a cotton filled box. Dolores looked up in surprise. "Nancy. What are you doing here? Aren't you visiting the in-laws?"

"Changed my mind. I'm going up to Memphis with you guys. What are you doing with your precious pot sherd?" Nancy replied, pointing at the Ramey rim sherd.

Dolores quickly closed the box and replied without looking up. "Oh this? Thought I would take it up to Chuck and Lisa and see what George Miller has to say about it — he's digging up there this summer."

Nancy squinted in suspicion. "Does Boss Man knows about this?"

"Sure," Dolores replied, "I told him last night."

"You mean when he was fall-down drunk?"

Dolores said nothing, just sipped her coffee in silence. She hadn't, in fact, mentioned her plan to Boss Man, but knew it didn't make any difference since he wouldn't have remembered one way or the other. She knew he would say no if she had asked, but she just had to show her find to someone who had seen a lot of Ramey sherds. George Miller was her man. He could tell her whether her sherd was from a true cosmogram vessel, made at Cahokia and then carried down to Hamblin's Fort, or if it was a locally made imitation — a faux cosmogram — still interesting and important, but not the same as a genuine Cahokia creation. And just as importantly, George Miller talked to a lot of people. Word would spread quickly that she had found a Ramey cosmogram at Hamblin's Fort. That would be big news, and Dolores wanted to make sure it was her big news, and that her name was associated with the find.

They made good time on the drive up to Memphis, with Tom and Nancy up front and the other crew filling the two rear seats of the Travelall. The Chucalissa site was crowded with tourists when they arrived, with only a small crew digging a few squares for the benefit of the curious onlookers. Dolores hurried over to where she saw George Miller standing in the shade waiting for her, and they then headed for the small museum at the site. There they would lovingly fondle the cosmogram sherd, talk temper, paste, and design elements, and discuss its origin — local or Cahokian.

The other crew members scattered. While most headed for the air-conditioned gift shop, Nancy wandered over to see what the small excavation was all about. It had attracted a small crowd, and when Nancy joined them, her curiosity increased. Whatever was going on, it was a mystery to her. A rectangular wall trench house measuring maybe fifteen feet on a side had been uncovered and a portion of the burned floor area adjacent to its central hearth had been carefully cut away, leaving a small still-intact pedestal of compacted burned clay. As Nancy watched, a man kneeling next to the pedestal extracted a small open-ended rectangular metal box or tube of what looked like aluminum from his toolbox and carefully lowered it down around the shaft of burned soil. He then slowly poured an already mixed cup of liquid plaster into the aluminum box, completely filling the space around the enclosed soil pedestal. As the plaster hardened, he oriented the open-ended aluminum square to magnetic north using a fancy looking compass attachment. Satisfied with his effort, the excavator visibly relaxed and sat back on his heels, looking up at the crowd of tourists close around him as he waited for the plaster to harden.

Nancy recognized him immediately and stood frozen in place, hoping he would not notice her. But he did. Standing up and stretching languidly, he smiled broadly and walked over to her. "Nancy. It's been a long time. How are you doing?"

Momentarily at a loss for words, Nancy replied in a subdued voice. "I'm doing OK, I guess, Matt. How about you?"

"Me too — I'm good," Matt replied, with a concerned look. "You look like you need cheering up. Just let me finish here and we can grab some lunch and get caught up."

Twenty minutes later they were on their way to the Peabody Hotel, where Matt had a room. He was so going to take a quick shower and change before they headed over to Corky's BBQ for lunch. They never made it to Corky's. Instead, they spent the afternoon in bed getting reacquainted. Matt and Nancy had been almost inseparable for more than a year when they were undergraduates and Nancy had figured they would get married right after graduation. She thought they had reached the mind-meld stage and would spend the rest of their lives together. But Matt was a year ahead of Nancy in the archaeology program and as his graduation approached, he became more and more reticent regarding their future together. Their final break-up was a sad, teary event, and Nancy never really bounced back afterward. Marrying Boss Man on the rebound was a mistake, she knew, and it was a whopper. But it never would have happened if Matt hadn't abandoned her. He said he wasn't ready for marriage. He told her he needed to find himself, decide what he wanted to do with his life. He was going to take a gap year to figure things out he said, and walked out of her life. But now he was back, and it seemed that their mind-meld was still intact.

Their sex life had always been good, and now, reunited in the Peabody Hotel, their lovemaking seemed to reach an entirely new level of intensity and intimacy. Maybe it was because Matt couldn't stop saying what a fool he'd been, and how he didn't want to lose her again. Pressing up against Matt in bed, Nancy talked about her miserable marriage, how she was desperate to escape, and how she had never given up the dream of sharing her life with him.

Later, after they dozed for a while in each other's arms, Matt talked about what he had been up to since he graduated. He had bounced around for almost a year before deciding to go to grad school out East and pick back up on his interest in developing a new way of establishing the age of archaeological sites. A few researchers at Oklahoma State and other universities had been toying with a way of using the changing location of the earth's magnetic poles over time to date burned clay deposits in archaeological sites. When such deposits were heated, it turns out, the magnetic minerals in the clay lined up with the earth's magnetic field and pointed to the location of the magnetic pole at the time. The little open-ended aluminum box filled with plaster that he had placed around the clay pedestal at the Chucalissa site captured the orientation that the magnetic minerals in the clay took when it was last heated, centuries ago, while the cube itself was precisely oriented to the current location of the magnetic north pole. Back in the lab, by comparing the two pole locations, the approximate age of the burned deposit could be determined. It would never be as accurate as radiocarbon dating, but the amount of charcoal or other organic material needed for carbon 14 dates was not always present in archaeological sites. In such cases, the new dating method would be very valuable. Armed with lots of the open-end aluminum boxes and a big bag of plaster of Paris, Matt was now crisscrossing the Southeast looking for Mississippian sites with burned clay deposits that he could sample for his dissertation research. So far, he had collected samples from more than a dozen sites.

Nancy was only half listening to Matt's account of his research project, but quickly tuned in when she realized that Hamblin's Fort had a number of burned clay features. Matt should come down and take some samples, while also, she hoped, scooping her up and riding away on his white horse. She suggested he visit Hamblin's Fort, and Matt thought it was a great idea. His enthusiastic agreement with her idea was influenced to a considerable extent by the activity of Nancy's right hand under the sheets.

While Nancy and Matt were spending the afternoon in bed up in Memphis, Denny and Josh had been digging in the hot sun. When they got back to the crew house late Saturday afternoon they were tired, filthy, and quietly ecstatic with their discovery of an apparent ritual pit on the summit of the Red Mound. The Hamblin Mansion was almost empty. The rest of the crew was not back from Memphis yet, and probably wouldn't be till quite late, but Cecelia was there.

She was sitting on the veranda swing with a small wiry man who was wearing mirror sunglasses, a sweat-stained cowboy hat, a faded blue pearl-button snap shirt, and a holstered revolver on his hip. Denny cautioned Josh before they got out of the truck. "That's Sheriff Hogg. It's a big family in these parts. Lotta local Hoggs. Don't fuck with the man Josh. Seriously. Best to stay off his radar and on his good side. He's going to decide in the next minute or two if he likes you or not. So don't comment on his name and don't be a smart ass. Paste a dumb smile on your face, give him a little 'yes sir, no sir,' and shuffle your feet a bit. He'll know it's an act but will appreciate the kowtow and will promptly forget about you."

Sheriff Hogg was in his mid-sixties, with the leathery skin and slow movements that reminded Josh of a lizard. He smiled broadly as Denny and Josh climbed the steps to the veranda, exposing stained and crooked teeth. He waved them both over to the wicker chairs by the swing where he sat rocking with Cecelia.

Taking off his sunglasses and staring at Josh intently with close-set piggy eyes, the sheriff handed Josh a beat-up envelope, then spoke in the raspy, phlegmy voice of a life-long pack a day man. "Found this on the floor right under where I'm sitting. It's addressed to you, Josh, from your university, and looks like it has been here a while, judging from the footprints on it. Cecelia thinks it probably fell out of Boss Man's pocket. He was pretty hammered last night."

Josh gave a quick, puzzled thanks and stuffed the still unopened mystery letter in his back pocket for reading later.

The sheriff smiled again. "How do you like it down here Josh?"

Putting on what he hoped was a sincere expression, Josh nodded enthusiastically. "I like it a lot, Sheriff Hogg. It's quiet. I like the crew and the project. It's going to be a good summer, I think, sir."

Hogg put his head back and roared with laughter, easily seeing through Josh's little act.

"Good answer there Josh. I think we're going to get along fine. You like weed?"

Josh wasn't sure what the right answer was, and Cecelia chimed in. "Josh is a big-time stoner, Harry. Should be a good customer."

Josh nodded vigorously, working hard to keep a smile off his face, knowing that Harry Hogg, the sheriff, and the cannabis source for the crew, was watching him closely for any reaction to hearing his full name — Harry Hogg.

Satisfied that Josh didn't appear to find his name amusing, Harry put his arm around Cecelia's shoulder and continued. "Cecelia was just telling me that you've discovered an energy vortex in the mound out at the Hamblin place where some treasure hunters dug a pothole. She tells me that there's some powerful, maybe dangerous, crimson currents coming out of the mound. Sounds exciting."

Turning serious, the sheriff continued. "I also been hearing from some other folks that you might have discovered something valuable out there — something mysterious and hush-hush. That's why I stopped by. Cecelia says it's just a broken piece of pottery. Once these rumors start it's good to shut them down fast, before you start getting a lot more night-time digging out there."

Thinking of the mystery pit waiting to be excavated, Denny looked at the sheriff with an anxious expression. "What do you think we should we do, sheriff?"

"Well, Cecelia and I talked it over, and it sounds like the best thing would be to let some of the most interested locals visit the site and see what you are doing, maybe show them the piece of pottery that's caused the stir. They won't be interested in a broken pot. They like fancy whole pots and other finery — the stuff usually put in with burials. Let them see what you're finding and how boring your work is, and they will soon lose interest."

The sheriff checked his watch, decided he had to head out, and gave Cecelia a gentle peck on the cheek as he got up from the swing. Turning as he walked over to his car, a ten-year-old Chevy Bel Air with a blue bubble gum light duct-taped on the roof, he called back. "Don't forget to tell Tom that I got some excellent product for him."

After the sheriff drove off, waving out the window of his car, Cecelia waggled her bare legs on the swing and answered the question Josh hadn't asked. "No, I don't fuck the sheriff. That peck on the cheek is all he ever gets, which is pretty much OK with him. He mostly just wants his buddies to think he's getting it on with me. But I have to be careful — he can get nasty quick if he thinks he's being laughed at." She paused then, rearranging her diaphanous dress on the swing, and asked Josh about the envelope.

Josh pulled out the crumpled envelope, which looked like it had been walked on a good bit and tore it open. As he read the enclosed letter, Josh looked more and more puzzled and handed it to Denny with a question. "Is this some sort of joke?"

Denny read it and then, with an excited fist pump, explained. "No joke, dude. It's a form letter from the university — boilerplate signed by the director of the museum. You must have impressed him in the archaeology class last fall. You, my man, have been anointed from on high. You've been awarded an undergraduate research grant. It's only five hundred bucks for supplies or whatever. But the important thing is it gives you the opportunity to pursue your own research project this summer, as long as it doesn't get in the way of other ongoing research efforts."

Josh stayed silent for a while, and then with a slight grin, looked at Denny, put his hand on his cheek, and asked. "I can't quite decide what kind of project I should undertake this summer. I was thinking maybe some excavations on the temple mound, Cecelia's Red Mound…. What do you think Denny?"

Denny stared back at him with a blank expression. "That's all up to you Josh. It's your decision. I sure as hell won't tell you what you should do. But Boss Man probably wouldn't approve you digging the temple mound anyway. You don't have the experience."

Josh responded. "Maybe if I had someone working with me that knew what she was doing."

Denny shook her head wistfully. "Boss Man and Dolores will make sure that never happens."

Observing the interchange, Cecelia thought to herself. "I'll mention it to daddy, I bet he can pull some strings."

8.
THE MAN WITH A MULLET

Denny woke early on Sunday morning, worried about the possibility that pothunters had dug into the Red Mound at Hamblin's Fort overnight. She had slept fitfully after being roused by Dolores, back from Memphis, who stumbled into their bedroom in the dark sometime after midnight. Creeping downstairs in the early morning light, Denny was surprised to see Nancy sleeping on the couch in the living room. She was supposed to be up in the Ozarks with Boss Man. Grabbing the keys for the Travelall from the hook in the kitchen, Denny slipped quietly out the back door, anxious to check on her temple mound excavation.

Everything seemed quiet at Hamblin's Fort when Denny arrived. She wasn't that surprised to see Cecelia once again enthroned and motionless in a lotus position on the summit of the conical mound, but the sight of Black Dog on top of the temple mound froze her in her tracks. The dog was lying down on the back dirt pile adjacent to their trench, right next to the location of the red ocher pit. Its front legs were casually crossed in front of it, and its head was up, ears cocked, gazing directly at her. It continued to calmly watch her, seemingly unconcerned, as she climbed the side of the mound and approached it.

As she slowly moved closer Black Dog stood up, wagged its tail a few times, sniffed her hand, and lay down again. It was an old male dog, Denny noticed, weighing maybe seventy pounds, with sad eyes, a graying muzzle, and arthritic hips. Noticing that Black Dog had been lying next to where they had discovered the red ochre pit feature the day before, Denny wondered if he had been there all night, keeping watch. Black Dog had in fact been guarding the mound all night and had scared off the pothunter, who returned, as Denny had feared, eager to continue his search for confederate gold in the mound. He had beaten a hasty retreat, however, when confronted by a black snarling beast.

Satisfied that the Red Mound was undisturbed, Denny headed back to the crew house. She found Nancy awake now, sitting at the kitchen table with Tom and Dolores. All three were nursing coffee and hangovers. Tom was unusually quiet, brooding over having missed out on the sheriff's visit yesterday and a chance of scoring some fresh weed. Nancy and Dolores were both uncharacteristically upbeat — Nancy because she was secretly celebrating having reconnected with the love of her life, and Dolores because of the Nancy and Boss Man upheaval and the good news that she had received from George Miller — her Ramey incised sherd had definitely been made at Cahokia. It was a genuine Cahokia cosmogram. Dolores thought her personal and professional lives were looking up on this Sunday morning.

Denny was also in a great mood — excited about the discoveries she and Josh had made the day before — the burned clay feature and the red ocher pit. She described what they had found, and also mentioned the undergraduate research grant that Josh had been awarded. When she had finished, Nancy looked pleased and Dolores went ballistic.

"There's no fuckin way that frat boy fuck gets to fuck around in the fuckin temple mound. He's digging for me. Wait till I tell Boss Man about this." Abruptly standing, knocking her chair back, Dolores stormed out of the kitchen.

Nancy stood as soon as Dolores left and with an unexpected warmth asked Denny if she'd like a cup of coffee. After placing a mug of fresh brew in front of Denny, Nancy slipped Matt's card across the table to her. "We bumped into this guy up in Memphis," Nancy began. "He's got some amazing new way to establish how old burned clay deposits are. Maybe he could get some dates for your burned clay feature on the mound. You think we should call him and see if he'll drop down and take some samples?"

Tom grabbed the card. "I've heard about this new archaeomagnetism dating method. Far out. Let's call him up and get him down here."

Denny looked skeptical. "Shouldn't that be Boss Man's call?"

"Naw," Tom replied, oblivious. "It's a no brainer. Boss Man will be thrilled. It's something for nothing and it puts us on the cutting edge of new technology, the New Archaeology. And you can never have enough dates." Tom walked over to the wall phone and dialed the Peabody Hotel phone number that Matt had scribbled on the card. Nancy was almost squirming with pleasure. She hadn't thought it would be quite this easy. Matt picked right up when the front desk called his room, and after a short conversation, Tom ended the call. "My man Matt will be crusin on down tomorrow or the next day, see what kind of burned clay features we have, and sample them if we're interested."

Later that afternoon, the Sunday croquet game was well underway when Boss Man pulled into the driveway, back from the Ozarks. Zack had just driven Paula's croquet ball deep into the vegetable garden, egged on by encouragement from Tom and Nancy, who were watching from the porch swing, calling out — "Okra. Okra."

When he reached the veranda Boss Man paused briefly to glare at Nancy, who silently stared back with a blank expression.

Tom broke the awkward silence. "Hey, Boss Man, up in Memphis we ran into a guy who's lookin for Mississippian sites with burned clay features that he can sample for archaeomag dates. I called him up and he's comin down tomorrow or the next day to check out Hamblin's Fort. Cool, right?"

Tom's report barely seemed to register with Boss Man, who appeared out of focus and agitated. He turned and walked in the front door without replying. Finding Dolores on the back porch, Boss Man unloaded. "I got a phone call from our dissertation advisor Professor Shetler this morning at my folk's place. He said he'd heard that you'd found a Ramey incised sherd here at Hamblin's, and that George Miller has confirmed it's from Cahokia. What the fuck, Dolores. How about including me in your announcements to the world."

Dolores tried to respond, to explain, but Boss Man interrupted. "Shetler also said he was excited about the red clay feature Josh and Denny uncovered, and that he thinks Josh's undergrad research award is a perfect fit for excavating the temple mound. It seems the administration is looking for some high visibility projects to raise the profile of the undergraduate experience at the university, and excavation of a temple mound sounds perfect. What the fuck? My bitch of a wife blows me off, a couple of undergrads are digging whatever they want on my excavation, a hippy shovel bum is inviting people to come date my site, and you, Dolores, are blabbing to the world about your big discovery."

Taking a closer look at Boss Man, Dolores noticed with growing concern that he had been drinking, and was uncharacteristically unkempt. Usually clean-shaven and decked out in crisply creased khakis, Boss Man was sporting a two-day stubble and was wearing the same clothes he had on when he left for the Ozarks on Saturday morning. There were food stains on the front of his shirt.

Fearing a male ego meltdown, Dolores jumped up and after closing the kitchen door she hurried to embrace Boss Man. Ignoring his strong body odor, she whispered soothingly in his ear. "It's OK. It's OK. Hamblin's Fort is your site, right? Your excavation, right? Let them dig the temple mound. Whatever they find, it's your site, your discovery. And if we can get archaeomag dates from Hamblin's Fort it will be a big feather in your cap. And what about the Cahokia connection, along with our courtyard excavations — it's going to make a big splash. Let's just focus on our research, and this other stuff will work out fine." Dolores was tempted to also point out how Boss Man would be much better off if he dumped Nancy but figured that the marriage looked to be imploding quite nicely without any further help from her. She did, however, make sure to caress his neck as she moved away from him.

Out front, Paula was still looking for her croquet ball in among the okra. She had in fact already located her ball but was pretending that it was still lost. She was going to keep looking for a few more minutes, then quit playing the game. She hadn't wanted to play in the first place but had been afraid to say no when Zack challenged her. He had been acting sorta weird lately, flirty toward her with aggressive overtones, and teasing her about the nature of her relationship with Wilma. Tomorrow, early, she would be driving up to Kansas City for a week-long visit, and while she would miss Wilma, Paula was looking forward to getting away from Zack. He was definitely creeping her out.

Heads turned as a rusty pickup with a loud exhaust came up over the rise and slowly approached the house. At first Tom thought it was the sheriff, who said he would drop off some weed this afternoon after church. It wasn't the sheriff. Several ditch hounds were riding in the bed of the truck. It was hard to see the driver, but the man riding shotgun was massive, with a mullet haircut, a stars and bars tattoo on his upper arm, and a graying beard. His right arm hung out the passenger side window and he had a large automatic pistol dangling in his hand.

The car paused in front of the house. Paula slowly dropped down into the shelter of the okra. Cecelia crouched, and Zack stood slack jawed as the two men in the car appeared to exchange a few words. The man riding shotgun gestured toward Boss Man's truck with his pistol, and they drove closer to it before coming to a stop at the end of the driveway. The man with the mullet lazily raised the pistol and pumped two rounds into the tailgate of Boss Man's truck. Then they drove off. The croquet players hustled up on the porch as the rest of the crew piled out of the house to find out what was up.

The sheriff arrived maybe a half an hour later. After handing Tom a paper bag that reeked of weed, Hogg sat across from Tom and Nancy on the porch swing and offered an explanation for the earlier shooting of Boss Man's truck, along with a warning.

"That was Cletus who popped a few into Boss Man's truck. He waved me down this morning by the K Mart in Forrest City and said somebody in a truck that looked a lot like Boss Man's was driving around taking potshots at any dogs running loose. You don't want to be doing that. Shoot somebody's dog around here and there's gonna be trouble. Serious trouble. Cletus was just making that point." Taking the opportunity to pat Nancy's leg before getting up from the swing, the sheriff turned to her. "I have to go find your husband Nancy, offer him some good advice. But I have to say, you are looking radiant today, positively glowing."

Nancy smiled in agreement. She did feel radiant. She pointed toward the kitchen. "He's in there."

Standing with Dolores in the kitchen, Boss Man denied he had been taking potshots at dogs, but Hogg knew he was lying, and Boss Man didn't care. It had felt good when the gun recoiled in his hand and the dogs scampered away in fear. He might do it again, he thought. But it was Black Dog he was really gunning for. The weight of the revolver in his fanny pack felt good, made him feel powerful.

After repeating his warning about shooting at strays, the sheriff bluntly suggested Boss Man ought to go home, get cleaned up, and get his shit together. Still in an alcoholic daze, Boss Man decided that was good advice, and as he passed Nancy on the porch he told her to get in the truck, they were going back to Forrest City.

Nancy didn't move from her place on the porch swing and didn't respond until Boss Man turned around to confront her. Nancy beamed at him, still basking in the sheriff's earlier complement, and before Boss Man could speak, she calmly refused his request.

"No, I don't think so. I'll be staying here for a while. Paula's got a wedding to go to in Kansas City. She's going to be gone for a week or so and said I could crash in the trailer with Wilma until she gets back. If you could bring my stuff over tomorrow, that would be great." As soon as she finished the sentence, Nancy immediately turned and started talking to Tom, in effect dismissing Boss Man. Looking only a little perturbed, Boss Man shrugged and walked off to his truck without another word.

Listening to Nancy, the bag of cannabis clutched close to his chest, Tom felt the swing move slightly from side to side and wondered if Nancy was causing it. But then he noticed that the water in a glass on the table was also gently sloshing, and realized it was just another of the small tremors they had been getting a few times a day ever since they had arrived. Bopper noticed Tom looking at the swaying water glass and piped up with his favorite doomsday prediction.

"See that water glass sloshing? That's gonna be us when the big one hits.

Josh looked at Bopper with a puzzled expression. "You talkin about earthquakes Bopper? This ain't California you know."

As soon Josh finished speaking, Zack piped up. "Oh, Jesus suffering fuck, Josh, did you have to say that? Now Bopper's gonna rehash his high school senior honors thesis for us. Again."

Bopper cackled as he turned to Josh. "You don't know shit Josh. Ever hear of the New Madrid Seismic Zone, or as I like to call it, 'the zone of death'?" Not waiting for an answer, Bopper carried on, standing now and waving his arms with excitement. "Right now, Josh, you are sitting on top of a major fault system that zig-zags 125 miles from central Arkansas all the way up into Illinois. You've apparently never heard of it, but over a period of a little less than two months in 1811-1812 this fault system produced a series of seven earthquakes with a magnitude greater than six, with four of those measuring greater than seven, including the three strongest ever recorded east of the Rockies."

Zack had fled the porch as soon as Bopper started talking, and when he paused to catch his breath Cecelia and Tom also snuck off. Not seeming to notice, or care, Bopper launched again into his arm waving soliloquy.

"Even scarier Josh is what earthquakes in the New Madrid Seismic Zone are like. They are not California pussy quakes — they're way worse in a lot of ways. That's because the faults are not close to the surface — they're buried under 200 feet of soft river sediments. And when these faults shift, the overlying sediments react in strange and scary ways, turning the area into a hellscape."

Pausing for dramatic effect, Bopper then lowered his voice and described what such a hellscape would look like, accompanied by even more dramatic arm waving.

"Skies turn dark with earthquake smog. The air, which smells bad and is hard to breath, is filled with loud explosions. Wildlife totally freaks out. Lights flash from the ground due to intense compression of quartz crystals. Massive sand boils spew water and sand out of large fissures. Forests and riverbanks collapse.

Some areas are uplifted and others suddenly subside, with water flooding in to fill the void."

Pausing again to catch his breath, Bopper grinned broadly and delivered his clincher. "But my favorite part of this hellscape is soil liquefaction. That's when the solid ground beneath you suddenly turns into quicksand. Let's say that you're standing in the front yard here on a bright sunny afternoon, admiring the bean fields. All of a sudden birds become disoriented and fly up in agitated swirls. Then huge spurts of sand and water shoot out of the ground down by the garage, lifting vehicles skyward. The air turns dark and foul smelling, and you hear distant booming sounds. Trees in the front yard crash to the ground and a large section of the street abruptly sinks out of sight. Then soil liquefaction comes for you. What before was solid ground beneath your feet suddenly turns to quicksand, and in the blink of an eye you sink soundlessly into oblivion." Raising his arms above his head, Bopper bends forward into a deep bow and sits down, quite pleased with his performance.

Josh turned to him, still skeptical, and raised the obvious question. "But that was over a hundred and fifty years ago. How often do earthquakes happen here?"

Bopper nodded. "Good question. The geology geeks think maybe every 500 to 1,300 years or so, which might lead you to believe we're safe. But the truth is, nobody knows. The faults are so deep they're difficult to study, and surface evidence of past quakes has been largely erased by erosion or new soil formation. There's some evidence from archaeological sites of quakes dating back thousands of years — displaced skeletons and stuff, and Native American myths suggest temblors are caused by dark forces and monsters of the underworld. Sounds like as good an explanation to me – monsters of the underworld. Maybe you're completely safe, or maybe tomorrow — liquefaction. Something to think about when you feel the gentle temblors in the night."

The next morning everything seemed oddly to be pretty much back to normal. Boss Man arrived at the site freshly shaved and once again dressed in crisp khakis, mirror sunglasses, and his pith helmet. He acted as if nothing unusual had happened the previous day, and managed to project confidence and authority, surprising the crew, who had been wondering if he would even show up.

Calling the crew together he announced Josh's undergraduate research award, making it sound as if he had in fact arranged it all. With guidance from the museum director, he had decided that Josh would be allowed to conduct excavations on the temple mound as his summer research project, with Denny as his direct supervisor. He would monitor them daily and have overall responsibility for their work.

While Josh and Denny were digging the mound, Boss Man said Dolores and her crew would continue stripping the plow zone from the southeast house cluster area where they had found the Ramey sherd, and he would start exposing the courtyard area at the northeast corner of the central plaza. Paula had left early that morning for Kansas City, and Boss Man assigned Nancy, Bopper, Cecelia, and Tom to work with Dolores while he would take Zack, Richard, and Wilma with him to start the excavation of the northeast courtyard. If both courtyard crews made a serious effort to strip plow zone the next few days, he added, the researcher that he had arranged to visit to take archaeomagnetism samples could target three different areas of the site.

After they had split up into three crews, Cecelia pulled Boss Man aside for a brief conversation and then joined Josh and Denny on the temple mound. Denny welcomed her with a vigorous handshake and an excited cry — "gimme five," while Josh, looking puzzled, asked. "I thought Boss Man said you would be digging with Dolores on the courtyard."

Cecelia shook her head. "Boss Man's not the boss of me. I do what I want, and I need to be over here with you guys, diggin the Red Mound."

9.
MOOD RING

The three excavation crews worked hard right up until 4 o'clock, when Boss Man called out an official "Quittin time." Nancy had been glancing up every few moments throughout the day, looking for Matt's car to pull into the parking lot. But he didn't appear. It wasn't until the afternoon of the next day that he showed up at the site. By then they had burned clay features at both house cluster locations, as well as on the Red Mound, ready for Matt to sample.

Nancy held her breath as Boss Man and Matt shook hands, then exhaled in relief as she watched the two men strike up a friendly, animated conversation as they inspected the three now exposed burned clay features. Boss Man clearly didn't realize that Matt was her ex-lover. She had talked about Matt on numerous occasions with Boss Man over the years, and he had even seen photos of him. But the fool didn't have a clue. He'd never been a very good listener. Matt had changed some, of course, Nancy admitted, smiling. He had gotten into serious weight training and had put on maybe twenty pounds of muscle.

Matt grabbed his tool kit and decided to start with the Red Mound, where he cut away at one corner of the burned clay feature, creating a small pedestal about the size of a half-stick of butter. He then placed the open-ended aluminum box down over the pedestal, oriented it to present-day magnetic north, and poured in some plaster of Paris. Giving the plaster a half hour to dry, Matt then gently snapped off the box with its imbedded clay sample, labeled it, and carried it carefully to his car. There it went into a padded case in the trunk. He decided to wait until the next day to take the clay samples from the house cluster locations. It was late and he didn't want to delay the end of a long workday for the crew. Stopping briefly to check in with Boss Man, Matt thanked him profusely for the opportunity to conduct research on the site and said he was at the Green Door motel up the road and would be back in the morning to sample the courtyards. Nancy overheard the exchange and watched him drive off, feeling both excited and apprehensive, wondering how things would turn out in the morning. As soon as she got back to the crew house, she called the motel she had overheard Matt mention and left a message for him. "Pick me up."

She was sitting, waiting, on the veranda with Tom, Dolores, and Bopper when Matt drove up to the crew house half an hour later. Nancy got up from her seat before the car came to a full stop, and without saying anything, walked down and climbed in the passenger seat. Nancy and Matt briefly embraced and then drove off. Jaws dropped on the veranda. Bopper and Tom stared at each other, gob smacked, while Dolores was visibly alarmed. She suspected that Boss Man might be carrying a handgun in his fanny pack, and in spite of his seemingly stable demeanor the last few days, she knew he was still very fragile. He could easily freak out.

Matt dropped Nancy off at the crew house early the next morning before continuing on to the site. He wanted an early start on getting his last samples and getting the fuck out of Dodge. As soon as Nancy climbed the veranda steps, Dolores and Tom started asking her to open up about what was going on. She just smiled and reassured them not to be concerned. It would all work out OK. Others on the crew were not so sure. On the drive out to Hamblin's Fort, Bopper predicted that Boss Man and Matt would get into a scuffle and there would be some brief bitch-slapping. Zack thought it would be more violent, with maybe a headlock or some serious face-punches, and Boss Man going down. Dolores was afraid to mention the possibility of Boss Man pulling a handgun from his fanny pack and doing something stupid.

The crew were all keeping their heads down and paying unusually close attention to their tasks when Boss Man arrived at the site. Denny, Cecelia, and Josh were working on the north-south trench on the mound summit and the others were digging the house clusters. Boss Man looked sober. That was a good start. There was an uneasy silence as he approached the northeast house cluster excavation where Matt was just finishing up labeling the last of his samples. Boss Man started to sense from the mood of the crew that something was off and noticed with surprise that up on the mound summit Cecelia was wearing a quite subdued dark dress, one that she reserved for formal occasions.

Boss Man turned to Richard with a puzzled expression, about to ask what was up, when Dolores called out in an excited voice from where she was carefully scraping with her trowel to better define the outline of a pit they had uncovered the day before in the southeast house cluster area. "Oh my God. Oh my God. You gotta see this."

Boss Man led the rush over to where Dolores's crew was crowding around her, jockeying for a better view of what she was now turning over in the palm of her hand. It was a small red object that was the size and roughly the shape of her thumb — nothing very impressive at first glance. Grabbing it from Dolores, Richard looked at the object and declared in an authoritative voice. "Catlinite. Pipestone. Probably from Minnesota. Part of a pipe — not really a big deal, Dolores."

Grabbing the object back, Dolores laughed in a mocking bray. "Close Richard, but no cigar. It's not catlinite, or any form of pipestone, and it's not from Minnesota. It's bauxite - Missouri fire clay or flint clay, from the St. Louis area, and it's a huge fucking deal. What you are looking at here is a figurine fragment — part of an arm, I think. And bauxite figurines, or fragments of them, have mostly been found in the Cahokia area, where they almost always occur in ceremonial or ritual contexts. Missouri fire clay figurines and fragments have been discovered a dozen or so times outside of Cahokia, at other mound centers scattered across the Midwest and Southeast. Like the Ramey sherd we found earlier, this little arm provides compelling evidence of a strong connection between Hamblin's Fort and Cahokia, and a connection that involved ceremonies and a belief system introduced from Cahokia, almost 400 miles north of here."

The fire clay arm fragment was passed around, and Boss Man had tears in his eyes as he caressed it gently before handing it back to Dolores. As soon as she packed the arm away safely in a cotton lined plastic container, Dolores returned to the pit she had been working on and cautioned the other crew members working on the southeast house cluster.

"Careful with your trowels. If you hit anything hard, switch over to your wooden tools so you won't damage any figurine fragments you might encounter. There's a good possibility that the rest of the figurine is still here, in this pit or nearby, broken into fragments. The arm fragment indicates the figurine might have been ritually killed — broken up, at the conclusion of a ceremony."

Nancy and Matt hadn't joined the crowd around Dolores and her new discovery. They remained standing close to each other where Matt had collected his final burned clay samples from the northeast courtyard. They briefly watched the crew gathered in their celebratory huddle around Dolores, and then Matt took Nancy's hand. Smiling at each other, they walked over to his car and drove away. It was a little over four hours north to St. Louis, and they could easily make it by dinnertime.

As the miles rolled by, Nancy talked about how miserable she had been, and how she felt like she had just gotten out of jail. Then a giddiness bubbled up inside them and they were soon singing along with the radio and acting like it was the first day of summer vacation.

Stopping for ice cream at a tourist trap an hour north of Memphis, they sat outside at a picnic table and tentatively started charting their future. Matt still had to finish his dissertation research, and Nancy's options were wide open. As they finished their ice cream cones, Matt suddenly turned serious. Taking Nancy's left hand, he slowly removed her wedding ring, and after looking to her for an OK, tossed it into the tall grass. Reaching into his pocket, he produced a cheap plastic "mood ring" he had just found inside among the assorted gee-gaws, and slid it onto her ring finger. He asked, she answered, and they kissed. The fact that she was still technically married to Boss Man didn't really matter. Not at all. She and Matt were the future, Boss Man was in the rear-view mirror.

Boss Man joined Dolores in carefully removing the dark fill from the small pit that had yielded the figurine fragment, screening the soil through window screen so they would not miss any small fragments. They found another piece — part of a shoulder, several inches down, and then nothing until they reached the base of the pit. There, they found most of the rest of the figurine. It was about a foot tall and broken into four large fragments and several smaller pieces. They cleaned away the soil sufficiently to photograph it in situ before lifting it from the pit and into a waiting cotton-lined container.

Leaving the rest of the crew at the site to finish out the workday, Dolores and Boss Man rushed back to the crew house with their prize. It was a beautiful object and in excellent condition, apart from being in fragments. The Hamblin's Fort figurine was very similar to the "Birger figurine," which would be discovered two decades later in a shrine at the BBB Motor site near Cahokia. Like the Birger figurine, the Hamblin's Fort figure was of a kneeling woman with a large serpent coiled around her on the ground. The kneeling woman's left hand rested on the snake's head while her right hand held a short-handled hoe, the blade of which was imbedded in the snake's back. The snake's tail turned into a vine which grew up the kneeling woman's back and ended in a pair of large gourd-like fruits. Like the Birger figurine, the Hamblin's Fort figure could be interpreted as being an expression of the Earth-Mother concept — a goddess of life and death and the creator of people and plants. With the help of the "Earth Serpent," symbol of death and the underworld, the Earth Mother was the source of the agricultural crops that people relied upon.

Giddy with their discovery, Boss Man and Dolores sat on the front porch at the crew house and talked excitedly about what this might mean. Maybe Hamblin's Fort represented a "budding-off" of a segment of the elite from Cahokia who had relocated south 400 miles to Hamblin's Fort. Maybe Hamblin's Fort was a Cahokian satellite ceremonial center, established and maintained to spread Cahokia's world view and cosmology south into the lower Mississippi Valley. Maybe the southeast house cluster wasn't residential at all, but part of a ritual precinct, a shrine. Whatever it turned out to be, Dolores and Boss Man had hit the jackpot.

After a few beers Boss Man called Professor Shetler, their dissertation advisor, to report their discovery of the figurine and to make sure that this time the good news came from him. He and Dolores then talked a bit about Nancy and Matt running off, which Boss Man seemed to have barely noticed and didn't seem too disturbed about. As they gazed at the beautiful, oddly compelling bauxite figurine, nested in its cotton cocoon, Dolores held his hand and told him what a good man he was, and how the end of his marriage to that bitch Nancy was a good thing. Then she led Boss Man up to her room for a lay-back, and by the time the crew returned, Boss Man appeared in good spirits. After a few more beers he was remarking on how fantastic it was to be rid of that "harping bitch" Nancy.

Later in the evening Boss Man paused in his steady consumption of Griesedieck to caution the crew about keeping the discovery of the figurine secret. He warned that If word got out, they would be overrun with locals wanting to dig at the site. By the end of the evening Boss Man was fall-down drunk again and clearly couldn't be allowed to drive back to Forrest City. Dolores deposited him in her room for the night, banishing Denny to the now vacant bed in Wilma's trailer, with Paula still up in Kansas City. Denny agreed but made it clear that it was for one night only. Josh had hoped Denny might opt to join him in the attic, but after briefly pausing to seemingly consider his invitation, she declined. Josh wasn't surprised, and took her momentary consideration of his proposal as a very good sign. She seemed to be warming up to him.

Boss Man's fears that word of their discovery of the figurine would get out, and what might happen as a result, seemed to be happening anyway. About ten the next morning a convoy of four pickup trucks arrived at the site, and the sheriff led a group of five middle-aged men up to greet Boss Man and get a quick tour. The visitors didn't introduce themselves and they all looked shifty. But it turned out that they hadn't heard anything about the figurine. They were there as part of the sheriff's plan to pre-emptively discourage pothunting by demonstrating that nothing of value was to be had.

Boss Man and the sheriff emphasized to the visitors that they were conducting scientific research at Hamblin's Fort and were interested in trying to reconstruct the way of life of this ancient society, not in the recovery of items of value. A variety of uninteresting objects they had recovered were shown to the visitors, with no mention of the Ramey cosmogram sherd or the figurine.

After watching the crew carry on with what was clearly mind-numbingly boring work in the hot sun — scraping and screening dirt, mapping pot sherds and other discarded objects of everyday life, the visitors eventually wandered back down to the air-conditioned comfort of their trucks. The crew thought they were all getting ready to leave, but only the sheriff drove off. The other three pickups remained, with the occupants just sitting there, gazing out through their windshields. Josh was the first to figure out why they were sticking around. He and Denny and Cecelia had been skimming down the north-south trench on the Red Mound summit, but were going to start excavation of the red ocher pit after lunch.

It had been Cecelia's turn to work the shaker screens that morning. She happened to be wearing one of her flimsier frocks and noticing the visitors' interest she decided to turn the Red Mound summit into a platform for expressing both her strengthening spiritual connection to the Red Mound and her belief in the almost sacred nature of dance. In a bizarre coincidence, Cecelia's spiritual gossamer dances on the Red Mound summit echoed the ritual performance carried out there some seven hundred years ago by four Native American priests.

Cecelia didn't just dance, but wove her leaps, twirls, and hand dancing in with her shovel, wheelbarrow, and screening efforts. Her audience wasn't particularly interested in the spirituality of her performance, however. Gazing up at her, with the bright morning sun backlighting her slim body, barely covered in thin gossamer, the visitors were admiring other aspects of Cecelia's graceful movements.

Denny eventually pulled Cecelia aside and threatened to bar her from working on the mound if she didn't stop, pointing out that the men in the pickups were creeping people out. Cecelia somewhat reluctantly agreed, and she and Josh traded places. Soon after, her audience departed, honking their horns and waving, as Cecelia waved back.

10.
POOCH IN THE PIT

Things settled down pretty quickly after the departure of Nancy and Matt and the discovery of the Hamblin's Fort figurine. Work at the site was progressing at a good pace. Several new structures had been uncovered at the northeast corner of the central plaza, and excavation of one of them had begun. Nothing interesting had been found so far.

The crew were getting along with each other for the most part. Cecelia's local fans were showing up three days a week at noon, when Cecelia had agreed, after talking with Sheriff Hogg, to offer twenty minutes of scheduled expressive dance on the summit of the Red Mound. The sheriff thought it would be a great way to curry favor with the local community and tamp down the anti-hippy, anti-Yankee, anti-pointy-head resentments that were always just beneath the surface. Cecelia found she enjoyed the opportunity and the appreciative audience, and the sheriff was getting excellent reviews from Cecelia's fans.

Paula had returned early from the wedding in Kansas City and Zack had started in harassing her again. She was pretty much fed up, and complained to Boss Man, but he just laughed at her. Bopper was complaining to anyone who would listen that Tom was being stingy with his weed. Richard was beginning to wear on people with his seemingly constant defense of old-style archaeology with its primary emphasis on placing sites in space and time and establishing their degree of similarity or cultural closeness to other sites.

This was accomplished, Richard would explain at length, by comparing pot sherd assemblages collected from sites across broad regions. He could go on for hours about what kinds of temper, paste, vessel form, and decoration were diagnostic of different pottery types, from "Parkin Punctate" to "Old Town Red." That was the primary research goal in archaeology, in Richard's world view — using pot sherds to situate sites in the space-time-social framework, not looking for feasting debris or community organization.

Boss Man and Dolores were quite the couple now, with frequent PDAs during the workday and Dolores increasingly spending nights with Boss Man over in Forrest City. She had talked him into ditching the fanny pack and stashing his revolver in the glove box of his truck. Nobody on the crew noticed the change except Cecelia, who soon after the fanny pack disappeared pulled Dolores aside for a rare hug and a whispered thanks for her ongoing wrangling of Boss Man.

Josh and Denny were excited by Dolores's discovery of the bauxite figurine, confident that it indicated that more evidence of ceremonial activities involving Cahokian ritual paraphernalia would be uncovered at Hamblin's Fort and that the summit of the Red Mound was an excellent place to look. The top eighteen inches or so of soil across the entire summit of the mound appeared to consist of a clean white sand, no doubt carried in from nearby natural levee deposits. This white sand layer, Denny thought, represented a ceremonial closing of the mound — a final curtain to the centuries of activities that had taken place on its summit.

At some point during the addition of this final layer to the mound a pit had been dug into the white sand adjacent to the red clay feature, and it had been filled with a darker soil flecked with red ocher. What the pit contained was still to be determined. Denny could tell that the pit was not recent. It hadn't been dug down into the white sand layer from the present-day mound surface but rather had been created during the final white sand capping of the mound.

Cecelia sat on the backfill dirt pile next to the sifting screen, enveloped by the powerful red vortex she felt rising out of the pit where Denny and Josh now knelt as they carefully removed the soil from the red ocher pit. After maybe ten minutes of digging, Denny's trowel hit something hard. Switching to her brush, she carefully cleared some of the soil away before looking up and blurting out "Bone. It's bone. We've got a burial."

Cecelia stood and called out the news to the crews working on the house clusters, who hurried over to check out the burial. Given the placement of the interment on the mound summit it was undoubtedly going to be a highly ranked individual, Josh thought, perhaps a religious leader associated with the ceremonies that had been carried out, or the chief whose death had precipitated the closure of the mound. But there was something off about the burial. It didn't appear that they had been buried with much ceremony — just a small pit as part of the white sand capping of the mound.

It only took a few more minutes, and a little more brushing away of the overlying soil, before it was clear that they had found something quite unexpected. Denny paused, looked up, and said what most of the watching crew had already figured out. "It's not human," Denny said as she exposed the top of the skull of the burial.

"Looks like a dog to me," Bopper added.

Denny brushed away more soil around the skull and replied. "Too big for a fox. Definitely a canid. Dog or wolf, hard to tell before we take a closer look. I'll get the forms we'll need, and the camera." Denny stood and shuffled down the side of the mound, followed by the rest of the crew except for Josh and Cecelia.

Everyone knew that finishing up the full excavation of the skeleton and any associated artifacts would be a slow, meticulous process — not worth hanging around for.

It took Denny almost twenty minutes to return with all the necessary forms to record the burial, and she was stunned on her return to see that Cecelia had been joined by Black Dog, who was now lying down next to her with his head in her lap. He slapped the ground with his tail a few times as he looked up at Denny.

"He showed up soon after you went for the forms," Cecelia explained. "Now we know why he was hanging around the mound. I'm sure he's linked somehow to the pooch in the pit. This dog has some powerful juju flowing through him. I can feel it." Cecelia rubbed Black Dog's belly and the dog responded by licking her hand.

Looking alarmed, Josh raised the obvious question. "What's Boss Man gonna do when he sees Black Dog. He still got that gun?"

Cecelia stood up, looked at the dog and told him to stay. Black Dog remained in place as she skipped down the side of the mound and walked over to Dolores and Boss Man. They talked for several minutes, with Boss Man looking over at the Red Mound summit and crossing his arms on his chest in full pout mode. Dolores put her arm around him and led him off toward the trucks as Cecelia came back to where Josh and Denny were digging

"What's up?" Josh asked.

"It's all sorted out. Easy-peasy. I told Dolores and Boss Man that I'm adopting Black Dog. He's my dog now. Under my protection. If Boss Man messes with him, I'll mess with Boss Man. He knows I can make trouble for him, so we agreed that Black Dog is welcome on the site." Cecelia settled back down next to Black Dog, talking quietly to him about energy vortexes and auras, as Denny and Josh went back to excavating the canid burial.

They had completely uncovered the burial by mid-afternoon and took several photos, filled out a burial form, and drew a sketch map of the skeleton before removing it for transport back to the crew house. It looked to be a complete skeleton, and in good condition given the length of time it had been in the ground. Denny was eager to compare it to her modern domestic dog and red wolf skeletons to see how it matched up. It was either a red wolf, a very large dog, or some sort of a hybrid. Figuring out which wouldn't be all that easy. But she could already tell that it was much larger than most dogs recovered from Mississippian sites.

Whatever it was, Denny had never heard of a dog/wolf burial being found in a temple mound. And this canid's position in the burial pit was markedly different from that of other dog burials recovered from archaeological sites in eastern North America. Rather than being curled up on its side, like most dog burials, the Hamblin's Fort canid was lying on his belly, with his hind legs gathered under him and his front legs stretched out in front and crossed, with his head resting on his front paws, sort of sphinxlike. It was as if he was still watching, still alert and ready to respond to any trespass. Altogether a little strange, particularly when combined with the recovery of the Cahokian cosmogram and the mother goddess figurine.

At the end of the workday, with the canid skeleton safely packed away, Cecelia led Black Dog down to the parking lot, where it happily jumped in the back seat of the Travelall with her. Black Dog soon settled into his new life and became part of the crew. He hung out in Cecelia's tent, and would come with her every day to the site, where she set up a water bowl and small awning on the mound to give him a shady spot to watch them work and doze in the constant upwelling of the mound's misty red power vortex. In the late afternoon and evening he would lie at Cecelia's feet on the veranda back at the crew house, alert to any strangers that might approach. Often Black Dog would disappear at night, likely returning to Hamblin's Fort and the Red Mound. Boss Man and the Black Dog established an uneasy truce, and the crew noticed that Black Dog became quite protective of Cecelia, as she was of him. They had formed a very close bond.

Back at the crew house that evening after dinner Denny had laid the newly excavated canid skeleton out on the kitchen table and was taking measurements and examining the each bone for any evidence of trauma or other anomalies. She was alone in the kitchen and had the radio on low to a local country station. A bright gooseneck lamp illuminated her tabletop in the surrounding shadows. Humming happily along with the music, entirely focused on the bones, Denny was blissfully content. It didn't get much better than this. When she finished the cleaning and close inspection, she would pull out her red wolf and dog skeletons for comparison.

Picking up the mandible for cleaning, Denny looked surprised, then reached over and grabbed the modern dog mandible on the table and compared the two. The mandible of the canid recovered from the mound was missing all four of its second premolars, upper and lower. It could be the result of trauma or infection of some sort, but Denny wondered if it could be genetic — an anomaly passed down through multiple generations, particularly if breeding was limited to a small group of related individuals. That would be cool, she thought, and certainly something to mention in the journal article she was planning on writing on this unusual discovery.

She worked for another hour or so inspecting and cleaning the bones and then, even though it was getting late, she couldn't resist starting in on beginning to compare the ancient canid with the dog and wolf skeletons in her modern comparative collection. Her modern dog skeleton was a roadkill — one of the local strays they lumped under the general term "ditch hound" because they always seemed to be lurking in the roadside drainage ditches, ready to suddenly appear in pursuit of passing cars. She had shoveled it up and rendered it down the previous summer because it looked to be a rough match, size-wise, to what she thought might turn up at Hamblin's Fort. At first glance as she compared the two, she could see that the ancient canid was definitely larger overall than the modern ditch hound, with a longer muzzle and longer legs. The ancient canid, she thought, seemed to be about the same size as Black Dog.

Feeling a little silly, Denny had a far-out idea, ridiculous really, but Cecelia's constant chatter about energy vortexes and red auras had seemingly, subliminally, found a way around her scientist's world view based on objective reality and observable facts. She looked out the front door to see if Cecelia was on the veranda, but she and Black Dog had already retired to their tent. Checking her watch Denny realized she had lost track of time and it was almost midnight. Grabbing a flashlight and heading outside, she was relieved to see that Cecelia was still up, judging from the soft light glowing through the canvas side of her tent. Calling out a hello and flipping up the tent flap, Denny looked in, immediately waving away a dense cloud of cannabis smoke that floated up around her. Cecelia and Tom were reclining on opposite sides of the tent, clearly stoned. Tom was reading a Fabulous Furry Freak Brothers comic to Cecelia, who seemed to be enjoying it immensely. There was an open package of chocolate chip cookies between them on the floor of the tent. Black Dog was lying on his side next to Cecelia, snoring softly.

Denny sat down next to Black Dog and asked Cecelia if it would be OK to just take a quick look in the dog's mouth. Cecelia understandably looked puzzled, took another toke from the fatty Tom passed her, and nodded her head as she exhaled. Black Dog had opened his eyes and seeing Denny, he languidly repositioned himself for an expected belly rub. Instead, Denny gently grasped his muzzle and lifted his lip. Black Dog's teeth were in surprisingly good shape for a ditch hound — bright white, with healthy pink gums. He was, however, lacking all four second premolars.

Denny sat back, still not really believing it, and Tom asked her what she had been looking at. She recounted her recent examination of the ancient dog/wolf mandible, and how it, like Black Dog, lacked second premolars. She expected Tom and Cecelia to have the same reaction she had had — surprise and disbelief. But neither of them seemed particularly surprised.

Tom took another toke, nodded, and replied. "Far out, man, I dig it."

Denny was already starting to get a buzz on from the thick cloud of smoke as Cecelia sat up, assumed the lotus position, and offered more wisdom. "You gotta rip off your blinders Denny. Science, rational thought, all that rigid dogma, doesn't have all the answers. Open your mind. Think about your amazing discovery — one you will never be able to get published in one of your scientific journals. But it looks to me like Black Dog is a direct descendant of your ancient canid. He's not pure red wolf, of course. All those generations — more than 700 years, there would have been interbreeding with local dogs and maybe with coyotes, but he's still got some red wolf in him, along with a strong connection to the Red Mound's energy vortex."

11.
WHADDA GOT?

A light rain began later that night and continued for the next few days. Twice a day someone would drive over to the site to check that the tarps covering their excavations were still in place. Otherwise, the crew were all stuck indoors.

Denny spent the morning laying out the ancient canid skeleton and taking a set of standard cranial and post-cranial measurements. In terms of its size and morphology, she thought the temple mound canid looked to be a good match with her modern red wolf. It was intermediate in size between a gray wolf and coyote, and larger than any domestic dogs recovered from archaeological sites in eastern North America. Like the red wolf, which some researchers called the greyhound of wolves, it also had relatively long and slender legs, a narrow skull and a long slender snout.

After a quick lunch Denny went to find Wilma, who had a good personal library of books on Southeastern Native American tribes. Borrowing several, she settled down on the front porch for a drizzly afternoon spent searching for any discussion of red wolves. The Cherokee, she soon discovered, considered the red wolf to be a tribal guardian or protector. It was the companion of Kana'ti, the hunter and father of the Wolf Clan, the largest Cherokee clan, which traditionally produced war chiefs and other powerful individuals. Maybe her red wolf burial wasn't so anomalous after all. Maybe he was guarding the mound and its ceremonies, and perhaps even the burial of a powerful individual — a war chief or a ritual authority of some sort. Her planned journal article on the red wolf burial was looking better all the time.

Bopper, Tom, and Zack were spending the rain days engaged in a much more boring activity — catching up on the initial cleaning of artifacts they had so far recovered from the excavation of the southeast and northeast house clusters. Artifact processing was a mindless activity that involved removing artifacts — mostly broken pieces of pottery, bone fragments, and small flakes of chert, from their labeled paper bags, cleaning them off with brushes and a pan of water, and then placing them back on their bags to dry. By lunchtime the entire floor of the living room of the crew house would be covered with paper bags and drying artifacts.

Bopper quickly found a way to make their mind-numbing chore more entertaining. He and Tom were washing the material recovered from Dolores's southeast house cluster area, which had produced the Ramey sherd and bauxite figurine, while Zack and Richard were processing the artifacts recovered so far from Boss Man's excavation of the northeast house cluster.

Bopper decided to turn their boring work into a game of "Whadda got?" Every few minutes he would hold up whatever object he was washing and trumpet its magnificence, even when it was a lowly broken sherd from the body of an undecorated pot. Interspersed with these announcements he would challenge Zack to match the magnificence of his little beauties — "Hey Zack. Whadda got?" He would then laugh when Zack couldn't match what he had pulled out of a bag and finish with a taunt. "Zack ain't got Jack."

Bopper's beauties would usually top whatever Zack could produce, continuing a pattern that Boss Man and Dolores had already noticed — the two areas were yielding quite different artifact assemblages. Boss Man's northeast house cluster appeared, based just on its artifact assemblage, to consist of typical domestic structures containing mostly discarded household trash. Zack's bags yielded broken ceramic sherds from undecorated storage jars, bowls, and plates, small discarded lithic debitage flakes and blocks, and broken bone tools.

The two structures that had been uncovered so far in Dolores's southeast courtyard area, in contrast, were quite different from the northeast courtyard houses, as well as from each other. Bopper would laugh every time Zack or Richard pulled out another body sherd that was no match for what he was able to hold up from the southeast house cluster and wave in their faces. He was at his most obnoxious when he held up the often tiny, seemingly inconsequential pieces of shell that were turning up in their bags. The white shell fragments were not all that significant by themselves, but they held out the promise of something much more exciting that could still be waiting to be uncovered.

It was the thickness of the small shell fragments that was the giveaway — they were too thick to be from local river clams. They were most likely fragments from conch shells that must have been carried in from the Gulf Coast of Florida. Conch shell cups, often engraved with ritual symbols — water spiders and falcon warriors, winged snakes and other mythical creatures, had been found in a number of the more high-profile Mississippian sites including Cahokia, Moundville, and Spiro, and were another indication of the presence of high-status elite individuals and sacred ceremonies. The fragments of conch shell they were finding suggested that intact conch shell cups might be still waiting to be discovered.

Paula was particularly interested in the shell fragments that Bopper was crowing about, as well as the lithics that had turned up in the sifting screen. She had a hand lens and was sifting through the artifacts drying on Tom and Bopper's bags, picking up and peering closely at both the small conch shell fragments and the numerous small chert flakes that had been recovered. She was looking for, and finding, evidence that the southeast house cluster had witnessed the actual manufacture of conch shell cups. Several of the shell fragments showed evidence of engraving, and she had also identified maybe a half dozen of the quite distinctive lithic engraving tools used to decorate the ceremonial cups.

Every half hour or so Dolores would wander in from the kitchen where she and Boss Man were working to update records on the house cluster excavations and fill in new information on their maps. The differences she saw in the ceramic assemblages from the two courtyards was not exactly what she had been hoping for but was still a reason to get excited. They had not found any more Ramey incised cosmogram sherds, but her southeast house cluster had continued to yield a few decorated sherds — both incised and painted, along with undecorated ones. Some of the designs on the decorated sherds suggested Cahokian influences while others suggested connections to more nearby sites. Even the undecorated plain sherds from the southeast house cluster were different from those recovered from Boss Man's northeast area. The clay was harder, darker, and the ground shell fragments that had been added to temper the clay were much smaller — in archaeological terminology there were from "Bell plain" rather than "Neely's Ferry plain" ceramic vessels. On such distinctions were dissertations constructed.

The northeast and southeast house cluster excavation maps had been laid out next to each other on the kitchen table, and like the artifact assemblages, they showed the two areas to be very different in terms of the size and shape of structures. So far, they had uncovered two burned structures in the Boss Man's northeast house cluster, both of which were small square houses — typical domestic structures measuring fifteen feet on a side.

Each had a central hearth, numerous interior storage pits, and their floors were scattered with household debris.

On the other hand, the two structures in Dolores's southeast house cluster not only looked nothing like the domestic structures exposed by Boss Man's crew, they were also quite different from each other. One was a small T-shaped structure about ten feet across. Its interior yielded few artifacts and contained only a small, raised clay platform situated in the center of the structure. Dolores had reasonably concluded that this T-shaped structure was a shrine, and that the base of the bauxite figurine would be a perfect fit for the shallow indentation they had observed on the top of the central clay pedestal.

The second structure was larger than those uncovered at the northeast corner of the plaza, and its interior looked quite different. So far, about the only interesting objects they had recovered were the abundant conch shell fragments Bopper was bragging about. These seemed to be scattered randomly across the house floor along with numerous chert flakes, some of which Paula had identified as engraving tools. Dolores, Boss Man, and Paula's most fervent hope — what they would call their leading hypothesis, was that this structure was a workshop where specialized craftsmen made engraved conch shell cups for use in elite ceremonies. They were eager to get back to excavating the rest of the structure in anticipation of perhaps finding intact finished cups.

The two southeast structures had also drawn Wilma's interest. If conch shell cups were not only being manufactured at Hamblin's Fort, but also being used in a ceremonial context, perhaps in association with the T-shaped earth mother shrine or on the mound summit, then there might also be evidence of what was actually contained in the cups — "Black Drink." Derived from the leaves and stems of a native species of yaupon holly,

Black Drink was very high in caffeine and had been consumed in ceremonies by historic Native American groups across the Southeast. Evidence of the Black Drink holly — identified by botanists as _Ilex vomitoria_, would be difficult to find, Wilma knew, but she took soil samples from a number of concentrations of burned plant material in and around the T-shaped structure for later lab analysis. She was spending the rain days dry-screening the samples through window screen and then sorting the carbonized plant fragments she recovered under a low-power microscope, looking for anything that might be yaupon holly. So far, she had struck out.

Josh spent the rain days in the attic. He had scrounged a beat-up coffee table with hundreds of cigarette burns out of a trash pile in the back yard and turned it into a desk. Sitting on the floor with the attic chimney at his back and the coffee table pulled up to his waist, he had by lunch time the second day brought the north-south trench excavation forms, maps, and profiles up to date.

Now he was thinking about doing some digging on the mound on his own. He knew Denny had pretty much finished up the analysis of the red wolf burial and would be pushing to start back on excavation of the north-south trench to extend it across the entire mound summit. But they had also talked about digging some more 5x5 test squares on the summit, just to show they had done a thorough investigation of the mound.

Josh was going to propose that Denny and Cecelia begin back on excavation of the north-south trench, and he would start digging a few 5x5 test squares. He likely would find little except clean white sand, but it would be fun to do it using randomly placed excavation squares.

Boss Man and Dolores were also considering how best to proceed with excavation of the house clusters. They had pretty much decided to pause work on Boss Man's northeast structures and shift Zack, Richard, and Wilma over to Dolores's excavation area — it was much more interesting, and, as they framed it, had far greater research potential.

While the rest of the crew were getting caught up with artifact processing, record keeping, and planning for what came next, Cecelia was off in Memphis with a new man. He had first shown up at the site a week or so ago — just another pickup truck there to watch Cecelia's dance recital. After a few days of just watching from the comfort of his truck, he started sitting on the hood.

Cecelia liked what she saw. He was younger than her other fans and seemed well mannered. Tall and thin with long blond hair in a ponytail, he was clean-shaven, wore bell-bottom jeans and tie-dyed T-shirts, and had a calm blue aura. When he finally climbed up the side of the mound the day before it started raining, bouquet of flowers in hand, to introduce himself to Cecelia, she could tell right away there was a connection. His name was Jake, short for Jacob, he told her, and he played blues guitar with a band at one of the clubs up in Memphis.

Word of the strange woman doing dances on an Indian mound out in the boonies had reached some of the clubs in Memphis, and hearing the stories, Jake decided on a whim to check her out. He was sure that it would be a waste of time, and he would end up watching some drug crazed spaz stagger around in a daze. What he found at Hamblin's Fort was not what he had expected. Cecelia was very talented, he thought, and very well trained. He saw a dancer with a distinctive style, a sensual yet refined sense of movement, and a certain mysterious something that made him want to get to know her. Plus, he couldn't fail but notice she was easy on the eye.

Cecelia accepted the flowers he offered her and his shy invitation to lunch. She and Jake stopped by after their two-hour lunch just long enough for her to introduce him to Denny and Josh, and noticing the dark clouds building in the west, to say she would be away up in Memphis for a while and would be back when the weather cleared. Josh and Denny agreed to take care of Black Dog during her absence.

12.
FAT HENRY

After two rainy days the sky cleared and work resumed at Hamblin's Fort. Cecelia returned from her getaway up to Memphis with Jake and was welcomed warmly by Black Dog, who seemed to take to Jake well enough. Cecelia let Boss Man know that Jake would be spending some time with her and would be lending a hand on the Red Mound excavation. Boss Man was clearly reluctant to agree to having a stranger with no experience join the crew, even temporarily, but couldn't really say no to Cecelia, given her father's influence with the museum director. Josh and Denny, on the other hand, were eager to have an additional person to help with their work.

It soon became clear, however, that Jake and Cecelia would not really be making much of a contribution to the ongoing Red Mound excavation efforts. They spent most weekends, and even some weeknights, up in Memphis. And when they did show up at the site it was usually only for a few hours in the afternoons. Jake had asked Cecelia to cancel her impromptu dance recitals and give up her gossamer frocks, so now she was wearing much more modest attire — usually jeans and T-shirts. Jake was certainly having an influence on Cecelia, and the crew wasn't sure exactly what to make of it. Tom, of course, was crushed by Cecelia's new romantic relationship and became withdrawn and sulky when she and Jake were around. The others watched Cecelia's apparent shift closer to something considered normal with surprise and skepticism — how long would it last?

With Cecelia slacking off and Jake not much of a help, Josh and Denny appealed to Boss Man for a more equitable division of crew labor. There were eight people excavating the house clusters while it was pretty much just Josh and Denny excavating on the temple mound. Boss Man, puffed up now by the cosmogram sherd and bauxite figurine discoveries and the resultant upturn in his own prospects, responded with a nasty laugh and a smiling shake of the head. There was no way they were getting any help, particularly now that Cecelia seemed distracted by her new boyfriend and less likely to rush in to get daddy to support work on the Red Mound.

Undeterred, since they hadn't really expected Boss Man to provide any help, Josh began staking out some of his test pits and Denny had started in on extending the north-south trench toward the south edge of the summit and her goal of then stepping the trench down the mound slope looking for feasting debris.

Denny first removed the rest of the white sand layer from the 5x10 excavation unit that had contained the red wolf burial pit. She now had a good view of the two edges of the red clay feature exposed in the bottom of the trench, and they appeared to form straight lines parallel each other across the trench, maybe three feet apart, with the red burned area extending into one of the side walls of the trench. She guessed that if the side walls were cut back the feature would be revealed to be a deliberately formed rectangular clay floor or platform, three feet wide by five or so feet in length. It was certainly worth investigating when time allowed, but right now Denny was determined to continue the trench southward toward the edge of the mound summit.

By mid-afternoon Josh had finished one test pit — another dry hole yielding only white sand, and had begun to strip the sod from his second 5x5 when he noticed an area several feet away where the sod appeared torn up and the ground surface seemed disturbed. It was roughly circular and looked to be maybe three feet across. Curious now, he flipped up all the loose sod, exposing what appeared to be another pit, this one clearly dug down from the current ground surface through the white sand layer. When exactly it had been dug was anyone's guess, but the disturbed sod suggested it was recent. Maybe somebody else had been looking for Civil War gold, Josh thought, smiling to himself. Not sure how to proceed, he asked Denny, who then called in Boss Man, who in turn gave the go-ahead to excavate the newly discovered pit.

"Don't waste time," Boss Man admonished, since it was intrusive and probably wouldn't yield anything other than some trash that pothunters may have left behind. Josh began shoveling out the pit fill and quickly noticed that it was a recently churned mix of white sand from the capping layer and darker soil from the underlying layers of the mound. After digging down several feet he hit something soft with his shovel and stopped. Black Dog had walked over and joined him in gazing down into the pit, growling softly. There was a bright red item poking up from the loose soil. Josh reached down and tugged on it, then dug around it with his shovel before dislodging it and pulling it out of the ground. It was a red leather jacket — the kind motorcyclists wore, with zippered pockets and some sort of design on the back. Shaking the soil off the jacket, Josh took a closer look at the design. It showed a coiled snake — a water moccasin with bared fangs, encircled by the words "Swamp Rebels MC." Josh climbed up out of the pit with the jacket, and only then noticed a strong smell of decay wafting up from the hole.

Boss Man was called over. After jumping down into the pit and briefly digging with his trowel, he suddenly stood up, gagged, and vomited, barely missing Josh. Wiping his mouth with the back of his hand, clearly shaken, Boss Man called off work for the day. "Quitting early today. Gotta call the sheriff. Looks like we got something fresh down there."

Sheriff Hogg's reaction to the news of the red leather jacket and bad smell unsettled Boss Man even further. "You found what? Red Leather? Swamp Rebels?" There was a short silence on the other end of the line, and then Boss Man heard the sheriff talking in a muffled voice to someone else before he came back on the line.

"OK. Here's what you need to do," the sheriff said. "Drop the jacket back in the hole and close down whatever you're doing. I'll take care of this. I can't say too much, but I think it's part of an ongoing investigation, and needs to stay quiet. It's best forgotten. I'll stop by in the morning and fill you in. But nobody talks about this. You got that, right?"

"Yes sir," Boss Man replied. "I can assure you, as far as we are all concerned, it was an empty pothole."

As soon as he ended his call with Boss Man, Hogg dialed a number he knew from memory. "Hey Skeeter, looks like Fat Henry finally surfaced. He and his old lady didn't skip town with that shipment back in the spring like we suspected. He's been takin a dirt nap in an Indian mound." Hogg paused, listening to Skeeter's reply, and then continued. "No, it sounds like him — red leather jacket with Swamp Rebel logo. If we're lucky his old lady Candace, that prune-faced bitch, got planted with him. Take Junior with you and go dig em up. He's in the flat-topped mound out at the old Hamblin place. I cleared the hippy diggers out so nobody will get in your way. And take some heavy-duty garbage bags and rubber gloves — it sounds like he's pretty ripe."

Hogg paused again, listening, then responded. "It's gotta be the Outlaws out of St. Louis again. Still tryin to squeeze us out of the weed market in Memphis. They got no clue we're cutting in on their meth dealing. Planting Henry in the mound is their idea of a joke. They musta heard I hang out with the hippy diggers and the dancing chick, so they decided to let them find Henry for us. Get the word out and watch your back."

True to his word, Sheriff Hogg stopped by the crew house the next morning and updated Boss Man. "I sent someone out yesterday afternoon, and as you suspected, they found a body. We're pretty sure it's a local drug dealer who went missing a while back. It's a gang related killing. The Outlaws, a biker gang up in St Louis, has been trying to shut down a smaller local outfit — the Swamp Rebels, that has encroached on their Memphis meth market. But there's no real call for concern. They never target civilians, just their competition in the drug trade. It's sort of a constant low-level turf battle. A body or two shows up every six months or so."

Boss Man leaned back and exhaled. "So we shouldn't be concerned?"

Hogg laughed. "No, no. No reason for concern. Y'all got nothin to worry about. Best to just forget about it and get on with what you're doin. But we gotta keep this quiet. There's an undercover operation going on and we need to keep a lid on things for now." Hogg hurried off after bringing Boss Man up to speed. Why stick around? Cecelia wasn't around to chat with, and anyway, Hogg had heard from her former dance fans that she had stopped her impromptu mound summit performances and had hooked up with some guitarist that played with a Memphis blues band. He was anxious to check out this new guy Cecelia had taken up with, but right now he had other things to attend to.

Despite his assurances to Boss Man, the sheriff thought that the hippy archaeologists were now caught in the middle of something that could get out of hand in a hurry. The crew had plenty to be worried about if the Outlaws suspected them of being involved in moving drugs. And picking the Red Mound as the place to plant Fat Henry sure suggested that they did. Hogg had flown under the radar for almost a year now and had made modest inroads into the Outlaw's methamphetamine monopoly in Memphis. He had been moving weed across the river in West Memphis for a number of years, but meth was where the big money was, so he had added it to his portfolio, making sure to keep it separate from his cannabis dealing and very quiet. Only Fat Henry, Skeeter, and Junior were in on the crank operation, and things had seemed to be going smoothly until Henry and Candace had abruptly disappeared several months ago.

The sheriff could care less, however, about what Fat Henry's mound burial might mean in terms of putting the archaeology crew in danger. They weren't his problem. But he was worried that the Outlaws might be close to figuring out who was the source of the meth that had been reaching Memphis and impacting the Outlaws' profits.

Meth could be cooked in small labs, and the Outlaws had probably assumed that their competitor's lab was hidden in a trailer or RV somewhere in the backswamps of southeast Arkansas. But they could look all they wanted and would never find a land-based lab. The sheriff's nephew Clete had built their meth operation a few years ago on an old houseboat which he frequently moved from location to location along the numerous tributaries and sloughs, large and small, that joined the Mississippi River downstream from Memphis. Rather than moving the meth by land, which had become increasingly dicey, his nephew carried it by boat to well-hidden drop-off points where Hogg, Junior, or Skeeter would be waiting for the delivery.

Hogg, however, was no longer sure just how safe their secret drop-off locations were. The Outlaws buried Fat Henry in the temple mound for a reason. But why? Was it simply because they saw Hogg as a rival weed seller that needed to be taught a lesson? Or was it more serious? Did Fat Henry tell them anything before he died? He could have given up the general location of the transfer points, one of which was only a few miles or so east of Hamblin's Fort. Shortly after the disappearance of Fat Henry the sheriff had taken a number of precautions in case there had been an information leak, including changing their drop-off locations, pausing the movement of newly arriving shipments from his nephew into Memphis, and stashing his meth inventory in a variety of safe places where it could be easily retrieved.

As Hogg backed out of the driveway Boss Man called the crew together on the veranda and repeated the sheriff's story of rival drug gangs and an ongoing undercover investigation. He emphasized that they would all have to keep what happened quiet and not mention the dead body in the mound to anyone, particularly anyone associated with the university. The last thing they wanted was for their project to be shut down by some weak-kneed dean worried about student safety. Boss Man assured the crew that what was going on really didn't involve them or their excavations. They were not in any danger, Boss Man assured them, and could carry on with their work.

Those crew members with a stake in the excavations, since their academic and scholarly futures depended on it, were happy to swallow this story line. Boss Man, Dolores, Paula, Wilma, Denny, and even Josh were eager to get back to the site and continue their work. At the same time, Cecelia actually seemed to welcome the corpse since it could explain the mound's aura being a sinister shade of dark red. Otherwise, she seemed unconcerned.

Not everyone was happy, however, with the back-to-work order. Zack and Bopper had been hoping for a few more days away from the heat and humidity, and Richard remained skeptical of Boss Man's assurances about their safety. He was also seriously considering cutting his summer on the crew short. He was excited about what they had been finding at Hamblin's Fort, but the crew was too radical, he thought, in their approach to how you do archaeology. They were not very well versed in the deep historical roots and long-established tradition and practice of doing research in the Mississippi Valley. They also seemed almost proud of their lack of knowledge and liked to badmouth the "old fogey" professors and "young fogies" like him that followed the established, traditional way of doing archaeology.

Figuring out the age of a site had long been a central challenge for archaeologists. The development of radiocarbon dating in the late 1940s and its widespread application by the 1960s, however, pretty much solved the problem of determining how old an archaeological site was — all you needed was a chunk of anything organic, anything that had once been alive, and a radiocarbon lab could tell you how many years had passed since it died. Preserved plant material or bone were now essential in establishing the age of an archaeological site.

With the application of radiocarbon dating and a steady increase in the excavation of sites across eastern North America, the construction of developmental sequences for many different regions of the East had, by the 1960s, progressed far enough that this general goal of traditional archaeology had in many respects been achieved. New approaches were emerging, new research questions were being asked — it was the beginning of the "New Archaeology."

While many of the new ideas and approaches that were lumped under this general label of "New Archaeology" would soon mostly fizzle out, one that seemed to have staying power was the "ecological approach" which focused on the place of ancient societies in the environment. Long relegated to appendices at the end of excavation reports, descriptions of plant and animal remains recovered from sites began to receive much more interest and attention. It was sometimes termed "the revolt of the appendix people," as plant and animal remains began to gain equal analytical status with lithics and ceramics, and their analysis was included more into the main body of site reports rather than appendices. Denny and Wilma were part of this new trend, and eager to make their mark.

Richard was not the only one thinking about an early exit from the crew. Although he managed to outwardly maintain his laid-back persona, Tom was totally freaked out. The discovery of a drug gang murder victim at Hamblin's Fort made him wonder if he might be next. He hadn't thought much of it when Sheriff Hogg had handed him a shoe box wrapped in duct tape a few weeks ago and asked him to hold it for him. But now he wondered who might be coming for the box and for him. The box was safe, he thought, hidden under the old chicken coop with his weed stash, but not that safe.

Tom was no stranger to the drug trade. Like Josh, he had grown up in Detroit, and while he had never been a victim of violence, he had heard numerous accounts of drive-by shootings and had witnessed enough violence himself close-up to understand the randomness and collateral damage that surrounded such incidents. Sheriff Hogg's assurances and those of Boss Man that the crew was in no danger were, he knew, total bullshit.

As soon as he got back to the crew house after the discovery of the body of Fat Henry, Tom had packed a go-bag and stashed it under the spare tire in "Songbird," his station wagon. He'd given the car the name of Sky King's plane several years ago following one night's high-flying evasion of the Michigan State Police. Songbird might once again be called on to carry him safely away into the night. The go-bag didn't contain much — a few changes of clothes, a few hundred dollars in cash, toiletries, and a few moon pies.

13.
TONGUE-TAPPIN

The crew was understandably subdued the next morning on the drive out to Hamblin's Fort. They all trooped up to the summit of the temple mound to check out what the aftermath of the corpse removal effort looked like, and were pleasantly surprised. Fat Henry's burial pit had been filled in and there was no remaining evidence of Fat Henry or any lingering smell of decay. Cecelia sensed something of a change in the mound's aura, but it was still a dark brooding red. It wasn't just Fat Henry's decomposing body that had been causing the unsettling red vortex. Something else remained. Something dark.

Jake had headed up to St. Louis for some gigs and Cecelia had opted in his absence to help out again with the excavations. But she thought she would steer clear of the Red Mound for a while, until its aura settled down a bit, so she joined Dolores' excavation of the southeast house cluster. Josh was surprised when Black Dog stayed on the Red Mound rather than follow Cecelia, then remembered Boss Man's enmity toward the dog, as well as Black Dog's continued fixation with the mound.

Josh was also a little uneasy about continuing with his excavations so close to Fat Henry's burial pit, and he was losing interest in his test pits into the mound summit. There didn't seem to be any other features — nothing but an empty white sand layer and mound fill beneath. Maybe he should switch back and help Denny with her trenching. He walked over, squatted down next to where she was digging, and floated the idea.

"My test pits are gonna be dry holes, Denny. Maybe I could switch back and lend a hand digging your trench for a while. Whatdaya think?"

Denny looked up, a smudge of dirt on her forehead, surprise clear in her eyes, and hit him with one of her blazing smiles. Stepping up out of the trench, she dropped her trowel and pulled him into an embrace. Josh felt her breasts pressing up against his chest and was so surprised that Denny managed to give him a too brief but quite memorable kiss and pull away before he could react.

The embrace did not go unnoticed by the rest of the crew, however. Bopper was on his way up the side of the mound to ask about borrowing one of their soil-sifters and witnessed the embrace and the quick kiss. Bopper's jaw dropped in surprise but he quickly recovered. Cupping his hands around his mouth he excitedly bellowed out the news to the crew digging down on the plaza below. "Josh and Denny doin some serious tongue-tappin up here — right in the middle of the workday."

Denny and Josh tried to ignore the scattered shouts of derision that drifted up from the crew as they told Bopper to take the sifter and fuck off. Still somewhat dazed by the embrace, Josh turned toward Denny, who looked equally surprised, and apologized. "Sorry, Josh. Shouldn't have done that," she said, but she smiled as she said it.

Josh decided to act as if the embrace and kiss was no big deal. He returned her smile and replied as he reached down to pick up his trowel. "I'll take that as a yes. But I think we need to work on the kissing thing."

Every few minutes Denny would sneak quick glances in his direction, and Josh made sure to stay intent on his troweling. But he couldn't help the feeling of simple happiness that welled up inside him. Things were looking up.

By the time Boss Man called out "Quittin time," Denny and Josh had made progress in extending the north-south trench toward the south edge of the mound summit. They were both eager to continue toward the goal of trenching down the mound slope but were nervous that Boss Man would amble over and discover what they were up to. They quickly pulled the tarp back over their trench and secured it before hurrying down to join the rest of the crew.

Fortunately for Josh and Denny, nobody seemed interested in what they were up to. Dolores had found a small piece of conch shell with a few engraved lines on it late in the day, and this discovery dominated conversation most of the evening. Bopper made a few crude comments about tongue-tapping, but nobody picked up on teasing Denny and Josh. More importantly, there were no questions asked about what progress was being made on the mound trenching. Somewhat surprisingly, any lingering concerns the crew may have harbored regarding the murder of Fat Henry seemed to have had quickly faded away.

As usual, Wilma and Paula had gone out to their trailer right after dinner, and the rest of the crew had gathered on the porch to down a few beers and trash talk. Dolores and Boss Man were leaning in and whispering to each other, probably fantasizing about their next big find. Richard was quietly getting hammered. Bopper was hogging the fatty he and Tom were passing back and forth and was happily surprised that Tom wasn't calling him out with his usual complaint — "Hey Bopper, don't Bogart the joint, man." Concerned about Tom's recent moodiness, Cecelia tried to get him to recount one of his Fabulous Furry Freak Brothers tales, but Tom didn't pick up on the invitation, just smiled ruefully.

The sun had gone down and it was cooling off a bit when the quiet of the evening was split by the roaring exhaust of a vehicle approaching up the road to the crew house. A beat-up pickup with only one headlight, on high beam of course, turned into the driveway, briefly lighting up the porch. Denny stood and excitedly hurried toward the truck, calling out as she rushed down the veranda steps. "Hey Catfish, what you got for me tonight?"

Josh stood and watched Denny approach the truck, puzzled by Zack and Bopper's muttered obscenities as they quickly stood and rushed into the house. Josh soon realized what had spooked Zack and Bopper. A rancid odor emanating from the newly arrived truck rolled across the yard and enveloped him on the porch.

"Jesus," Josh blurted out as he briefly wondered if they'd turned up another corpse. Then he remembered. Denny had somebody local collecting dead animals for her to render down for her comparative skeletal collection. It must be Catfish.

Following Denny down to the truck, Josh was introduced to Catfish, who turned out to be an attractive black woman, probably in her early twenties, wearing overalls and a T-shirt and sporting an impressive afro. Catfish and Denny clearly were good friends, based on their easy banter. A variety of dead animals were scattered across the bed of the pickup in various stages of decomposition.

Catfish pointed to and identified the dead critters as Denny and Josh looked on. "Got you a couple of swamp rabbits and a gray fox, but mostly it's waterfowl this trip - a black duck, a lesser scaup, a wood duck, and a double-crested Cormorant. I should have a bunch more for you next week, I think, but I wanted to get these to you before they got too ripe."

Denny and Catfish good-naturedly haggled over the cost of the animals, settling on thirty bucks, based mostly on the gray fox, which Denny agreed was a great specimen. It wasn't Denny's money, anyway — she had research funds from the university to cover the cost of building up the archaeology museum's comparative skeletal collections.

Josh grabbed a shovel and wheelbarrow from the garage and hurriedly wheeled Catfish's rancid cargo into the garage for storage overnight. Tomorrow he and Denny would individually wrap the new acquisitions in window screen and bury them in the back yard for initial rendering down before being given a final cleaning.

Wondering what the back story was on Catfish, and how Denny knew her, Josh asked the obvious question as they watched the one-eyed pickup rattle away down the road.

"Isn't it dangerous for her to be in the county after dark? What about the sundown rule? No blacks are supposed to be in the county after dark, right?"

Denny shook her head and replied. "It's only a half mile to the county line. Catfish is OK doing a quick in and out like this, and anyway, Sheriff Hogg lets Catfish slide on the small stuff. She's a good vendor for Hogg's product — sort of his outreach to the black community. But there's still a lot of other folks around, crazy cracker white trash, who wouldn't hesitate to harass her if they caught her here after sundown, particularly since both her brothers are still working in the Ford plant up in Ypsitucky, and not around to protect her."

When he had first heard Catfish's truck come roaring up to the house Tom had briefly thought that this was it — a drug gang was coming for him and that package he was holding for the sheriff. He was freaked out and the weed he had been smoking helped to generate a sudden spike in paranoia. He had shared many a joint with Catfish the summer before, however, and his fear quickly dissipated when he realized who it was.

Zack and Bopper returned to the front porch and sat down again after assuring themselves that the rancid odors had dissipated. Zack was unusually quiet this evening, a stark departure from his usual unending stream of commentary about whatever sprang into his head. Bopper had explained to Josh that Zack had a "throat brain" in addition to his regular brain, and that it was often in control, allowing him to talk incessantly without really engaging any higher-level cognitive functions.

Zack claimed to have American Indian ancestors going way back, including a great-grandmother who was Cherokee, or maybe Choctaw — his story changed from one week to the next. He was of average height, maybe five nine, stocky, with black beady eyes, a wide "gummy" smile showing yellow teeth and too much of his upper gums. He wore his greasy blond hair long, often in a braid, and would sport a leather headband on most days, along with a fringed rawhide vest that he thought showcased his impressive torso. After the first few weeks of the excavation season the vest began to offer a distinctive olfactory experience to anyone who came close to Zack, which he seemed not to notice or to care about. A pair of shorts, flip-flops, and a well-worn John Deer baseball hat rounded out his usual attire, along with a rawhide necklace holding an Egyptian Ankh symbol.

Zack had a lot of free-floating hostility and was quick to take offense at perceived slights. He was particularly attuned to anyone, particularly women, making jokes at his expense. He and Richard had a long-running practice of belittling the excavation skills and physical shortcomings of the women on the crew whenever the opportunity arose, and Zack considered himself the only one truly competent enough to operate the mechanical sifter. Paula in particular had drawn his insults and harassment, apparently because she had bluntly laughed at his advances.

"I'm gay, Zack. I like women. Wilma and I are a couple. Don't you get it?"

Zack apparently didn't get it. He thought it must be some sort of a phase, and that Paula would have to come around in time. All he had to do was wait patiently while at the same time reminding her both of his manliness and the proper place for women in archaeology — they should play a support role in the background. In the laboratory for example, washing artifacts and gluing potsherds back together — not in the field. Zack was not gaining any traction with his views on gender roles in archaeology, however, at least among the crew. They all pretty much laughed him off.

The phone started ringing in the kitchen and Cecelia jumped up and ran in the house to answer it. She was expecting a call from Jake up in St. Louis. It was Jake on the phone, judging from Cecelia's wide smile and raised fist when she picked up the receiver. Her smile quickly faded, however, and her arm dropped to her side. She listened for a few minutes, asked a quick question in a whisper, and nodding her head, blurted a quick "bye" and hung up. Strolling causally back out onto the porch, she motioned for Tom to follow her out to her tent.

As soon as they got around the side of the house Cecelia stopped and grabbed Tom's hand in both of hers, squeezing hard. "That was Jake. He heard from a contact he has that the Arkansas State Police might be planning a raid on us. They think we're involved in moving drugs into Memphis. He said he'd tell me the full story when he got back, but for now we need to hide the weed and anything else there might be. But it's just weed, right?"

Tom nodded his head rapidly. "Yeah, yeah. Just weed. And actually, not much of that. I've got the only stash. Bopper was down to seeds and stems last week and starting to mooch my supply. I'll move what I have left over the fence a hundred yards or so into the bean field." Turning quickly toward the garage for a shovel, Tom was off into the darkness to retrieve the shoebox the sheriff had given him for safekeeping from under the chicken coop. It would be safe buried out among the soybeans and he could mark its location with a rock or something.

Tom made a strange sight in the moonlight, loping silently across the yard with a shovel in one hand and the sheriff's parcel tucked under his other arm.

14.
RUNNING WAS A BAD IDEA

Tom was expecting the narcs to descend on them at any minute. He buried the sheriff's shoebox in the adjacent beanfield and then joined Cecelia in her tent, where they hunkered down in the darkness. They could hear the low sound of voices drifting across the yard from the front porch of the crew house, muffled by the walls of Cecelia's tent. Tom nervously poked around in the top pocket of his overalls — the one holding all his pens and a few fatties, and pulled out one of the joints, suggesting it might calm them down a bit if they took just a toke or two. They both agreed to not mention anything just yet about Jake's narc-raid tipoff. It might not happen, so why alarm the crew, they figured, and Cecelia didn't want her dad hearing about it — he would order her home in a heartbeat.

Soon they were well into a second joint, its glowing tip moving back and forth between them in the darkness. It was good weed and Tom and Cecelia alternated between giggling at their predicament and frozen silent in sudden paranoia whenever they thought they heard a car approaching. At some point after midnight Cecelia fell asleep with her head on Tom's chest. He lay awake for a while, listening to the night sounds and the slow steady rhythm of Cecelia's breathing.

Tom woke just as the sun was coming up. Cecelia was gone. He figured she was out at Hamblin's Fort watching the sunrise from the top of the conical mound. She would be getting quite a show this morning. The entire eastern sky was a deep fiery red. Tom figured it just meant that a low-pressure system and rain was coming, but he was curious to see what Cecelia would have to say.

Perched on top of the conical mound, Cecelia sat cross-legged with an aggressively erect back and her hands resting comfortably on her knees. She was trying to concentrate on her mantra but watched the deep red sky in the east with a growing sense of unease. Cecelia was still a little stoned from the night before and was not too surprised when she felt a brief vibration radiating through her body every few minutes or so. She couldn't tell if it was her or the mound beneath her that was the source of the tremors. Across the plaza the Red Mound energy upwelling appeared to be pulsing and growing stronger as the dark red vortex funneled up from its summit to join the red sunrise. Black Dog, who had followed Cecelia out to Hamblin's Fort, was also clearly agitated, and paced the summit of the temple mound, pausing often to seemingly listen to something Cecelia could not hear.

Cecelia was also worried about last night's phone call from Jake. She wasn't concerned about a narc raid so much as she was about the exact nature of Jake's connection to the Arkansas State Police. What was that all about? She was certainly grateful that he had called to warn her, she, but was he an undercover narc? Did he suddenly appear to watch her dance and then charm his way into her tent just so he could spy on the crew and their supposed drug dealing? Was it all an act? They had a lot to talk about if he ever reappeared. Jake had some serious explaining to do.

When the crew arrived at the site around eight, Tom joined Cecelia on the conical mound, wondering about the no-show on the part of the narcs and the question mark hanging over Jake. But he hesitated to say anything. Maybe it was better to just let things unfold. To let that sleeping dog lie. But he was dying to know. Was Jake a fake? A spy? Was he going to show his face again or not? Tom, of course, hoped Jake was history, and was standing ready to console Cecelia and perhaps make some progress with her.

Before Tom could sit down next to Cecelia, Boss Man called up to him from the southeast house cluster and waved him over.

"Tom, get your skinny ass down here, we need your skimming skills." As soon as Tom got close, Boss Man explained what he wanted, scratching his crotch and squinting in the bright sun.

"We got two structures here — the small shrine and the larger structure with the conch shell fragments, but we need to see if there's anything else associated with them. Are there any other structures, hearths, activity areas, pits, anything at all. I want you to sharpen up your shovel blade and start skimming out away from what we got. Any direction — let's see what you can find."

Tom had just started to sharpen his shovel when he noticed Cecelia moving quickly down the side of the conical mound. She was waving at him as she ran and pointing toward the parking area. Tom glanced over to see Sheriff Hogg just pulling up in his Chevy Bel Air. Setting his shovel down he walked over to where Cecelia and the sheriff were talking, no doubt about last night's phone call from Jake. As he reached them, the sheriff scowled at him and pointed to his car, growling.

"Get in."

As soon as Tom and the sheriff left, Cecelia trotted over to join Denny and Josh on the Red Mound.

"Hey Denny, I got a deal for you. I'll come back and dig my ass off up here for you guys, but can we fill in the trench over the red clay feature for now. It might calm things down. The energy vortex is getting stronger. Did you see the sky this morning? I think exposing the red clay platform and excavating the red wolf burial upset the balance in the mound somehow. And look at Black Dog — he's freaked."

Denny and Josh looked at each other, and both shrugged.

"Sure," Josh responded, and walking over, started shoveling dirt on top of the red clay feature. He continued until it was covered by six inches or so of soil and was surprised when Black Dog wagged his tail excitedly on the back dirt pile, clearly pleased by Josh's efforts.

Tom and the sheriff rode in silence back to the Hamblin mansion. Tom was frozen in fear as he listened to the sheriff muttering obscenities in a low menacing voice. When they arrived, Tom led the sheriff behind the crew house and into the soybean field. He was sure the stash was eight rows straight in from the broken fencepost, but the crossed sticks he had used to mark its location didn't seem to be there anymore. He freaked out for maybe fifteen long seconds as he tried to scan his surroundings without the sheriff noticing. Then he saw the empty hole where he had buried the drugs. Someone had dug them up.

"This is bad," he thought, "really bad. I'm fucked." Tom was having trouble catching his breath and he noticed that his hands were shaking. He briefly considered making a run for it but looking out across the vast expanse of the soybean field he realized that running was a bad idea. Really bad. He wouldn't get far. The sheriff had showed off his shooting skills with his pistol several times at the crew house, shattering beer bottles to the great enjoyment of Zack and Bopper.

Just as Tom was about to turn and tell the sheriff about the missing stash, he saw something several rows away. It was the shoe box the sheriff had given him, lying on the ground. Tom rushed over and picked it up. It was still intact except for one corner where a critter had chewed away the cardboard and sampled some of the product. An off-white powder trickled out of the opening in the shoe box. Tom turned and nervously shoved the box into the sheriff's hands with a muttered explanation before hurrying past him, back to the house. "Looks like a woodchuck or something got into it, sheriff, but he didn't eat much." Tom said, half expected to hear the sound of the sheriff drawing his pistol for a shot to the back of his head, but he had only taken a few steps when Hogg cackled loudly and replied.

"You're right son. He didn't eat much. And I bet he's dead or seriously fucked up right now. This is some good shit."

After warning Tom again to keep his trap shut if anyone, including the crew, started asking questions, the sheriff dropped him off back at Hamblin's Fort. Relieved that he didn't have to worry about safekeeping the sheriff's package anymore, Tom checked in with Boss Man and returned to his skimming. He was already thinking of some snappy responses for any questions the state cops might ask if they came calling. Cecelia walked over to find out what had happened and went up on her tiptoes to give him a light kiss on the cheek when he indicated that the drugs were gone. They were clean. Everything was copacetic.

Tom was so focused on the potential answers he might offer the police, if need be, he was slow at first to notice the foot-wide darker strip of soil his skimming had uncovered. When he did, he stopped briefly, surprised, and then hurriedly took a few more strokes with his shovel.

"I got a wall trench here. It's a big one," Tom reported. Boss Man and Dolores hurried over, trailed by the rest of the crew. "What the fuck" was the general reaction from the sweaty, dirt-covered group that crowded around Tom as he exposed more of the wall trench. A substantial wall feature didn't seem to make much sense in this location. The crew got bored after a few minutes and drifted back to work. Tom uncovered five feet or so of the wall trench — enough to establish its general direction, and then moved another ten feet forward along the line the trench was taking and skimmed again, finding the trench feature just where he expected.

Continuing this strategy of looking for the darker soil of the wall trench every ten feet or so, it took Tom less than an hour to trace its entire length. It formed a square in outline, maybe fifty feet on a side, with the small shrine that had yielded the bauxite figurine at its center, and the larger "conch shell" structure about halfway between the shrine and the wall trench. Judging from the width of the trench it had held large posts and based on its large size and the lack of any evidence of interior support posts, it had to have been a free-standing wall, not part of any sort of building. There was a single opening in the wall, six feet or so wide, on the side that faced the Red Mound.

Tom spent the rest of the day first shovel-skimming to expose the rest of the trench, and then cross-sectioning it in several places to record its depth and width. It was consistently about a foot wide and more than two feet deep. Their cross-section digging also indicated that the trench had been dug down through a number of earlier, underlying houses, indicating that it had been constructed very late in the occupational sequence of the site, and was not part of any organized community layout.

One of the cross-section pits also contained a gallon or so deposit of clay that had apparently been packed around several loose posts in order to stabilize them. The presence of packing clay immediately drew the attention of Wilma, who elbowed Tom aside and carefully removed the clay fragments and placed them in a cotton-cushioned box. She would look at them in more detail back at the Hamblin Mansion that night, but she already was beaming as she checked out one of the fragments with a hand lens.

"It's got red cedar bark impressions." Her announcement produced smiles all around and an impromptu series of dance moves from Cecelia.

Watching from the summit of the Red Mound, Josh wondered why red cedar was such a big deal, but didn't want to look ignorant by asking. Denny saw the puzzled look on his face and sidled up next to him with an explanation.

"Red cedar wasn't used much for everyday construction Josh. It was usually a marker of a ceremonial or high-status setting, like a chief's house or a temple. Finding a cedar wall around the shrine and the conch shell structure means there was some serious stuff going down in there. It was a physically and visually restricted space."

Even with the exciting find of the red cedar enclosure, discussion on the Hamblin Mansion porch after dinner was somewhat subdued. The T-shaped shrine and conch shell structure, along with the enclosing red cedar wall, were exciting finds, but after an initial flurry of excitement that evening, Bopper abruptly ruined the mood.

"We're finding some cool shit, no question. But what does what we're doing have to do with discovering social organization by analyzing pot sherd designs. Isn't that why we're here?"

Once Bopper asked the question, it was pretty obvious to everyone that the exciting finds had drawn them off-course. They had made little actual progress so far toward collecting the data they needed for their dissertation research. While certainly important, the red cedar enclosure and its contents — the bauxite figurine, Cahokia ceramics and lithic and shell debris, did nothing to advance their understanding of Hamblin's Fort social structure. They couldn't even be sure that the enclosure had anything to do with the Hamblin's Fort community.

If the Cahokian presence they had discovered represented any sort of influence and interaction between Cahokia and the local Hamblin's Fort community, including perhaps a religious visitation, they should be seeing more intermingling of material culture, more evidence of actual interaction between locals and the delegation from Cahokia. But so far, the Cahokian presence seemed completely isolated from the rest of Hamblin's Fort.

They couldn't even be sure that Hamblin's Fort had been occupied when the enclosure and its structures were built. Maybe the site had been abandoned by the time the Cahokians arrived.

Boss Man proposed that they finish up work in the Cahokian enclosure, which in any case was pretty much completed, and turn their attention to other areas of the site and other structures — ones that were clearly part of the Hamblin Fort community. Dolores immediately agreed, and Paula and Wilma also voiced their support. The Cahokia Enclosure was a great find and would result in several journal articles, with a shot at getting published in *American Antiquity* or another high-profile publication. But they were all under pressure to collect sizable data sets from different areas of the site to compare and contrast for their dissertations, and they needed to get on with it.

Richard piped up from time to time, voicing his total agreement, but also suggesting they should be sure to excavate Tom's wall trench more thoroughly in case ceremonial objects may have been deposited as dedicatory offerings during its construction, particularly at the corners and the enclosure's single opening. Bopper strongly supported Richard's suggestion and offered to join him in the trench digging.

"You and me tomorrow morning Richard — we're gonna dig the fuck out of those corners and find something amazing."

Richard was surprised by Bopper's encouragement and offer of help but nonetheless pleased by the support for his idea. Boss Man blessed the search for offerings, but told Bopper and Richard to make it quick, as they were needed for the new excavation that they would be opening up at the southwest corner of the plaza. Denny and Josh added nothing to the conversation about shifting focus away from the shrine and red cedar enclosure. They stayed silent, holding their breath, worried that Boss Man might try to stop them from continuing to work on the summit of the Red Mound.

15.
DEFINITELY TEOTIHUACAN

Bopper was up early the next morning and off to Hamblin's Fort on foot. After a brief stop for a Coke and bag of chips at the corner store, he got to the site maybe a half-hour before the rest of the crew. As soon as the rest of the crew arrived Boss Man shifted most of them over to open up another block excavation at the Southwest corner of the plaza. Bopper and Richard stayed behind to look for ritual offerings in the enclosure wall trench that Tom had discovered the day before. The Red Mound crew stayed under the radar.

Bopper had cleaned off two of the corners of the wall trench and was sharpening his trowel. Clearly, he was ready to start looking for any ritual objects that might had been deposited when the enclosure wall was built. Richard picked one of the corners Bopper had cleared and set to work while Bopper started in on the other. Richard had only dug for a few minutes before he stopped troweling, reached for his soft-bristled brush, and after a few seconds cried out in excitement.

"Oh my God, Jesus."

Bopper rushed over and Richard, uncharacteristically at a loss for words, pointed down into his small excavation unit and gave Bopper a wide smile. Bopper had never seen Richard's full-toothed smile before and he recoiled at the jagged jumble of yellow chicklets on display. Looking down into Richard's freshly dug hole, he could see a dull greenish-hued object about the size of a beer bottle. Looking closer, he could see it was a carving of a standing human figure.

Richard suddenly jumped up and yelled across to the southwest corner of the plaza where Boss Man and the crew were opening up the new block excavation unit looking for house structures.

"We got another human carving here, Boss, but this one looks Mesoamerican. It's Teotihuacan I think." Richard suddenly sat down hard and lay on his side for a few moments before reviving. Bopper would later describe it as a "swoon" when he recounted the episode for anyone who would listen.

Moving back to the small hole he had dug down into the wall trench Richard continued cleaning off the small human figure, crowing loudly in a stream of consciousness jabber.

"I told you. It's fucking jade. It's my sweet little Teotihuacan priest. I'm the man. I AM the man. I fucking found it. Check it out!" Ignoring all professional procedures for proper recording of the statue in situ, Richard pulled it from the hole and held it at arm's length out in front of him. He slowly moved the statue back and forth in front of the gathering crew as he turned serious.

"You all have the great privilege of witnessing a historic event. The statue I am holding in my hand is the first solid artifactual evidence that proves that there was contact between Mesoamerica and eastern North America. Think of it. Cahokia and Teotihuacan. The Valley of Mexico and the American Bottom. And I'm the one who discovered it." Pounding his chest with his free hand, head thrown back, he screamed to the heavens: "I fucking found it." Dropping his free hand back to his side, Richard brought the figure up close for another assessment. "Oh yes, definitely Teotihuacan."

Puffed up with his own wonderfulness, with the excitement of such a monumental discovery, Richard looked up and realized in sudden confusion that Bopper was holding a human sculpture identical to the one he had just uncovered.

"Hey look, I found one too," Bopper said. After a long blank stare at Bopper's statue, Richard noticed that Paula, Wilma, and Zack were now crowding around and all of them were holding copies of the same statue. The light bulb went off in Richard's overheated brain that he'd been had. It was all a prank. Hefting his statue briefly before heaving it in a long arc toward the conical mound, Richard stalked off to the sound of Zack's high-pitched bray-like cackle.

Up on the Red Mound, Denny, Josh, and Cecelia watched the drama unfold.

"What's up," Josh asked. "Why was Richard freaking out? First screaming something about Mexico, then falling down, then getting up and more shouting, and finally throwing something off into the distance.

"I knew something was going on but wasn't really sure what they were up to until this morning," Denny replied, laughing. "Now I get it. They must have found some bogus statues at the Chucalissa site gift shop during their Memphis weekend. Bopper buried two statues, knowing whichever corner he picked, Richard would find a statue. Bopper then quickly dug up the second statue to have it ready to show. They figured Richard would trumpet his big discovery. They're poking fun at him and his constant claims that the Mississippian temple mound builders here in eastern North America had their origins in Mesoamerica, one way or another — maybe a migration, maybe religious outreach and the introduction of a new belief system, maybe trade networks. Mesoamerica has long been a simple answer for anyone looking to explain away any number of different developments that occurred in the East — pottery, agriculture, mound building, you name it."

"I don't remember any discussion of Mississippian — Mesoamerican connections in our archaeology class last fall," Josh replied, looking puzzled.

"That's cause nobody has ever found any artifacts from Mesoamerica in archaeological sites in the East," Denny responded. "Richard's 'south of the border story' and other similar 'big arrow' explanations have been around for a long time, but they don't cut it with a lot of younger archaeologists. Many of us consider them actually to be non-explanations since they conveniently side-step the challenge of figuring out how Mississippian mound builder societies independently emerged in the East, without any influence from Mesoamerica. They're a cop-out."

Josh watched as Richard walked rapidly toward the parking area and then kept going, heading down the road back toward the crew house. Bopper and Zack muttered "slip me some skin" and exchanged a few elaborate hand slaps before returning to the new block excavation being opened up at the southwest corner of the plaza. Paula and Wilma followed, still holding their bogus Teotihuacan statues up in the air and making them dance. As the four of them reached the block excavation, Zack turned, and pretending the statue was his penis, waved it at Paula a half-dozen times or so before dropping it to pick up his shovel.

"Did you see that?" Denny asked, pointing toward Zack.

Josh nodded, adding "He's a weird dude — kinda creepy if you ask me."

"He's more than creepy," Denny replied. "Zack's scary. He's got this free-floating hostility toward women in general, and Paula in particular. He tried to chat her up last year before he realized she was a lesbian. She blew him off at the time — laughed at him, and ever since he looks for ways to antagonize her. He likes to wonder aloud why women would prefer each other to a man, and ask what's wrong with him? He thinks his lack of a girlfriend is because women are shallow creatures, always looking for someone good looking, with status, power, or money, always looking to climb the ladder, not able to see all his admirable qualities."

"He's sketchy," Josh responded. "What are Paula and Wilma gonna do?"

"Right now, they're trying to just ignore his behavior and not provoke him. And that doesn't seem to be working too well. Wilma told me she thinks he's been peeking in their trailer windows at night. They asked Boss Man to do something but he just laughed it off, telling them not to be so sensitive, and that they should work it out with Zack themselves. In case you haven't noticed, Boss man's not exactly a feminist."

Denny smiled and lifted her eyebrows in concern as she continued. "I asked Wilma if she had any ideas of how to deal with Zack. She's so shy, I figured she would just suffer through. You know what Wilma told me? She smiled, patted my shoulder, and said that since Boss Man gave her the green light on Zack, she just might have to fuck him up."

Josh laughed. "Quiet Wilma? I would like to see that. Does Zack harass you?"

"He did a bit last summer, but gave up, I guess. Probably figured it was no use — decided I wasn't into men, was a boring nerd, and too smart-ass. Then after the science reporter did a face plant in the bonfire, he got fixated on Paula.

Smiling innocently, Josh replied. "It'll be interesting to see how Zack reacts when he realizes we're a couple."

Smiling as she pushed Josh away, Denny pulled her trowel from her back pocket and walked back to the trench they were extending toward the edge of the mound summit.

By noon Boss Man, Dolores, and the rest of the crew except for Denny, Josh and Cecelia — the Red Mound crew, had made good progress stripping the plow zone from the new block excavation unit at the southwest corner of the plaza. They had partially uncovered one house structure and part of a second structure, as well as several pit features. Although they were not screening the dirt as they removed the plow zone, since anything they found was already in a disturbed context, Dolores still managed to recover several dozen plow zone pot sherds and was quite encouraged by what was turning up.

Even though the sherds had been churned up from their original location by the plow, it was still safe to assume they were from somewhere in the vicinity of the new houses the crew were excavating. Dolores thought this small ceramic assemblage from the new excavation looked different from the ceramics recovered from the test pits they had dug the previous year into two houses just inside the north side fortification wall, as well as the ceramic assemblage recovered from the northeast house cluster. She couldn't wait to get back to the crew house and compare these new sherds with those of the earlier excavated houses — it looked like the internal variation in ceramics at Hamblin's Fort that they had been hoping for might actually exist.

Dolores was already fantasizing about some sort of north-south differences in ceramic traditions that would mark a major social division dividing the community into two equal parts — a moiety. Both of the newly uncovered houses also appeared to contain a crisscrossed jumble of burned wall posts that had collapsed inward when the structures burned. Burned wall posts had also turned up in the two structures tested the previous year, as well as in the northeast house cluster, raising the possibility that there had been a major fire that ravaged the entire settlement shortly before it was abandoned.

The piece of pottery that particularly caught Dolores's interest that morning was a handle sherd from what would have been a large storage jar. The handle was in the shape of a frog, with its head protruding above the rim and its two front legs grasping the lip of the jar. The ass-end of the frog formed a rivet through the wall of the vessel. "Rim riders" like the frog handle were not uncommon in Mississippian ceramic assemblages, but it could still reflect a particular social subset within the larger Hamblin's Fort community — perhaps it represented the Frog Moiety.

That evening Dolores started to carefully clean the remaining dirt from her new discoveries. After laying the sherds out to dry on the kitchen table she went into the pantry where they had stored the artifacts recovered from the test pits excavated in north side houses the previous year. Retrieving the bags containing last year's ceramics, she laid them out on the kitchen table next to the newly recovered sherds from the northeast and southwest house clusters and started comparing them. The ceramic assemblages were different in a number of ways, but Dolores wasn't sure exactly what the differences meant.

Most of the sherds in all three assemblages were from storage jars, and most were body sherds, from below the rim and shoulder areas of the vessels. Body sherds carried little useful information, being typically undecorated. But Dolores noticed a surprising difference in the composition of the clay used in the different groups of ceramics. Those recently recovered from the southwest corner of the plaza had a typical Mississippian ceramic paste — the clay had been mixed with ground up pieces of burned mussel shell to temper or strengthen the vessel walls. The sherds from the two north side assemblages also contained ground-up mussel shell as a tempering agent, but also showed the occasional inclusion of "grog" — ground up fragments of pottery.

Jar rim and shoulder sherds, far fewer in number than body sherds, also exhibited some differences between the three assemblages. The north-side jars had somewhat shorter rims and more abrupt shoulder angles, along with chevron design motifs, while the southwest corner vessels had taller rims and more curvilinear designs. A single large piece of a flat-bottomed large plate — a "salt pan," was also recovered from the southwest corner plow zone, along with the frog handle.

Dolores was stroking the frog handle sherd and gazing out the kitchen window, lost in thought, when the wall phone rang. She got up, walked over, and answered. She listened briefly, and then setting the phone down on the counter, walked out on the porch to find Josh, calling loudly so everyone could hear. "Hey Josh, you got a phone call. Said her name was Charlotte and you know her."

Josh got up from his place on the porch swing next to Denny and hurried into the house without looking at her. Dolores took Josh's seat next to Denny and smiling sweetly, provided additional color commentary. "Definitely a recent girlfriend, all breathless and gushy."

Zack and Bopper, still caked in dirt from a day of shoveling, watched Denny for a reaction to this news, while Richard and Boss Man continued their animated dialogue at the other end of the porch, paying no attention to Dolores or her announcement.

Denny's expression didn't change as she glanced at Dolores and shrugged, disappointing Zack and the Bopper, who were hoping for some drama. Not getting the rise out of Denny she had hoped for, Dolores got up, and collecting Boss Man, went back into the kitchen and her sherd assemblages. As they entered the kitchen, Josh stretched the phone cord and slid into the pantry and closed the door, hoping for a little privacy.

Dolores and Boss man sat down at the kitchen table with the three ceramic assemblages and Dolores outlined what she had found so far. They knew full well that the differences between the ceramics from different locations at the site could mean a number of different things. Maybe the houses the ceramics came from were occupied at different times during the occupation of Hamblin's Fort, with ceramic designs and temper changing over time. Grog temper was a common marker of ceramics from pre-Mississippian times, so there was some indication of possible temporal difference between the two locations, with the north-side houses perhaps being earlier in the occupational history of the site. Standard dating methods like paleomagnetism and radiocarbon dating wouldn't help to establish contemporaneity of the ceramic assemblages — they weren't accurate enough.

The simple fact that many of the houses they had exposed so far contained burned wall posts certainly suggested they were all contemporary and had all burned in the same fire. Wilma had even floated an interesting possibility for further consideration of the burned wall posts — comparing their tree-ring records. The carbonized posts, if well enough preserved, might contain tree-ring growth records that could be compared and potentially be matched up with each other, showing if they were harvested within the same short period of time.

Boss Man and Dolores also had to consider that the differences between the ceramic assemblages might be due to status differences between the households in question, with those situated closer to the plaza and the conical mound having higher social rank. So far though, the houses they had excavated seemed to have quite similar artifact assemblages and were similar in size and construction - so status differences did not, so far, seem to be a factor.

They fervently hoped that the differences they had so far seen in their admittedly small ceramic assemblages did in fact reflect internal social organization rather than temporal or status differences. Sitting at the kitchen table, eager to see evidence of social organization in their piles of pot sherds, Boss Man and Dolores worked to convince each other that what was laid out on the kitchen table met the "proof of concept" of their hypothesis that their dissertation advisor had demanded. What they needed now, of course, was more ceramics. But it wasn't just more ceramics. They knew that if they were going to make a compelling argument for their impressive claim — that you could get at social organization through spatial pattern analysis of intra-site variation in ceramic design and construction, they would have to demonstrate that they had collected the ceramics in a scientifically rigorous manner.

Since they didn't have the time or resources to recover all of the ceramics from every corner of the site, they would have to settle for analyzing a part of the total — a sample. The key challenge Boss Man and Dolores faced would be to demonstrate that the ceramic sample they had recovered by the end of the field season, and on which they would be basing their analysis, was "representative" of the entire site assemblage — that it reflected the larger whole in terms of the spatial distribution of different ceramic types.

They both had taken an "Analytical Methods in Archaeology" graduate seminar the previous year. Taught by Professor Shetler, who chaired both of their dissertation committees, the "Anal Methods" course included a lengthy consideration of various forms of sampling design that could be employed to ensure the recovery of representative samples from archaeological contexts. Shetler, who was a strong proponent of the "New Archaeology" and considered himself an authority on the application of quantitative methods to archaeology, had spent several afternoons that spring working with Boss Man and Dolores, brainstorming different possible ways of sampling the Hamblin's Fort ceramics in a scientific manner that would yield a representative sample.

After more discussion and pot sherd fondling, Boss Man and Dolores convinced each other that they had, in fact, satisfied Professor Shetler's "proof of concept" standard and were ready to get the go-ahead for the next phase of their ceramic collection efforts at Hamblin's Fort. They would shut down the southwest house cluster block excavation before it really got started and begin their scientific ceramic sampling from across the entire site. As soon as Josh got off the phone with Charlotte, Boss Man would call Prof Shetler and let him know they had attained "proof of concept" status and it was time for him to drive down and give final approval for their total site ceramic collection sampling design.

16.
TRY OUT THE COUPLE THING

Josh was in the pantry on the phone with Charlotte for almost half an hour and Boss Man and Dolores had moved back out to the veranda by the time he emerged into the kitchen again. Walking back out onto the porch he found Denny where he had left her on the porch swing, now sharing it with Bopper. He could hear Cecelia and Tom's voices drifting across the lawn from Cecelia's tent, which was softly illuminated from within. Wilma and Paula had retired to their trailer. Zack and Richard were well into a raucous back and forth about Mesoamerican influence in eastern North America. As soon as Josh came through the door, Boss Man jumped up and rushed in the house to call Prof. Shetler with their good news. Watching Denny out of the corner of her eye, Dolores probed Josh for information.

"Charlotte seemed like a really nice girl, Josh. Sounds like she misses you." Josh sat down and popped open the beer he had brought from the kitchen. Slumping in his chair, stretching his legs out, he took a sip of beer and replied offhandedly.

"She's not a girl, Dolores, and it's not really any of your business."

Dolores was quite pleased with the apparent tension in the air and doubled down.

"Hey Denny, did you hear that Boss Man is calling Dr. Shetler as we sit here, and we'll be shifting over now to our total site ceramic sampling approach. I'm thinking Shetler will be coming down in the next few days to review and bless our efforts. He'll probably want to pull you and Josh and Cecelia off the temple mound to help us. It's all-hands-on-deck now, no more undergraduate flights of fancy. This should be fun. He's got quite a thing for you, I hear. Kinda grabby, isn't he? Didn't you complain about him at some point just this spring?" Dolores smiled sweetly, waiting for a response, and snickered when Denny stood up, returned Josh's gaze with a quizzical expression, and walked into the house without saying anything.

Wilma's suspicions about Zack peeking in the windows of the trailer that she shared with Paula were well founded. Later that night, Zack was again sneaking out the back door of the crew house and quietly creeping across the side yard to their trailer. One of the windows provided a good view of the bedroom, and Zack was excited to see Paula lying in bed reading a book. It was another hot and humid night, and Paula was naked with a sheet pulled up to her waist. It was like she was displaying herself for him, Zack thought. He couldn't believe his luck and was savoring the view when he thought he heard someone whisper "Okra." He turned toward the sound just as Wilma pasted him just behind the left ear with one of the croquet mallets, bouncing his head off the side of the trailer and dropping him to the ground. He was unconscious for a minute or so, and when he looked up, Wilma and Paula were looking down at him. Wilma was twirling the croquet mallet in her right hand.

"How did that feel Zack?" Wilma asked in a calm voice. "It sure felt good on my end." Stepping closer, Wilma continued. "You think you know me, but you don't. There's more where that came from Zacko, my boy — just let me know. Mess with Paula anymore and you will get an encore performance." Zack tried to move, but his head was pounding and Wilma quickly pinned him to the ground by pressing her foot down on his head, right where the mallet had landed. Moving the mallet up against Zack's face and tapping it gently against his nose and mouth, Wilma smiled down at Zack. Then she and Paula turned away and climbed back into their trailer, leaving Zack where he lay.

A little later in the evening, Josh was lying in bed in his boxers, trying to ignore the heat and humidity, and reading "In Cold Blood" when he heard someone climbing the stairs to the attic. Denny peeked over the top of the stairs and then continued up. Standing right below the overhead light, her face in shadow, she stuck her hands in the pockets of her overalls and asked in a quiet voice.

"What's the deal with your ex-girlfriend?"

Glancing at the bare lightbulb, which was swaying slightly again, Josh set the book aside. "Charlotte dumped me a few months ago, but now is having second thoughts. Her summer's not going well, and she wants to drive down and spend some time with me."

"That sounds nice," Denny replied, and waited for a response. When she got no reaction from Josh, she prompted. "What are you going to do?"

Looking a little surprised by Denny's questions, Josh paused before answering.

"I'm not sure. I told her I would have to clear it with Boss Man." This time Denny made no response, so Josh asked, "What do you think I should do?"

Denny scratched a bug bite on her arm, and then reaching up, she pulled the cord on the overhead light, casting the attic into total darkness.

"Why don't we sleep on it Josh? I think things will be much clearer in the morning."

Denny was gone when Josh woke up the next morning. He found her sitting at the kitchen table having coffee with Cecelia and Tom. Sensing his presence, they looked up at Josh with big

Cheshire Cat smiles. Seeing their expressions, Denny quickly spoke up, looking straight at Josh.

"So, I was just telling Cecelia and Tom that we're going to try out the couple thing for a while, see how it goes, that's all."

Cecelia laughed. "And how's it going Josh?"

Josh sat down and replied, with a deadpan expression. "Pretty good, I guess. One day at a time."

Dolores and Boss man had been staying at his double wide up in Forrest City for the last week or so, and on most mornings they showed up at Hamblin's Fort after the rest of the crew had arrived. This morning was no different, and they drove up just as the tarps were being pulled back from the excavation areas. Seeing Josh and Denny on the summit of the platform mound, Dolores jumped out of the pickup, eager to let Denny know that Boss Man had checked in with Prof. Shetler the previous evening and that he would be driving down tomorrow. Dolores had made sure that Boss Man had told Shetler that Denny was off on her own excavation on the temple mound with an undergrad rookie.

Laughing to herself as she thought of how much fun it would be to watch Denny evade Shetler's determined gropes and advances, Dolores trotted up the side of the mound. She stopped suddenly, however, as she reached the summit. Denny had seen her coming and was now standing next to Josh with her arm around his waist and leaning into him. She smiled broadly as Dolores froze upon seeing them, and then went up on her tiptoes and gave Josh a lingering kiss on the neck before telling Dolores her news.

"Hey Dolores, check out my new squeeze. What do you think?" Speechless, Dolores quickly turned and descended the side of the mound, unwilling to give Denny the satisfaction of seeing her expression.

Josh didn't say anything, just smiled at the retreating form of Dolores as she scurried down the side of the mound. His phone call with Charlotte the night before had in fact mostly consisted of him listening to her complain about how bad her summer was going. She hated her job and was bored. Most of her sorority sisters had left campus for the summer. Rather than telling Charlotte that he would have to check with Boss Man about her visit, Josh had told her straight out that she shouldn't drive down to spend time with him, and that he would look her up in the fall. He had told Denny a slightly different story, hoping that the possibility of Charlotte driving down to visit him would elicit some sort of a response from Denny.

It clearly had worked. Josh also figured that the looming arrival of "slimeball" Shetler, as he was known among the grad students, had also played a role in her decision. Shetler might cause real difficulties for Denny. How could she fend off his advances without potentially complicating her dream of a doctorate degree and an academic career in archaeology? By adding Josh to the equation, Denny had solved that problem. Shetler would still creep her out but would keep his distance with a boyfriend in the picture. And for Denny, there was of course the added bonus of having outmaneuvered Dolores in impressive fashion.

Josh, Denny, and Cecelia were all in good spirits after watching Dolores stalk off and turned back to their excavation of the north-south trench, with Cecelia running the sifter. They had almost reached the south edge of the mound summit, but so far hadn't encountered any additional features, just the clean white sand layer capping the mound. Denny had been telling Cecelia and Josh, for probably the fourth time, her plan for extending the trench down the south side of the mound, which would involve the long-established practice of "stepping" trenches down the sloping sides of earthen mounds.

She was well into her description of the stairway they would be digging down the side of the mound when Josh held up his hand, shaking his head. He had been thinking about Denny's plan for the mound slope excavation for the past day or so.

"Maybe I'm wrong here Denny, but when this trench reaches the mound slope, if there is feasting debris deposited down the side of the mound, wouldn't it be better to remove the sterile white sand layer that caps the mound in a manner that follows the slope rather than stepping the trench?"

Denny frowned, shaking her head in response as Josh continued.

"I know I'm just the undergrad frat rat, but that way we would come down on the debris layer all at once. If we step the trench — making a stairway up the side of the mound, we'll end up first exposing only a small bit of any feasting trash where the steps cut deepest into the sand layer. That's no good. We need to get a more complete exposure all at the same time."

Denny looked askance at Josh. "No way. Nobody digs sloping excavation trenches down the side of a mound. It just isn't done. Stepping a trench allows you to keep control of the vertical stratigraphy. That's Archaeology 101. You couldn't do that with a sloping trench."

"Yes, you could," Josh countered, "and don't forget, at this point we don't have any stratigraphy — any soil layers, anyway, just a solid white sand layer that needs removing. Why not remove the sand layer without cutting steps, and expose a larger portion of the slope all at the same time?" Denny stayed quiet and Josh continued. "Let's not be young fogies here, like Richard. The New Archaeology is about asking different, more interesting questions, and trying out new theories and methods, right? Excavation methods should be tailored to the specific situation being investigated. Looking for mound slope feasting remains is a very new idea, and the best way to uncover it hasn't been developed yet. We could do that right here at Hamblin's Fort."

Josh paused. Denny still stayed quiet, and he decided to offer his final point.

"Think of it this way — once we expose some portion of the mound-slope refuse layer, you're gonna want to expand the area that's been exposed to see more of it, right? So why not plan for that larger exposure area now. We can come down on it all at once, as much as we can."

Denny looked over to where Boss Man was standing by the southwest corner of the plaza and thought about what his reaction would be to Josh's crazy suggestion of a sloping excavation trench. He would go ballistic, and Richard's head would explode. They would both come up with reasons why it was a stupid idea — the potential for erosion, problems mapping artifacts, and more than anything else, tradition. It just wasn't done that way.

But she liked Josh's idea, and his reasoning seemed sound — new research questions called for new approaches. You couldn't be locked into old ways of doing things. She leaned in close to Josh and whispered.

"Let's try it. If we're lucky we can find and expose some feasting remains before Boss Man sees what we're doing, and then a sloping trench will make sense." As Denny turned back to their excavation a sudden thought popped into her head — maybe Shetler, a New Archaeology zealot, would endorse their sloping trench idea. Having "slime ball" on their side could be critical. Denny and Josh continued removing the white sand layer from their north-south trench, discussing different scenarios of how they might get Shetler to back their search for mound slope feasting debris.

Cecelia had been feeling a little under the weather since she got up that morning, and soon lost interest in her task of screening the soil coming out of the Red Mound. She decided to escape the heat and head back to the crew house. Dropping the soil sifter, she apologized to Denny and Josh before leaving.

"Sorry for quitting on you guys, but I feel like shit. I need to get out of the sun, maybe treat myself to a little AC."

Walking over to where the rest of the crew had started backfilling the block excavation unit at the southwest corner of the plaza, Cecelia let Boss Man know she was heading back to the crew house and listened patiently as he told her that Josh and Denny would be coming down from the mound and joining the rest of the crew tomorrow in digging random test squares across the site, and that she was welcome to join them. He also asked Cecelia to check on Zack, who had stayed back at the crew house that morning, complaining of a bad headache.

Cecelia stopped to tell Denny and Josh the bad news, then started walking back to the crew house, skipping every few feet, stirring up dust from the road. She whistled and called up to Black Dog, who stood watching her from his usual spot on the Red Mound but didn't join her. Cecelia called again but Black Dog stayed where he was. That was surprising to Cecelia as well as to Denny and Josh. Black Dog usually stuck close to her.

She was almost to the crew house when a familiar pickup crept up next to her from behind, and Jake rolled down the driver's side window, clearly nervous. "I can explain Cecelia. Honest." Frowning now, Cecelia walked around the front of the truck and hopped in the passenger side, and the truck drove slowly past the crew house and headed north toward Memphis.

Boss Man and Dolores were excited about the next phase of their research. As soon as the backfilling was finished, they would start to in on their plan to dig a site-wide sample of 5x5 squares aimed at recovering representative ceramic assemblages from a sizable number of different house structures across Hamblin's Fort.

Under Prof. Shetler's guidance earlier that spring they had developed a good initial sampling design that should yield a representative sample of ceramics from Hamblin's Fort. This general plan had been scrutinized and tentatively approved by their committees, and now that "proof of concept" had been demonstrated by the small assemblages they had recovered, they could move forward with implementation of their overall sampling design.

Using the established five-foot square grid system, they would first divide the site into different sections, or "sampling strata," and then excavate a randomly selected sample of grid squares from each section. First separating the site into north and south halves by drawing a line down the middle of the plaza, and bisecting the conical and flat-topped mounds, they would further divide each of the two halves of the site into three strata — close to the plaza, close to the outer fortification wall, and in between these inner and outer strata. Their sampling design could, of course, be modified and refined as they progressed, depending on what they found.

The random selection of grid units for excavation within each of the strata would be complicated by the need to recover ceramics from within structures, but Dolores was confident they could easily finesse that. During discussions with Shetler that spring she had proposed that when a randomly selected square was not located within a structure, they could simply extend some slit trenches outward from it until a structure was located, and then excavate a five-foot sampling unit. Her dissertation committee chair had blessed this wrinkle in their approach and was eager to see what they came up with.

Denny and Josh both realized that based on what Cecelia had just told them, this could well be their last day working on the Red Mound. Watched over by Black Dog, who had remained unsettled and would frequently come over to see how they were progressing, they completed the trench across the top of the mound summit just before noon. Rather than join the crew in the shade for lunch, Josh and Denny instead immediately started in on extending the trench down the side of the mound, anxious to be able to have something to show Shetler the next morning when he came to the site.

Lying on their sides on either side of the trench, they had by late afternoon worked their way about six feet down the side of the mound. They had troweled away maybe 18 inches of the white sand layer and sould be coming down on ceremonial debris soon if there was any. They had uncovered nothing of interest, and were hot, hungry, and out of sorts.

Just then Denny's trowel made a distinctive snick as it hit a hard object. Denny and Josh looked at each other across the trench. Based on the feel and sound of what she had hit with her trowel, Denny blurted out "bone" before even looking down again. Setting her trowel aside and picking up her boar bristle brush, she gently cleared some of the sand away from her discovery. It was shell fragment and appeared to have black lines engraved on it. Josh grabbed his brush and was ready to join in cleaning off their find when Denny grabbed his wrist.

"No. I think we should cover it back up and let Shetler uncover it tomorrow. If we can get him involved in the discovery, maybe we can avoid digging test pits for Dolores."

Josh was surprised. "Don't you want to know what we found? You've been obsessing for weeks about what was on this mound slope. Now you want to let "slime ball" get to do the big reveal?"

Denny brushed sand back over the shell fragment, stood up, and reached out to help Josh up.

"I already know what we've found Josh. It's good news. It's a cup fragment. And I'm betting if Shetler finds this he definitely will want to see more."

Boss Man and Dolores were expecting Prof. Shetler to arrive late in the afternoon and had reserved him a hotel room in Forrest City. They planned on meeting him for dinner and Boss Man had gone all out for the occasion — knife-edge creased khakis, a white button-down shirt, and a paisley tie. Dolores wore a yellow sleeveless summer dress along with a little eye makeup and pale pink lipstick. But they ended up eating alone. Shetler called about the time he was supposed to arrive and apologized for running behind schedule. He said he would stop in Jonesboro for the night and catch up with them at the site in the morning.

Shetler had been delayed in starting his drive south when his early morning meeting with the Anthropology Department promotion committee had run much longer than he had anticipated. He was still two years away from his tenure review, which would determine if he became a permanent faculty member at the university, or if on the other hand his contract would not be renewed. It was up or out. He had thought his morning's meeting would be a brief check-in with the committee, since he had updated and submitted what he considered to be an impressive record of his accomplishments since joining the faculty three years ago.

But the committee was not as sanguine as Shetler regarding the strength of his case for making tenure, and had presented him with an outline of what they thought he needed to prioritize over the next two years. His teaching was OK and his service for the department had been sufficient, but they thought he was underperforming in his research. At the top of their list of recommendations was for him to publish more articles in high impact journals. So far, much of his output was in regional journals like *Southeastern Archaeology* or even in the state journals. Unimpressive. A brief report of his in the flagship journal *American Antiquity* certainly helped a bit, but the clear and blunt message he had received from those self-important asses on the committee was clear — he needed something solid, and soon. The elephant in the room, of course, was his dissertation, completed nearly five years ago but not yet published. Why, they wanted to know, hadn't it seen the light of day?

17.
BAD PEOPLE

Tom was freaked out when Cecelia was not at the crew house that evening and breathed a sigh of relief the next morning when he found her once again perched on the summit of the conical mound at Hamblin's Fort. His mood crashed, however, when Cecelia told him where she had been.

"Jake showed up, finally, and explained everything that has been going on. He drove us over to Jonesboro, where his mom lives, and I met his mom Betty and his sister Doris. They were very nice, but both were pretty scared. Doris told me how she got pulled over for speeding a few months ago by the state police. The cops smelled weed in the car and nailed her for possession with intent to distribute. When Jake showed up and they realized that he was around lots of sketchy people in the clubs in Memphis where he played — that's when they offered a deal. If he agreed to get information for them on suspected drug gangs they would drop all charges against Doris. We were his first assignment but when we turned out to be just low-level stoners, not raid-worthy, Jake was pulled off of us and given some other targets that were suspected of moving crank into Memphis."

Tom looked at her with poorly concealed apprehension. "Jesus, Cecelia, this guy's bad news. Good thing he's history."

"History? Not really. Jake said he's got a few loose ends to tie up but will swing back around in a few days to pick me up. We're getting outta Dodge — got a big road trip planned. I want to show him Chaco Canyon and the sun dagger. Maybe we can find a hippy commune to hook up with for a while."

Tom was going to try to get Cecelia to change her mind, maybe tell her some drug war horror stories from growing up in Detroit. But she glanced over his shoulder and then abruptly jumped up and hurried down of the side of the conical mound. Tom looked past her and saw the sheriff driving up in his Chevy Bel-Air patrol car with the blue bubble gum light on the roof. It looked to be sagging a bit on the passenger side. Sheriff Hogg was driving, and his sumo-sized deputy Skeeter was riding shotgun — literally. Cecelia hurried over to the sheriff's car and leaned on the driver's door, listening intently to what Hogg was telling her. The sheriff turned his gaze toward Tom, and Cecelia waved him over with a few nervous jerks of her arm.

Cecelia looked back with wide eyes at Tom as he approached, and he saw why as he reached the patrol car. In addition to his holstered revolver, the sheriff had what looked like a Glock 9mm pistol on his lap, and Skeeter was cradling a newish-looking sawed-off Remington pump shotgun with a pistol grip. Skeeter was a big fan of B.B. King, and the name "Lucille" was engraved into the side of the shotgun's receiver. An open box of #1 Buck shotgun shells was sitting on the floor between his feet, along with a pile of empty soda cans and discarded fast food containers.

Tom thought the sheriff looked like he hadn't slept in a few days, and the body odor that accompanied the cool air-conditioned air wafting out of the driver's side window added to Tom's rapidly growing sense of unease and looming threat.

"The sheriff's looking for Jake," Cecelia blurted out. "But I haven't heard from him since he called about the possible raid. Have you?"

Tom immediately picked up on Cecelia's not-so-subtle cue and shook his head. "Haven't seen that prick since he skipped out on us. Good riddance."

The sheriff stared at them, and after a pause, replied.

"Well OK. We can leave it at that. If Jake calls or shows up, you tell him I'd like to talk to him. It's important. Some other people are also trying to find him. Bad people. Could be tough on Jake if they find him first. And call me if anybody you don't know comes sniffin around. Cecelia has my number."

Hogg started to roll up his window, then stopped and asked another question.

"How about Catfish? You seen her? She's made herself scarce and she owes me." Cecelia and Tom both shook their heads. Clearly angry now, Hogg rolled up his window and the patrol car pulled away. Turning to Skeeter, the sheriff sounded off.

"Cecelia's a lying little bitch. If we had time, I'd like to stake this place out. Jake is going to show up here soon I bet. He and little Miss Cecelia are planning a runner. I'm sure of it."

Sheriff Hogg and Skeeter headed south toward Helena, and after driving for maybe twenty minutes, wary and watchful, they turned off on a dirt road winding east toward the Mississippi River. Reaching an isolated spot on a small slough, well screened by a stand of willows and a sizable cane break, they waited for Hogg's nephew Clete to rendezvous with them and pass on a sizable new shipment of crank for the burgeoning Memphis market.

They were right on time, but Clete was not there waiting for them. Hogg's nephew was never late for these hand-offs, and the sheriff had called him repeatedly over the past few days, with no success. This was not good. They waited for more than an hour before giving up and retracing their route back along the dirt side road. Soon after turning north on the main road Skeeter called out to the sheriff in a high squeaky voice.

"Hey Harry, that red pickup we saw earlier is on our tail again, and it's coming up fast behind us. He's got a white van right behind him."

The sheriff increased his speed and watched as the truck gained on them. As the red pickup got closer, Skeeter squealed again.

"I see guns, Harry."

Still about thirty yards back, the red truck pulled across the center line into the opposite lane to come up beside them on the driver's side. The sheriff quickly swerved in front of them, blocking their move. The red truck immediately countered by moving back into the right-hand lane, and when the sheriff didn't try to block them again, they accelerated to draw even with the patrol car on the passenger side.

They were within twenty feet of the Bel-Air's back bumper, and coming fast, when Skeeter turned in his seat, slid the barrel of his shotgun up onto the bottom edge of his open window and pumped three quick rounds into the windshield of the red truck. After a long few seconds, the red truck drifted off the pavement. When it hit the soft shoulder, it rolled over several times and came to rest upside down, half submerged in the roadside drainage ditch.

The sheriff slowed and stopped fifty yards up the road. There was no movement from the truck in the ditch. No sign of life. One tire spun slowly. The white van had slowed to a stop next to the truck in the ditch. Sheriff Hogg watched the van in the side mirror. If anyone in the white van had rifles, their best chance was to make a run for it. If they were just armed with handguns, Skeeter had the upper hand. The white van did not move. They waited a long minute. No shots. That meant no rifles. Hogg languidly slid his left arm out the driver's side window and waved the van forward. Rather than accept the sheriff's invitation, the van pulled a quick U-turn and drove away.

Sheriff Hogg dropped Skeeter off back at his place in Palestine, a few miles west of Forrest City, and told him to lay low for a while. Then he headed over to his mother's old house in Forrest City. She had died a decade ago, and he rented it out now, but held on to the large garage for storage. Swinging open the garage doors, he pulled the patrol car in next to a parked vehicle covered with a tarp. Taking a pump shotgun and a box of buckshot from a large, locked gun safe, he loaded the gun and pulled the tarp off a rusted pickup — a tan-colored early '50s Ford. Placing the shotgun and shells on the passenger seat where he could reach them easily if needed, he headed back south again to see what was going on with his nephew Clete. Stopping for gas and a Dr. Pepper, he found a pay phone and called Catfish again. This time someone picked up, but it wasn't Catfish. Before the person who picked up could say anything, Hogg blurted out "Lemme talk to Catfish."

After a pause, a refined voice responded. "I'm sorry, but Margaret — you call her Catfish, is not here right now. I can take a message, though, and pass it on. May I ask who's calling?"

"It's Sheriff Hogg, Elizabeth. You know damn well it's me. Now where is she?"

"Oh sheriff, I thought it might be you. I can tell you where she is. She's gone up to Michigan to pick up her big brother Henry — wrongly imprisoned for far too long. Henry is coming home and we're throwing a huge welcome home party for the boy. Not sure if you were on the invitation list, but you are sure welcome to come. Margaret is guaranteed to be there — she's Henry's favorite you know."

The sheriff was about to respond when the line went dead. Here was something else for Hogg to worry about. Henry, Catfish's older brother, must be getting out early, and coming back to make the sheriff's life more difficult in a variety of ways.

A little over an hour later the sheriff pulled into his nephew's driveway. Clete lived in a small run-down house with a variety of rusted appliances and old tires decorating the yard. His shiny new pickup was parked in the driveway. Hogg climbed the front steps and knocked on the door. No answer. He tried the door and it was locked. Cutting around the side of the house he looked in windows but saw nothing unusual until he glanced in a kitchen window and saw an overturned chair and a shoe lying in the middle of the floor.

Hogg tried the kitchen door and it was unlocked. He stepped into the house and just as quickly retreated back out the door. The stench of death was overpowering. Covering his nose and mouth with his shirt sleeve, he reentered the kitchen and stepped over to the arch into the living room. His nephew Clete was lying on the couch, missing a shoe, with his hands at his sides and his head resting on a dark red throw pillow. Clete had been dead for a few days at least, the sheriff guessed. Crossing the room, he realized the throw pillow's dark red color was from Clete's blood. He had been shot once at close range in the middle of the forehead.

Walking over, the sheriff took a closer look. He noticed two things — two fingers had been snipped off Clete's right hand, and there was something stuck in the entry wound in his forehead. He reached down and pulled what he guessed was a large chunk of crystal meth out of the wound. A clear message from the Outlaws. And the severed fingers suggested that Clete had been reluctant to tell them things they wanted to know. Hogg pocketed the meth crystal and walked back out the kitchen door and around the side of the house. As soon as he saw the back garden and the uprooted tomato plants, he knew Clete had given up their cash stash. No doubt he had also told them where the floating lab was moored. Getting back in his beat-up truck, Hogg drove another fifteen minutes south to confirm the boat was missing, then started the drive back north.

Hogg wanted to stay as far away as he could from his nephew Clete's death and the investigation that would be initiated.

Somebody else could discover and report his murder. When Clete's mother Judy called with the terrible news in the next week or so he would pretend to be shocked and angry and would make a solemn promise to conduct his own investigation into Clete's killing. But fending off Judy's suspicions that he was somehow involved in her son's death was the least of his worries.

He was sure the Outlaws out of St. Louis were behind all this. They had now taken out Fat Henry and Clete, along with hijacking the floating lab. His attempt to grab some of the crank market in Memphis was clearly over, and he had no real plan of what to do next, other than to keep an extremely low profile, try to stay alive, and hope the Outlaws eventually turned to dealing with new challenges and forgot about him. He figured that the body count was about equal now, and the Outlaws had also killed his kin, shut down his operation, and taken over his houseboat lab. That should be enough of a pay-back for them.

Turning west, Hogg headed for his fishing shack in the Ozarks, up along the Buffalo River, a few hours away. He would call in to the office along the way and let them know he would be gone for a day or two — that he had some out-of-town business to take care of. Skeeter would alert the other members of the Swamp Rebels to watch their backs. Gazing at the seemingly endless expanse of rice fields through a bug-spattered windshield, he briefly thought about warning the archaeologists digging at Hamblin's Fort that the Outlaws could be a problem. He might have called if that hippy girl Cecelia had been more welcoming of his attentions. But given her numerous refusals, Hogg figured they could fend for themselves. Cracking a smile, he wondered if Boss Man might get a chance to use his handgun in a real shootout.

18.
SHETLER'S GAMBIT

The air conditioning unit in Professor Shetler's Jonesboro hotel room was not only loud, but it also seemed to cycle on and off every ten minutes or so, making for a miserable night. Even with the AC running it was still muggy and warm in the room when he woke. Feeling particularly bitchy because of the heat and humidity, Shetler called Boss Man and Dolores and changed plans — he would meet them at the crew house to go over their sampling strategy in detail before visiting Hamblin's Fort. They should pull all their ceramics and maps and plans together and be ready to present their case. He would see them in a few hours.

Professor Shetler was of medium height, a little pudgy, with brown eyes and straight brown hair. He had a bearing and wardrobe that fully embraced a "professor" persona, but with an effort to also project an edgy '60s vibe. This involved sandals and black jeans paired with a tie-died T-shirt or turtleneck, often accompanied by a corduroy sport coat with elbow patches. And for good measure, he topped it off with a pipe. His hair was also fashionably long, and rapidly receding in front. But his most memorable feature was his mustache. It was magnificent. Not a handlebar or something else extreme, just a thick, vibrant, well-groomed mass of hair above his upper lip, like a majestic hood ornament. Shetler made sure it was always carefully trimmed and occasionally used a little product to enhance its gloss.

To fully appreciate Shetler's persona, his presentation of self, you needed to witness him in his "Method and Theory in Archaeology" seminar sessions, sitting around a table with graduate students. From behind a dense cloud of pipe smoke he would tell stories about the leading lights of the "New Archaeology," most of whom he claimed were his close friends. Shetler's dissertation research, which had involved the analysis and interpretation of status differentiation and social structure in a Mississippian society, was also one of his frequent seminar topics.

Shetler hadn't actually done any excavation at the Mound City site that was the subject of his dissertation. Instead, he had spent over a year in an air-conditioned collections curation facility in Georgia, sorting through the grave goods that had been recovered from several hundred human interments excavated at Mound City in the early 1950s. The excavated burials and associated grave goods had been carefully described at the time in field notes and burial forms, and the skeletons and objects buried with them were then stored away in cabinets and carefully curated in case future researchers with new questions might want to restudy them from any number of new perspectives.

For Shetler these Mound City site burials and their associated grave goods represented a rich data set for looking at the ways in which political power and social standing were structured within this major mound center society. And it didn't require any digging on his part, or any dirt, or any sweating. Shetler didn't mind being tagged as an "armchair" archaeologist by his detractors — he considered himself a theoretician and original thinker not bound by traditionalist attitudes. He was a brilliant scholar blazing new frontiers of insight and interpretation, not a lowly shovel bum. He would leave the grunt work for others.

Listening to the Goldberg Variations — Glenn Gould of course, and puffing on his pipe in air-conditioned comfort, Shetler had worked through the curated collections of the Mound City site and tallied up the various types of artifacts that were interred with each of the hundreds of burials, their location within the mound center, and their age and sex. Based on his analysis of this massive data set, he then described a number of different categories of social ranking and identified the distinctive political structure of a chiefdom level society.

Because of the massive size of the data set Shetler had pulled together — thousands of artifacts, complex spread sheets and various statistical analyses, his dissertation would need further polishing and re-formatting as well as rigorous independent peer review before appearing in print. That would take time. Eager to spread the word of his breakthrough interpretations, Shetler had quickly produced, with considerable fanfare, a short article summarizing all of his results and conclusions while leaving presentation of his supporting data for later, in his "soon to be published" dissertation.

This impressive analysis of the Mound City burial population, even sans supporting data, was a significant factor in him being hired in a tenure track assistant professor position at a major university. That was five years ago now, and his seminar stories and condescending bluster were wearing thin with the other faculty, not all of whom shared his "New Archaeology" perspectives. It was crunch time now, and Shetler would need to buckle down and tackle the dissertation.

He seemed to have a straightforward and well-worn path to the security of tenure — just turn the dissertation into a book. A book would be his ticket to tenure. As the months passed, however, it was becoming increasingly difficult for him to play the "soon to be published" card, and he noticed some of the graduate students rolling their eyes when he discussed his research. Was Shetler just lazy, the rumor mills were asking, or might there be problems with his massive data set?

Shetler had been looking forward to this site visit for a number or reasons. He was hoping that Boss Man and Dolores would come up with something that would reflect well on him as their major professor. In addition, he was hoping he might be able to make some headway with that hot graduate student, Denny something or other. And of course, the bauxite figurine and Cahokia cosmogram sherd that had been found at Hamblin's Fort were also of great interest to him. He had been doing some reading and thought that they could make for a high-profile journal article.

But he could do without the heat and humidity. His dislike of heat and sweat was ironic in that his area of expertise was Mississippian societies — the temple mound builders of the brutally hot and humid river valleys of the Southeast. Watching the heat shimmering on the asphalt as he drove east toward Hamblin's Fort, Shetler hoped he could sort out Boss Man and Dolores and their sampling design quickly, check out the figurine that had been found, and maybe get Denny back to his Forrest City motel to discuss the path of her graduate research. With luck he could be out of this hellhole of heat by the day after tomorrow.

Boss Man and Dolores met the professor on the front porch of the crew house and led him back to the kitchen table, where they had laid out all the ceramics that appeared to show spatial variation in manufacture and design across the site. A Hamblin's Fort site map with the different sampling strata outlined in red was thumbtacked to the kitchen wall next to the stove.

The first thing Shetler noticed as he stepped through the front door of the Hamblin Mansion was the lack of air conditioning and the food smells that floated on the stale humid air of the living room.

"Jesus, how can they live like this?" he thought to himself. The kitchen was a little cooler, with a box fan running in the window. It had been there for quite a while, judging from the grime it had collected. Pulling out one of the chairs at the kitchen table, Shetler settled in for what he anticipated to be several grueling hours of back and forth with these two, both of whom he considered as a little lacking in brain power. Pulling out his pipe and lighting up, he realized that he had already broken a sweat and his shirt was sticking to his back.

Boss Man went first, outlining again the stratified random sampling design the three of them had settled on earlier in the spring. Stepping to the Hamblin Fort site map, he pointed out the six areas of the site designated as different sampling strata, and how they would go about collecting ceramics from each of these half dozen site sectors. Within each of these six areas a series of 5x5 foot squares or sampling units would be randomly selected for excavation and a crew member would be dispatched to shovel down through the plow zone and presumably encounter a habitation structure. A basic map of artifacts in-situ on the house floor would be made and they would be collected and bagged for later analysis. All the ceramics encountered would become part of Boss Man and Dolores's dissertation projects.

Boss Man's dissertation would position their research in a broader context, starting with a general characterization of Mississippian societies and current theories regarding their sociopolitical organization and community structure. This would be followed by a description of Hamblin's Fort. A second major section of his dissertation would consist of a lengthy discussion of sampling design and how it can be appropriately applied in archaeology. The sampling strategy selected to address the question of social organization at Hamblin's Fort would then be briefly discussed along with their overall data collection plan, and the location of sampling squares and number of ceramics recovered would be presented. A final chapter would lay out in general terms what Dolores's analysis of the recovered ceramic assemblages seemed to show in terms of the community structure and sociopolitical organization of Hamblin's Fort.

Dolores's dissertation, in contrast, would be much more tightly focused on the description and analysis of the ceramics they recovered, and would pair up nicely with Boss Man's overview. She would first provide some summary historical background on the discovery and characterization of Mississippian ceramic assemblages from across the Southeast, followed by a discussion of the various types of vessels typically found in Mississippian sites — large-mouthed jar-form vessels, plates of different sizes, bottles, etc. Then the different types of ceramics recovered from Hamblin's Fort during their excavations would be described in some detail before turning to the key question of what the recovered pottery sherds had to say about social organization.

In order to attempt to tease out social organization and community structure, Dolores would be using style differences — variation in the designs observed on ceramics that occurred across the site, along with differences is vessel shape and clay composition, to identify distinct subgroups within the Hamblin's Fort population.

She would open this section of her dissertation with a historical summary of past discussions in the literature of how such ceramic stylistic traditions might be expressed, along with illustrative ethnographic examples. This would be followed by a recounting of how other archaeologists had tried to use design elements to discern social patterning. She then would present all of the design elements and vessel form and clay composition differences that were observed on the Hamblin's Fort ceramics, followed by a lengthy presentation of how all the stylistic variables were expressed across the site. This was the crux, the core of their entire research initiative. Did these variations in ceramic design and manufacture occur in spatial patterns that reflected different social sub-groups?

Shetler was pleased with Boss Man and Dolores's presentations and nodded appreciatively between energetic puffs on his pipe. When Dolores finished, Shetler complemented them both and then the three of them looked at the ceramic sherds that Boss Man and Dolores had laid out on the kitchen table. Shetler was disappointed at the relatively limited number of distinct design differences that so far could be seen from different parts of the site, but did agree that there was potential. All three hoped that the patterning in the distribution of design elements across the site would come into clearer focus as the number of recovered sherds increased over the next few months of digging.

Shetler listened to Boss Man describe how a single individual should be able to excavate one of their ceramic-recovery 5x5s in a day or two, and with all eleven crew members involved they should be able to recover an impressive sample of ceramics by the end of the field season. With Shetler nodding his approval, Boss Man then segued into a request that Shetler pull Denny, Josh, and Cecelia off the mound excavations and assign them to digging grid squares to recover ceramics. Dolores smiled broadly when Shetler concurred, saying that he was surprised that Denny had been allowed to do an independent solo excavation on the mound. While agreeing to shut down the mound excavations, Shetler also started to consider ways in which he might be able to use this to manipulate Denny. As for Josh, Shetler was genuinely shocked to learn that an undergrad was digging on the mound with little supervision and no experience. He would most definitely put a stop to that.

Boss Man and Dolores were not exactly surprised when Professor Shetler then asked to see the bauxite figurine and cosmogram sherd, but they had been hoping he wouldn't show any interest. As soon as the two objects were placed on the kitchen table, however, Shetler pulled a hand lens from his pocket and started a lengthy close-up examination of the cosmogram sherd, all the while offering a narrative regarding Cahokia ceramics and their defining characteristics, particularly Ramey incised pottery designs and the cosmogram conceptual framework. As Shetler pontificted, Boss Man and Dolores slowly deflated, sharing the realization that Shetler seemed to be angling to help them out with the write-up of their big discovery. When he turned his attention to the figurine, Shetler launched into an even longer explanation of the meaning and significance of Mississippian figurines in general, and the Hamblin Fort figurine specifically. Boss Man and Dolores listened attentively to Shetler's lecture but made no response.

Shetler wasn't expecting his gambit to be met with immediate enthusiasm and took the absence of any response from Boss Man and Dolores to be a good start. It might take a while, but he was confident they would come around. After all, he was their dissertation advisor, and their fate was in his hands. He continued chatting them up regarding the sherd and statue and the depth of his understanding of such things on the drive out to the Hamblin site, undeterred by the stony silence as the three of them rode side by side in the cab of Boss Man's pickup.

19.
ENTWINED SNAKES

Boss Man was eager to impress Shetler during his visit and had been out at Hamblin's Fort first thing that morning to get the crew started on excavation of the ceramic sampling squares. He wanted them to be hard at work when Shetler arrived. Boss Man had not yet, however, tried to pull Denny, Josh, and Cecelia off the excavation of the Red Mound. He would let Shetler do that — he and Dolores could just stand back and watch the fireworks.

Shetler had not been to Hamblin's Fort before so as soon as they arrived Boss Man led him to the middle of the central plaza where he could get a good view of the six crew members digging away at widely scattered ceramic sampling squares. They then climbed the conical mound and Boss Man pointed out the shallow palisade trench that encircled the entire site, along with the location of the small shrine structure, associated suspected shell workshop, and enclosing cedar wall.

Shetler was already feeling a little dizzy from the heat and humidity but was eager to see the shrine structure before continuing on to the temple mound and the confrontation with Denny. After slowly walking around the length of the shrine's enclosing wall, he crouched down by the figurine's clay platform, making a big show of serious contemplation accompanied by more energetic pipe puffing. Then he stood and turned back to Boss Man and Dolores and launched in again on his pitch.

"What we have here is a fantastic case study of a Cahokian visitation to Hamblin's Fort, a provincial mound center. For some reason they came all the way down here, constructed the red cedar enclosure wall, built the shrine, and enthroned the figurine. It looks like shell cups were engraved on site, suggesting black drink ceremonies. I think we can pull together a boffo article for a high-profile journal."

Dolores and Boss Man both failed to meet Shetler's eager gaze and neither responded to his entreaty. Turning, Boss Man started for the temple mound and Dolores quickly followed, with Shetler bringing up the rear. As they reached the mound summit, Boss Man and Dolores paused and let Shetler go ahead of them, then quietly retreated back down the side of the mound in anticipation of the coming confrontation between Denny and the professor.

Cecelia, Denny and Josh were hard at work on the mound summit. Josh was shoveling dirt into the sifter that Cecelia was holding and Denny was excavating the trench running down the south slope of the mound. Lying flat on the ground next to the trench, she was reaching down with her right arm and carefully troweling away the white sand layer. Glancing up over the edge of the mound, she saw the arrival of Shetler and got up and went to greet him.

Shetler had only ever seen Denny in her bulky overalls and had often wondered what her figure might look like underneath. Denny's outfit of shorts and a white T-shirt, smudged now with dirt and sweat, answered all of Shetler's musings, and left him momentarily tongue-tied. He was about to put on a stern professorial expression and begin to give her the bad news about having to shut down the mound excavations when two things disrupted his train of thought. Denny straightened her shoulders and hit him with one of her dazzling smiles as she held out a trowel for him to take, and at the same time he heard a deep throated snarl from his left rear, where Cecelia and Josh had been working the sifter screen.

Shetler turned to look and saw Black Dog now standing next to Cecelia. She had her arms wrapped around his neck restraining him. The dog was staring directly at Shetler and looked eager to rip out his throat — eyes blazing, body trembling, lips curled back and canines flashing.

"What the fuck is that?" Shetler blurted out, clearly freaked.

"Oh, that's just Black Dog. He's harmless," Denny replied as Cecelia pulled the dog down the side of the mound and tied him to a tree in the shade where they kept his water bowl. Drawing Shetler's attention back to her smile, her white T-shirt, and the offered trowel, Denny continued.

"And that's Josh and Cecelia. Josh has an undergraduate grant to conduct research on the mound, and Cecelia is working with us." Denny paused, noting Shetler's momentary confusion, and quickly continued. "It started as a clean-up operation here on the temple mound, but then we uncovered some interesting things. And based on what just turned up this morning, I think we can justify Boss Man and the Archaeology Museum director's support for us pursuing a second line of research up here on the temple mound."

Looking puzzled, Shetler took the offered trowel and followed Denny as she turned and walked back toward the mound slope excavation trench.

"We've developed a new "no-step" trenching approach and wanted to show you how it's working out. With the sloping trench, following the incline of the mound, we can come down on feasting debris all at once. Here at the top of the trench, just off the summit, we are now all the way down through the sterile sand cap that sealed the mound, and ready to finally find out if anything was discarded down the mound slope. Take a look at what just turned up."

Denny lay down again along the side of the trench and Shetler took a similar position on the other side. Denny picked up a small brush before handing it to Shetler. "You probably should use this," Denny remarked with another bright smile, and pointed down into the trench. Following her gaze, Shetler saw a small white object on the bottom of the trench. Reaching down with the brush he started to brush sand away from the object. As he uncovered more of it, he asked. "Is it shell?"

Denny's response was quick and succinct. "Conch."

Shetler abruptly stopped brushing and looked questioningly up at Denny across the trench.

"It looks too thick to be anything else," Denny explained. "I think there's more of it here, a lot more." As Shetler turned back to his brushing, tuning out the world as he slowly uncovered more of the fragment of shell that might, or might not, be conch, Denny crouched down next to him and excitedly filled him in on what other researchers had uncovered when they had looked for mound-slope feasting debris. She wasn't sure if Shetler was listening to anything she was saying.

The bottom of the trench was in shadow, but Shetler thought he saw several black lines on the shell fragment and leaned into the trench for a closer look. He quickly recognized what he was looking at. A design of two entwined snakes with crosshatched bodies had been engraved into the shell when still intact, and the fragment that remained showed a section of the snake's bodies.

Shetler cleared the remaining soil away from the conch fragment, paused briefly, and reaching over for the trowel Denny had given him, continued to clear soil outward from the shell fragment. He seemed oblivious to what was going on around him. Denny looked over at Josh and Cecelia and flashed them a smile before joining them.

"I think he's hooked," Cecelia whispered to Josh and Denny.

Walking up the side of the mound from where he had been waiting for Shetler to lower the boom, Boss Man joined them, voicing his concern.

"What's going on?" he asked.

Deadpan, Josh replied. "Apparently Professor Shetler has discovered something of major importance."

Boss Man muttered an "Oh fuck," and walked over to the trench where Shetler was hesitantly troweling. Seeing the shell fragment with the intertwined snakes design, Boss Man opened his mouth to say something, then thought better of it and retreated back down the side of the mound in stony silence. Dolores saw the storm cloud expression on his face as he joined her and asked.

"What did she do now?"

Slowly breathing in and out several times as he clenched and unclenched his fists, Boss Man finally answered. "Shetler just found a conch shell fragment with an engraved design in Denny's trench — looks like snakes, maybe the Braden style out of Cahokia."

Dolores took a few steps toward the Red Mound, wanting to see the engraved shell for herself, but then stopped, realizing she couldn't face Denny's smug smile. Turning around, she retraced her steps back toward Boss Man, blurting out her suspicions before continuing on past him.

"I think she planted that shell fragment. Shetler's never dug anything up in his life. He'd be easy to fool. So would Cecelia and the frat boy. But she can't keep it up. She will be out on her ass when I expose her."

Shetler scraped away for another half hour or so without finding anything else. He was finally forced to stop as a heavy thunderstorm moved in, sending the crew scrambling to get tarps over their open excavations. Boss Man called "quittin time." On the short drive back to the crew house Boss Man and Dolores tried to engage Shetler, but he remained taciturn and distant.

When they parked next to his car Shetler paused only long enough to get his motel details from Boss Man and announce that he would be back in the morning.

Eager to look over what the day's excavation of ceramic sampling squares had yielded, Boss Man and Dolores collected the paper bags containing the day's finds from the bed of Boss Man's pickup and carried them onto the back porch. There they could decompress from their hectic day, have some beers, and wash up the newly recovered ceramics in search of distinctive design motifs. They washed ceramic sherds and placed them to dry on their labeled grid square bags in near silence for quite a while, occasionally identifying style or other elements with a brief word or two.

Boss Man broke the silence with a question that had been bothering him ever since Shetler had hurriedly taken off for his hotel . "How come Shetler split so quickly? I was expecting him to hang around all afternoon so we would have plenty of opportunities to invite him to join us please, please, please, in writing up the enclosure, cosmogram, and Hamblin Fort Figurine."

Dolores smiled ruefully. "Oh, I think I know exactly why he left so abruptly. And I'm guessing he heads straight back north tomorrow without stopping by here on the way." Picking up another soil covered sherd and starting to brush it clean, Dolores continued. "Our dissertation projects here at Hamblin's Fort focus on collecting and analyzing ceramics to get at community organization and social structure, right? Not the Cahokia enclosure with its cosmogram, figurine and shell cup workshop. You could say that discovering the enclosure was an accidental, incidental finding on our part. We uncovered the figurine and other stuff, but it's not within the parameters of our original research design. I think that means that while we have a reasonable claim on writing it up, our ownership of it is sort of provisional, and pretty tenuous. Shetler figured that given the tenuous circumstances he could probably step in and leverage us into granting him co-authorship."

"So what's changed?" asked Boss Man, taking a solid slug from his beer.

"Everything's changed," Dolores replied. "The shell fragment with the likely Braden style entwined and crosshatched snakes that Shetler found on the mound summit strongly suggests that activities there were also part of the Cahokian presence at Hamblin's Fort."

Looking puzzled, Boss Man still didn't get it. "So what?" he replied.

Dolores fought to keep her impatience from showing as she replied. "If you link the enclosure with Cahokia, and also the mound summit activities with Cahokia, then the question is — are the mound summit ceremonies and the enclosure activities linked to each other?"

Boss Man's mouth opened in realization as Dolores continued.

"Denny's been excavating the mound summit. That's her research project, and back on campus she's been jabbering to faculty and grad students about her ideas on mound feasting debris for some time. If the enclosure and the mound summit can be linked to each other and to Cahokia, then by extension, Denny has a good argument for folding the enclosure and what it contained in with the mound summit activities, under her overall research plan. But it also might make some sense for Shetler to be the one to take over a combined analysis of the Cahokian connection that folds the mound and enclosure into one package. Denny's just starting out, after all."

"But she salted the trench with that shell fragment," Boss Man countered. "You said so yourself."

"No, I was just pissed off. I'm sure it's legit. And my guess is that she's gonna keep finding more up there."

"So where does that leave us?"

"Well, I'm not sure." Dolores responded. "If Shetler now wants to hijack analysis of the mound and enclosure, the obvious play for us would be to knuckle under. Maybe we could argue that the three of us should get to write up the figurine and enclosure, and Denny can deal with whatever she finds on the mound. The critical issue, of course, will be how much more is there for her to find. If she doesn't find much, then she doesn't have much to link the Red Mound to either Cahokia or the enclosure, and the case for folding the Cahokia enclosure, cosmogram, and figurine into her research plan will be weak. On the other hand, the more she finds, the stronger the case will be for including the enclosure and figurine in her analysis."

Boss Man then brought up the other obvious issue — what was Denny's standing to take on excavation of the summit anyway? Sure, she had been accepted to the grad program, but she hadn't even taken any classes and didn't have a dissertation proposal accepted yet, let alone a dissertation advisor and committee set up.

"That's true," Dolores agreed, smiling. "She's in a weak position. But she seems to have the museum director's ear, and there's always Cecelia and her donor dad to think about. I have no idea how this will turn out. The good news is we don't have to do anything right now. I think Denny is going to be focused exclusively on finding more slope side debris from whatever activities were carried out on the mound. She's not that bright, and she won't be looking beyond her stupid trench. I doubt she has even thought about the possibility that the enclosure and mound should be considered together."

Boss Man nodded. "But she will soon I bet. If she finds more conch shell cup fragments up there, it won't take her long to connect the dots, if she hasn't already done so. Evidence of shell engraving in the enclosure, and engraved shell cups on the mound — it's a no-brainer."

Dolores picked up the narrative. "If Shetler is planning what I think he is, he needs to shut her down, and fast. He needs to make his move soon, and that will involve getting back on campus to gin up support for his hijacking of Denny's mound summit research along with our enclosure excavations. I'm not sure exactly how that would play out, but there would probably be some sort of closed-door faculty confab."

Later that night, after most of the crew had turned in, Tom was in the kitchen with a serious case of the munchies. He had just gotten a moon pie from the fridge, where he kept them cold, and was sitting down with a comic book and glass of milk when the phone rang. It was Shetler letting them know he would be heading back up to campus early in the morning — something had come up.

As he hung up the phone Tom saw headlights sweep across the front of the crew house as someone pulled in the driveway. Stepping out on the front porch and lighting up a joint, he saw Jake's familiar pickup pull up down by the garage. Getting out of his truck, Jake walked up to Cecelia's tent and went inside. Crestfallen, Tom sat on the front porch, watching the shadows playing across the side of Cecelia's tent, and puffing on his fatty. He figured she was packing, and that she and Jake would be back in his truck and heading out to California any minute. He was surprised when Jake came out alone a short time later, walked back to his truck, and drove away.

A minute later Cecelia came out of her tent and walked over. She was clearly upset as she sat down next to him and spoke in a low growl.

"Well, that was interesting. I can't believe that prick."

Tom's spirits lifted. "I thought Jake came to pick you up — that you were heading out to Chaco Canyon."

"Oh, yeah — that was the plan," Cecelia replied. "And he was stickin to the plan. He just added his mom Betty and sister Doris to the mix. It turns out they are coming with us. Or that's what Jake was planning on. They were down there in the truck."

Tom stayed quiet, and passed the joint to Cecelia, who took a long drag before continuing.

"Jake said his mom and sister were being threatened by some bad dudes that are after him. He figured they could hitch a ride with us as far as Las Vegas, where Betty is pretty sure she and Doris can crash with an old friend of hers."

Cecelia held onto the joint, took another long hit, and stayed silent. Tom said nothing, waiting for Cecelia to continue as he too held his breath. Cecelia passed the joint back as she exhaled and answered the question that Tom had been afraid to ask.

"There's no fuckin way I'm doin' a cross-country trip with those three. I was fool enough to think Jake is crazy in love with me and is dying to join me on a shared journey of personal, spiritual growth. Nope. He likes the sex, and he's good in bed, but clearly, I'm not the love of his life. But he thinks I'm gonna be his wallet, his golden goose. Those three are running low on funds, closing in on flat broke, and some serious criminals are after them. I'm their ticket out of town."

"What are you going to do?"

"They're stopping back at Betty's over in Jonesboro tonight and switching to her car before heading west. I gave Jake the five hundred dollars I had stashed in my backpack and told him I could send more when he needed it. The plan now is for me to fly out and meet up with them in Vegas as soon as I can get a flight."

Cecelia looked on the verge of tears as Tom asked the obvious follow-up.

"Are you gonna do it?"

"No Tom, we've seen the last of Jake. No really big loss, actually. He couldn't play the guitar for shit."

20.
SOMETHING BIG

While Boss Man and Dolores were washing sherds on the back porch Denny had taken a quick shower and retreated to her room, where she now sat at her makeshift desk — several planks straddling a pair of sawhorses. She was reading over a partially finished rough draft of her dissertation proposal that she had started back during winter term. It still read pretty well but there was a lot to do to finish it. The initial sections that covered the theoretical and methodological aspects of analyzing and interpreting mound summit ceremonial debris were all completed, as well as a description of her general research design for excavation of the temple mound at Hamblin's Fort.

Now she needed to add sections describing what she had accomplished so far this field season. She described their pothole clean up and the discovery of the red clay feature and the red wolf burial, and most importantly, the recovery of the conch shell fragment with the entwined snakes design. She left out any mention of the motorcycle gang corpse they found in the mound. She had also done a rubbing of the shell fragment — placing a thin tissue over it and gently rubbing with charcoal to capture the underlying design.

Denny was sure she had seen a similar design element somewhere but couldn't remember where. She knew the museum director would be able to pin it down from memory, however, and he would see this rubbing in just a few days. Denny was planning on working through the night if needed to finish her dissertation proposal, type it up, and mail it special delivery to the museum director first thing in the morning, along with the rubbing and an accompanying letter.

By midnight she had finished a final draft of the proposal and began typing it up. When that was finished, maybe an hour later, she started working on her cover letter. In it she first asked formally if he might consider serving as her major professor and chair her dissertation committee. This was pretty much a formality, as they had talked about it earlier when she had applied to grad school, and he had seemed quite amenable to the idea.

She then laid out her case that the mound summit activities and the adjacent enclosure needed to be considered together, as a single event. Denny proposed that toward the end of occupation of Hamblin's Fort, or soon after it was abandoned, a delegation arrived from Cahokia with a very specific agenda — one that had little or nothing to do with the inhabitants of Hamblin's Fort.

Upon arrival the Cahokians constructed the cedar enclosure — a restricted, ceremonial space, at the base of the Red Mound. Significantly, the opening in the enclosure's wall faced the mound, not the plaza. A small shrine was constructed inside the enclosure and the figurine installed and venerated for an unknown period of time before being ritually "killed" and buried.

In a second, larger structure within the enclosure, conch shell cups were apparently being engraved, and a fragment of one of those engraved cups had now been recovered from the temple mound, where it had been discarded down the slope of the mound.

In a concluding section Denny argued that the engraved shell cup fragment represented the first of many artifacts they would find on the mound slope, and that once recovered, all the additional discarded material would provide a rich data set from which they could decipher the nature and purpose of the Cahokian ceremonies that were carried out on the mound summit almost seven hundred years ago.

In a final few sentences Denny alluded to the underlying urgency in the timing of her dissertation proposal, asking that she be allowed to continue excavation of the mound summit and slope for the rest of the field season. By then, she argued, it would be abundantly clear whether or not her mound slope excavation plan was worthwhile and would yield a data set reflecting what the Cahokians were hoping to accomplish, and why they came to this seemingly recently abandoned provincial backwater mound center. The plea imbedded in these final few sentences was unstated, but Denny knew the museum director would recognize what she was asking — let me complete this excavation. In the fall a decision could be made regarding the dissertation. For now, just allow the excavation to continue, free from interference from Shetler.

Along with the dissertation proposal, rubbing, and cover letter, Denny included her undergraduate transcript indicating all the graduate level courses she had taken her junior and senior years, including the dreaded but required linguistics course, which now left her only a few course requirements short of her master's degree. She had been assured that she could finish those off in the coming academic year and therefore could be ready to formally start her dissertation in the spring.

Denny and Josh drove up to the Forrest City post office at the crack of dawn the next morning and Denny was the first customer through the door. She was assured that her bulky envelope would be delivered the next day. Before heading back, they stopped at a diner in Forrest City. Once they were settled in a window booth, Denny bought Josh a celebratory breakfast. The coffee sloshed gently in their mugs for maybe ten seconds at one point, but neither one noticed. They were just finishing their pancakes and sausage, with biscuits and gravy on the side, when Shetler drove past on his way north. It was at this point that the race between Denny and Shetler began. Would her proposal get to the museum director before Shetler, and be accepted, or would Shetler's lobbying succeed in hijacking her project?

Josh and Denny arrived at Hamblin's Fort maybe half an hour after the rest of the crew. Yesterday's storm had carried high winds and many of the small tarps spread over the ceramic sampling 5x5 squares had been blown all the way to the tree line. The squares were flooded. There was a lot of bailing and a lot of bitching coming from crew members crouched next to their flooded squares as Josh and Denny climbed the slope of the temple mound.

Cecelia was on the summit, over by the south-slope trench. She was beaming.

"The tarps worked great. Water ran right down the slope on top of the tarp, and the soil is dry underneath." Her smile grew even wider as she described Boss Man's scowl when he saw how well their slope-side excavation had held up. "He rushed right over when we got here, expecting the trench to have turned into a gully down the side of the mound. When I pulled the tarp back and revealed a perfectly clean and dry trench bottom, he barked out a quick "fuck," and scurried away."

Cecelia then filled them in on Shetler's abrupt change in plans and his return north, which did not surprise Denny, given her suspicions about his still unspoken hijacking plans. She and Josh were surprised, however, when Cecelia told them of Paula's new quest.

"She took off early this morning, just after you guys. She's heading over to the Arkansas Archaeological Survey in Fayetteville. Apparently there's a guy there who might be able to help her with identifying the source of some of the chert artifacts and debitage she's been getting from the ceramic sampling squares."

Josh looked skeptical. "I find that hard to believe. Are you saying it's possible to pin down where the raw material used for the lithic tools at Hamblin's Fort came from? It all looks the same to me — crappy and crude, nothing but small flakes and useless little chert chunks." Sliding her arm around Josh's waist, Denny jumped in with a little background information so Paula's excitement would make some sense to him.

"Josh, we are smack in the middle of the lower alluvial valley of the Mississippi River. The valley is about 14 miles wide here, and all the soil was deposited by the river. It's alluvium — sands, pebbles, and clays. No rocks you can make into tools. The nearest chert sources are west of here, on Crowley's Ridge and in the Ozarks — more than a day's travel on foot. That's where almost all of the Hamblin's Fort chert comes from. Occasionally we find some chert flakes from the sharpening of Mill Creek chert hoes that were traded down from southern Illinois, but mostly it's Ozark and Crowley's Ridge material."

"Cherts there occur as small cobbles, however, and about all you can do with them is knock off small flakes which can be used for cutting, but soon get dull and are discarded. Sometimes you see larger formal tool types — scrapers and knives, but mostly it's flakes and what's left over when the small cores are used up."

"So, coming back to your question Josh - the answer is a qualified yes: some of the cherts that occur in different areas of Crowley's Ridge and the eastern Ozarks look different from each other, allowing artifacts made from those cherts to be traced back to where the raw material used to make them was picked up."

Nodding impatiently at Denny's pedantic interruption, Cecelia continued. "All of a sudden Paula's super excited about this new research question she came up with. She's pretty confident that she's identified four different chert types among the lithics she's looked at so far, and that they appear to come from different parts of the site. She's hoping that this Fayetteville guy can link her four chert types to different source area locations in the Ozarks."

Cecelia unconsciously began to sway to a tune only she could hear as she continued the story. "Here's where it gets really far out. Paula figures, or 'hypothesizes,' that the different sub-groups comprising the Hamblin's Fort community, which Boss Man and Dolores are trying to discern, could well have each had different traditional hunting territories in the Ozarks and Crowley's Ridge. If so, when these different kin groups went hunting, they would also have taken the opportunity to collect chert cobbles. Once the cherts were brought back to Hamblin's fort and made into tools, the spatial distribution of different used up and discarded cherts should both indicate the distribution of different kin units across the site, and the location of their respective hunting territories."

Josh couldn't hide his skepticism. "There's a lotta 'maybes' in that story Cecelia. Do you buy it?" Cecelia shrugged her shoulders and replied. "Maybe. It's a good story."

Denny quickly offered a stronger defense of Paula's new research direction.

"That's what the New Archaeology is all about Josh. It's all about asking new questions, trying out new approaches to understanding the past." Josh nodded, not really listening as he watched Black Dog emerge from the tree line and trot up the side of the mound. The dog slowly scanned the mound summit and then the rest of the site where the crew was bailing out the ceramic sampling squares. Josh figured Black Dog was no doubt looking for Shetler so he could sneak up and try for a groin lunge. Apparently satisfied that Shetler was not present, Black Dog plopped down in the shade of a wheelbarrow and commenced his silent watching, with an occasional tail wag when anyone looked his way.

Denny was anxious to get back to excavating the trench down the south slope of the Red Mound. She was already worrying they wouldn't find anything. She and Josh had decided over breakfast that they should also extend their trench in the other direction, down the north slope of the Red Mound, to see if mound summit ceremony debris may have been dumped in that direction. Josh and Cecelia started staking out the planned north extension of their trench and Denny got back to work on the mound's south slope.

By lunchtime Josh and Cecelia had stripped the sod from the north slope extension of the trench and were starting to shovel-skim down through the white sand layer. Not surprisingly, they had found nothing of interest so far, and were noticeably fading in the building heat. Denny had now almost finished removing the white sand layer from the south slope of the mound all the way to the base of the mound but had found nothing more. With the exception of the single conch shell fragment Shetler had discovered the day before, the slope seemed devoid of any artifacts. After breaking for lunch in the shade, it was more of the same. By late that afternoon, with little sleep the night before, Denny was pretty much exhausted, and the first serious doubts started to creep in. Maybe there was nothing here and her grad career would crash and burn before it even started.

She had moved back upslope and was now near the mound summit, lying flat on the ground on the west edge of the trench with her right arm stretching down into it to trowel. She stopped, closed her eyes against the sweat and rested her head on her arm. The late afternoon sun was now brightly illuminating the vertical wall on the east side of the trench, across from where Denny was lying. Squinting and brushing the sweat away from her eyes, Denny leaned into the trench for a closer look at the opposite side wall of the trench. She noticed an area of faint mottling of the white sand layer down toward the floor of the trench - several red flecks and many more black flecks, like specks of charcoal, ran for a yard or so along the wall.

Denny closed her eyes again, took a few calming breaths, and glanced over to where Josh and Cecelia were working with their backs to her. Without giving it much thought Denny then did something that archaeology students were taught to never do. Easing down into the trench, Denny reached across to the opposite sidewall, and placing the point of her trowel in the center of the mottled area, she carefully pushed its blade into the sidewall of the trench. This was frowned upon among the ranks of professional archaeologists because one of the most obvious things that distinguished them from looters was that the holes that they dug were square and had straight vertical sides. And they called them "excavation units," not "holes." And one simply didn't go digging into sidewalls. Professionally excavated sidewalls were expected to display carefully troweled and perfectly vertical surfaces along with beautifully stratified soil layers, and perhaps some colored nails or tags marking the location of important discoveries. Sidewalls were to be admired and emulated, not subjected to the desecration of digging, of penetration.

Denny's trowel went into the sidewall about three inches and then hit something solid. Momentarily stunned, she pulled the trowel out of the sidewall, moved it a foot to the left of her first thrust, still within the mottled soil patch, and pushed the blade in a second time. Once again, the trowel hit something solid about three inches in. Suddenly elated, Denny giggled to herself, immediately thinking of the cosmic curse that was the flip side of the sanctity of sidewalls — horror stories abounded of the trenches and test pits that archaeologists had dug that somehow managed to come within inches of uncovering something amazing but were just a little bit off. Big discoveries could easily be missed, hidden inches away in the sidewalls. But not this time. No question, there was something in the sidewall, right at the interface of the white sand cap and the underlying mound surface. And it wasn't just another shell fragment. It was something big.

Denny walked over to where Cecelia and Josh were shovel-skimming the trench and after cautioning them to stay calm and not draw the attention of Boss Man, she dropped her bombshell. "There's something big hiding in the east sidewall on the south slope."

Cecelia reacted first, dropping her shovel, and doing a quick pirouette while clapping discretely. Josh wanted more details, but Denny interrupted. "Later Josh. Right now, here's what we're gonna do. You guys keep shoveling the north slope trench for now. I'll quietly stake out a five-foot eastward extension of the south slope trench along a ten-foot section where I saw some speckling in the east side wall. It's almost quittin time, so let's keep this quiet and tomorrow we can tackle expanding that part of the trench into a 10x10 block excavation and then do a careful and well documented excavation of whatever is in there."

Josh's dirt-covered sweaty face broke into a wide smile. "I'm thinkin a big pile of engraved conch shell cups would be nice."

21.
KEEP DIGGING

Paula got back from Fayetteville by about seven o'clock that evening after a long day of driving for the short hour and a half meeting with her lithics expert. But she was bubbling over with excitement as she accepted a beer from Wilma and joined the crew on the front porch. Sunset was still an hour off, but Zack and Richard were already in the bag and providing raucous entertainment. Zack had seemingly bounced back from his major migraine, which had kept him unusually quiet for the last day or so. With drunken enthusiasm he and Richard were mocking Bopper's pronouncement that he thought that he could sense that the mini-quakes, the temblors, were coming more frequently. Zack was crouching under his chair with his shirt over his head, saying he was hiding from sand volcanos, and Richard had taken a surfer's stance on the porch railing, saying he was ready to ride the floodwaters.

Bopper seemed to take the ribbing in stride, just shaking his head and repeating. "You'll see. You wait. We are disturbing the forces of the underworld with our digging."

Denny, Josh, and Cecelia were watching the entertainment with amusement but said little and maintained an attitude of solemn disappointment, while sneaking each other occasional grins. They were neither surprised nor disappointed that no one asked how things were going on the Red Mound.

Boss Man and Dolores seemed particularly pleased with the lack of announcement of any new discoveries on the Red Mound. Eager to fill the void, they had been waxing eloquent about the potential meaning of ceramic design elements and how they were distributed across the site. In the last few days they had identified several new designs on the sherds coming out of the sampling squares and wanted to add them in to their ongoing analysis. But not tonight. They were in celebration mode tonight — Denny's stock was way down and theirs was trending up. The new sherd assemblages coming out of the widely scattered ceramic test squares were yielding promising results — they might actually be on to something. And Paula's new research focusing on chert sources provided both additional support for their ceramic study and a much-needed boost to their confidence.

Paula enthusiastically shared their excitement. Her Arkansas Survey lithics expert had not only confirmed her four lithic groupings, but also told her that each of her chert types in fact came from different source areas, with two in the Ozarks and two on Crowley's Ridge. She was now going to go back through all of the lithics they had recovered this summer and last, picking out those items that matched any of the four chert types, and start recording their locations of recovery across the site. At the same time, she would try to stay on top of identifying the chert samples that would be coming out of the ceramic test squares in the coming weeks. Paula, it seemed, had come up with an interesting and innovative research direction that happily could be piggybacked on the ceramic sampling plan that was already in place.

Wilma, in contrast, was not yet convinced that the scattered ceramic sampling squares would provide her with a data set of plant remains that could answer any interesting research questions — anything much beyond the basic identification and quantification of what plants were collected, cultivated, and used for tools and construction. She was hopeful that she could come up with something, but did not share the enthusiasm and high spirits, both on full display and carefully hidden, of the other crew members on the porch that evening.

Bopper, Richard, Zack and Tom were celebrating tonight for reasons that had nothing to do with research questions and data collection. Now that they had all been assigned their own 5x5 grid squares for excavation that were scattered across the site, Richard had come up with the brilliant idea of constructing simple sunshades for their squares using their plastic tarps and cane poles cut from nearby stands. Before the shift to the ceramic sampling squares, their excavation areas had been too extensive for any sort of overhead sun protection other than hats. But now they would have shade, wonderful shade.

The enthusiasm and heightened hopes of the previous evening extended over into the next day, with the crew setting to work in high spirits. Bopper, Zack, Richard and Tom seemed particularly pleased as they walked to their now shady excavation squares. Denny, Josh and Cecelia immediately set to work on the mound summit. They stripped the sod from the 5x10 foot extension to the south-slope trench that Denny had staked out, and then began skimming down through the white sand layer, taking turns handling the sifter. Nothing had turned up in the first six inches or so, when they broke for lunch.

Cecelia had gone back to the crew house to apply the sunscreen she had forgotten that morning, and when she returned, she was carrying a message for Denny from the museum director. His secretary had called on the kitchen phone while Cecelia was getting a sandwich. She had written it down to make sure she got it right, as it seemed somewhat curt. Handing the message to Denny, she asked what it meant. Denny unfolded the piece of paper, sticky with jam, and puzzled over the message. "Keep digging. Shetler may advise." She shrugged in response to

Cecelia's question and handed the note to Josh, who gave her a silent "WTF?"

Not knowing what to think at first, Denny carefully parsed the wording of the five-word message and decided that it was good news. The director was saying she could keep investigating the mound and pursuing her research questions. No stopping, no takeover by Shetler. Shetler might be given the opportunity to advise, to comment on her work, make suggestions, but his effort to hijack her research had been blocked, at least for now. What the note also made clear, however, was that her dissertation proposal had been received, but was now in a holding pattern. The museum director, reasonably enough, would want to wait to see what she came up with before giving full approval for her doctoral research plan. That's all Denny had been asking for, and her urgent request had been granted. But Shetler would be lurking, waiting in the wings for any opportunity to elbow her aside. Denny was confident, however, that the Shetler threat would disappear once they uncovered what lay waiting, just inside the sacred sidewall of her south slope trench.

They finally encountered something about half an hour after lunch. Cecelia, Josh, and Denny were down almost a foot in the white sand layer and had switched from skimming to troweling. They were kneeling next to each other in a line at the edge of the 5x10 trench extension, facing the trench, and reaching out to trowel the white sand back toward their knees. It was easy digging, but they were going slowly. Cecelia was in the middle, between Josh and Denny, and had been seeing black and red speckles for a few minutes when her trowel hit something with a soft 'thunk.' All three stopped troweling and exchanged glances. Just from the sound the trowel made they could tell it wasn't stone, and probably not pottery. That was not the sound of something hard. It sounded like bone, or shell, maybe — and weirdly, it had a hollowness to it. Dropping her trowel, Cecelia reached for her brush and began to clear the sand away, fully expecting to see the bright white surface of a conch shell cup.

Josh spoke for all three when he blurted out a confused "What the fuck?" as the object was exposed. It wasn't white, it was dull black. Cecelia continued brushing outward until maybe a square foot of surface was exposed. It looked like a plate of dinosaur armor, with a raised ridge having a pointed knob on it, like an alligator's back. Cecelia stopped brushing and looked to Denny for an explanation, handing her the brush. Denny began brushing straight out sideways from the prominent ridge Cecelia had uncovered. Soon a second bumpy ridge came into view, parallel to the first one.

Smiling now, Denny sat back and rendered her verdict. "Looks like an alligator's back, right? It's not an alligator, but it's just as scary. This is the shell, the carapace, of an alligator snapping turtle. They can live to be a hundred years old, and the males top out at more than 250 pounds. You would not want to encounter one of these in the rivers around here. And this guy was huge. I will be amazed if the shell is complete, and I have no idea what it's doing here."

Josh got up and hustled down the side of the mound to invite the crew, particularly Boss Man and Dolores, to come on up and see what they had found. Boss man was in front when the crew straggled up the side of the mound. When he spotted their trench extension, he went ballistic.

"Who said you could expand the trench up here? You got no approval for this. You're in some deep shit now Denny." Cecelia, Josh and Denny stayed quiet as the rest of the crew crowded around and admired the alligator snapper carapace.

"Big deal," Dolores snapped, "you found a fuckin turtle shell. But you dug yourself right off the site, sweety, with this boner move."

Enjoying the moment, Denny replied in a calm voice.

"Settle down Dolores. The museum director got word to me today that I should continue my excavations on the mound, so I am following his guidance. He said that Dr. Shetler might be offering advice, but he didn't say anything about Boss Man, or even you, dictating what I do." Denny paused, smiled, and continued. "But I welcome any suggestions you might have."

Cecelia backed her up. "I took the message at lunchtime from Carol, the museum secretary." Boss Man turned to leave, swearing to himself, only to be confronted by Black Dog, snarling at him and looking ready to lunge. Cecelia grabbed Black Dog by the collar that they had put on him for just such occasions and pulled him away as Boss Man stormed down the side of the mound.

By the end of the day the carapace had been almost completely exposed. It was complete and in excellent condition, apparently because it had been exposed to fire at some point and partially burned. It was a remarkable thirty-six inches in length, larger than any specimen documented in the historic period. It looked solid but they would have to be careful in removing it to minimize the possibility of damage. Josh built a simple lean-to structure of cane over it, which they then covered with a tarp to protect the snapper shell overnight. As Josh was finishing, Black Dog lay down next to the lean-to, clearly settling in to guard the shell overnight.

Denny had an idea about what the turtle shell was doing on the mound summit but would have to see the inside of the carapace to confirm her suspicion. She was happy to expound on her idea that night on the porch of the crew house, however. Boss Man and Dolores had stopped briefly after work to unload shovels and artifact bags containing the day's finds but didn't stick around, probably not wanting to listen to Denny's celebration. They looked grim as they left.

"It's not all that much of a mystery, actually," Denny began that evening after dinner, beer in hand. "Just think about what

Mississippian groups used turtle shells for. The flat part on the bottom — the plastron, was sometimes cut up and used as gaming pieces, but the top part of the shell, the carapace, was used almost exclusively to make cups and bowls, depending on the size of the shells. Three-toed box turtles made great cups, and the larger aquatic turtles — cooters and sliders, were turned into shallow bowls. Sometimes the bowls are burned on the outside, showing they were used in cooking."

Denny paused for a healthy slug of beer, burped, and continued. "So that's what we got, I think — a big turtle shell caldron for boiling up some black drink as part of the ceremony that took place up there. The caldron likely didn't have a lot of black drink in it — I'm guessing it was probably a pretty small group of participants up here on the mound. After they were finished with the caldron, they deposited it here on the mound slope. When we lift it out of there, I bet we find black drink residue on the inside surface. Preservation should be good with that turtle shell protecting anything inside from moisture, so we might also find conch shell cups or other ritual paraphernalia stashed inside it."

Richard snorted. "I heard quite a few speculative leaps in there Denny. Quite a few. Where did you come up with that crap?"

Denny seemed unperturbed as she continued her speculation.

"So why such a big caldron for my hypothetical small group of participants? That's what I'm wondering. A smaller container would have worked just as well. But here's this huge alligator snapper carapace taking center stage. I think it's more than utilitarian, it's not just functional. They wanted, they deliberately selected, a fearful denizen of the darkness, of the unseen watery underworld, to use as a caldron, and one that was a monster in terms of its size."

Bopper seemed intrigued but skeptical. "That's kinda sketchy don't you think? You been getting into Tom's stash?"

Richard jumped in before Denny could reply. "Sketchy? You better believe it. Sounds like more of that New Archaeology arc-bark — makin shit up outa thin air."

Continuing as if there had been no interruption, Denny added another piece of supporting evidence. "Don't forget the design on the conch shell fragment Shetler found — entwined snakes. Snakes, creatures of the underworld, dangerous, elusive, deadly."

Cecelia laughed from the other end of the porch where she and Tom were sharing a joint. "I been tellin you all along. The mound's energy is dark, dark red, with a powerful energy vortex flowing up like a tornado. The Red Mound ain't no happy place."

Richard piped up with another snide question. "What does the New Archaeology say about getting that sucker out in one piece? That turtle shell is going to fall apart when you try to remove it."

Denny had been thinking the same thing. "I'm open to any and all ideas. How do you think we should do it Mr. Harvard?"

Richard started his reply before Denny finished speaking. "I'm glad you asked. It's a no-brainer. First thing — you cover the carapace with a thin cloth covering, then pack on the plaster of Paris. Once it dries and the shell is stabilized, you just lift it up by the edges."

Bopper snorted. "Nope. Not gonna work. You'll be adding considerable weight on top of the shell, which it won't support when you lift it. It'll just collapse into a million pieces."

Wilma, who rarely said much during the after-dinner gatherings on the front porch, spoke up. "You're coming at it the wrong way. Think about what comes next. If you lift the carapace while it's still on the mound, then what? You've exposed whatever is under it to the bright sun, heat, humidity, and dust. And if we're lucky enough to have perishables preserved inside it, what will you do with them? Are we ready to deal with that? No way, José. You need to take it all out in a block, working underneath it, not on top with plaster of Paris. Once the shell and whatever's underneath it are taken out as a block, we can bring it back here and set it up on the kitchen table. Hell, we should probably pick up a window air conditioner to control the humidity in the kitchen. Then the carapace can be lifted up in a controlled environment and we can take our time figuring out how to deal with any ritual paraphernalia hidden under it, assuming there is anything there."

Once the crew got over their surprise at Wilma, quiet Wilma, causally providing a well argued and well supported solution to the carapace dilemma, there was general agreement to follow her plan. They brainstormed for another half hour about how to actually go about removing the carapace as a block, with Bopper and Josh coming up with what seemed to be the best way to proceed. First, they would excavate down around the shell, isolating it on a pedestal of soil, then undercutting it on either side. The undercutting would not be extended too far — they wouldn't want the pedestal to fall over. At the same time the undercutting might indicate how far down below the shell any preserved materials might extend. The base of the block when they removed it obviously would need to be below the level of anything hidden under the snapper shell. But how far down might any ritual paraphernalia go? Was there a pit under the shell, or was everything tucked up inside the dome of the turtle's shell?

The best approach, Bopper and Josh thought, was to cut more of the river cane and use the poles to probe the column a few inches below the carapace. If the poles met no resistance, nothing blocking their progress as they were pushed through, they would eventually form a solid horizontal layer supporting the soil block and carapace. If any of the poles touched up against something as they were pushed through, then the location of the pole layer would be moved lower on the pedestal. Once the cane pole layer had been completed, a couple of 2x4x8s could be positioned under it on either side of the shell, allowing the carapace to be lifted up like a sedan chair carrying an important personage, and then transported back to the crew house. The crew particularly liked the image of the carapace being carried like a statue of the virgin Mary, and considered forming a procession of sorts for its journey from Hamblin's Fort back to the crew house.

While the crew were figuring out the best way to extract the alligator snapper caldron from its location on the mound, Boss Man and Dolores had just settled into watching Jeopardy on the TV in their double-wide when the phone rang. It was Shetler wanting an update. Boss Man started telling him about their exciting new design element discoveries and their impressive progress in digging the ceramic squares, but Shetler cut him off. He couldn't hide the frustration in his voice.

"Has anything else turned up on the mound?"

Boss Man paused, not wanting to be the one to pass on the bad news, but finally blurted it out. "She found the biggest snapping turtle shell I've ever seen and claims it's a caldron for black drink. She's totally lost it if you ask me."

Shetler threw the phone at the refrigerator in his apartment in frustration, but Boss Man could still hear his string of profanities faintly on the other end of the call. Shetler quickly picked the phone up, took a few deep breaths, and worked to project cool confidence as he dictated instructions to Boss Man.

"You tell Denny she should not do any more excavation — no digging, until I can confer with her. I will be back down there tomorrow by dinnertime."

Boss Man tried to explain about the "keep digging" go ahead Denny had received from the museum director, but the line was dead.

22.
A QUICK PEEK

When Boss Man and Dolores arrived at Hamblin's Fort the next morning Denny and Josh were busy taking the lean-to covering off the snapper shell on the mound slope, and the rest of the crew were scattered across the site working in their individual ceramic excavation squares. Cecelia had headed up to Forrest City to pick up a window air conditioner for the kitchen lab setup they were planning.

When Bopper learned that they were actually going to buy an AC unit he quickly moved his cot down from the room he shared with Tom to a primo location in the corner of the kitchen. It was a big kitchen, he figured, with room even for a few more cots. He was surprised when Tom didn't jump at the chance to join him in air-conditioned bliss. Tom had other plans. With Bopper moving down to the kitchen for sleeping he figured maybe this was his chance to get Cecelia out of her tent on the lawn and inside the crew house to share his room and his bed.

Dolores went over to check on the rest of the crew while Boss Man climbed up the side of the mound to pass on Shetler's message to Denny that they should stop digging and wait for his arrival that evening. Boss Man walked over to the edge of their excavation and delivered the bad news.

"Hey Denny. Shetler called last night. He wanted me to tell you he was driving down today, and that you should stop digging until he gets here." Denny turned and looked at Boss Man for a few beats before responding. She thought it interesting that Boss Man's attitude had changed. He didn't seem angry, and he didn't order her to stop digging. He was just passing on a message.

"How come Shetler called you?" Denny asked. "Why not call me at the crew house. He has the number. He called it the other night. So why did he have you deliver his order, rather than telling me directly?"

Boss Man shook his head. "I have no idea, Denny. I'm just passin on the message." Denny nodded, then asked. "What do you think I should do, Boss Man? On the one hand I have the museum director telling me to keep digging, and on the other hand I have Shetler telling me to stop. Shetler's an untenured assistant prof, a year or two away from an up or out tenure decision. Who even knows if he will still be around two years from now. But the museum director? We know he's not going anywhere. He's been the director forever. He's a full professor with a named chair and a big reputation, and I'm pretty sure he's agreed to be my dissertation advisor and chair my committee."

Boss Man smiled as he replied. "Shit, Denny, I have no idea what's your best move here. Looks like you're in a tight spot." With that, he scurried down the side of the mound.

Cecelia had bought a nice 5,000 btu window air conditioning unit and was just arriving back at the crew house mid-morning when Sheriff Hogg drove up and offered to carry the heavy AC unit inside for her. Once inside, after installing the unit and turning it on full blast, Cecelia and the sheriff brewed a pot of coffee and shared some day-old Danish while luxuriating in the blast of cold air filling the kitchen. Cecelia needed little prompting to bring the sheriff up to speed on the progress of the excavations at Hamblin's Fort, and he seemed particularly interested in the alligator snapper shell and what it might contain.

The sheriff also asked if she had seen any more of Jake, and Cecelia filled him in on the latest — that Jake had skipped town with his mother and sister and was probably in Nevada by now. Cecelia was surprised that the Sheriff didn't perk up at the news that Jake was out of the picture. He looked old and worn out, she thought, and jumpy. He kept glancing out the window as if expecting someone. Cecelia hitched a ride back out to the site with Sheriff Hogg, and her concern ratcheted up another notch when he had to move a sawed-off shotgun and box of shells off the passenger seat before she could climb in.

When they got to the site Cecelia was expecting the sheriff to follow her up to the Red Mound summit to see how Denny and Josh were doing. Instead, he asked her to tell Boss Man that he needed to talk to him. Cecelia stopped by and delivered the message before joining Denny and Josh on the Red Mound, and then watched as Boss Man walked over to the sheriff's truck and climbed in. They talked for several minutes, with the sheriff doing most of the talking, and Boss Man nodding his head as he followed along. Boss Man had his usual dour expression as he got out of the truck and walked back over and joined Dolores, apparently passing on what Hogg had told him.

The sheriff left as soon as Boss Man exited his truck. Hogg stopped at the first pay phone he saw and made a quick call, leaving a brief message. "Hey Pappy, gimmie a call. I might have a line on some really nice Indian artifacts — maybe some of those big shell cups and maybe a stone statue."

The turtle shell pedestal excavation had progressed down far enough by lunchtime that they could start pushing in the cane poles a few inches below the rim of the shell. The first few poles went in easily and didn't encounter anything on their way through, and the rest went in just as easily, forming a solid horizontal floor under the shell. After lunch the sedan chair

2x4x8s were moved into position under the cane poles, and with Josh, Denny, Richard and Tom at the four corners, they carefully, delicately, lifted the shell and whatever it contained free from the soil pedestal. Skipping and twirling, Cecelia then led the procession down off the Red Mound and over to the parking area, where they placed the carapace block in the bed of one of the pickups for the short trip back to the crew house. Cecelia drove, Black Dog rode shotgun, and the sedan chair carriers rode cradling their precious cargo in the bed of the truck.

Once safely positioned on the kitchen table, the sedan chair 2x4x8s were removed and the cane stalks withdrawn one by one. The snapper shell seemed to cry out to be immediately opened up to reveal its secrets, but Denny had decided it was better to wait for Shetler to arrive so he could witness the big reveal. It was still a few hours till quittin time, but the sedan chair carriers and Cecelia reached a quick consensus that their best course of action was to stay in the cool kitchen, have a few beers to celebrate the successful transfer of their prize from Hamblin's Fort to the crew house, and to try to guess what was still to be revealed that evening.

The celebration soon moved to the front porch and expanded when quittin time came and the rest of the crew arrived back at the house. When professor Shetler drove up a little before dark, Boss Man set his beer down and hustled down to meet him.

"Welcome back professor, how was the drive down?"

Ignoring the question, Shetler countered with his own.

"What's the status of the mound excavations?"

Boss man took a deep breath and offered the answer he had formulated after discussion with Dolores. "Nothing new has been found so far, but the turtle shell and whatever it conceals has been removed and brought back here. We've set up a lab in the kitchen." Shetler started to reply, but Boss Man continued.

"It wasn't safe to leave it exposed at the site another night. The sheriff stopped by today to warn us that there's been an uptick in drug gang violence lately, and some of it may be mistakenly directed toward us. We've also had some problems with nighttime pothunter visits to the site."

Shetler took a step back. "What exactly does that mean — drug gang violence?"

Boss Man squirmed, avoided Shetler's gaze, and decided he should not sugar-coat it.

"Well, you know Cecelia, I think. She's on the crew because her father's a big supporter of the museum and a long-time friend of the director. Her boyfriend, a guitar player up in Memphis, spent some time here with the crew, and he apparently had some association with a motorcycle gang involved in moving drugs into Memphis. The boyfriend has run off now, but the sheriff thinks we should still be cautious."

Shetler nodded, almost seeming to welcome the news of the threat to the crew, and patted Boss Man on the shoulder as he moved past him, heading for the house. The crew went silent as he climbed the steps to the porch. Richard and Dolores stood to greet him while the rest of the crew stayed in their seats. Shetler brushed by Dolores and Richard without a word and headed for the kitchen. Denny jumped up to follow him and the rest of the crew crowded into the kitchen behind them, eager to witness the big reveal. Black Dog was curled up in a corner and lifted his head to growl at Shetler when he entered the kitchen. Bopper and Tom sat on the Bopper's cot, and the rest of the crew lined up around the walls.

Shetler stood next to the kitchen table looking down at the turtle shell as the crew filed in, and when they went quiet, he took the time to fill his pipe and light it, basking in the attention being paid by his audience. As the hanging bare bulb over the table swayed erratically, casting moving shadows across the faces of the crew, Shetler praised them all for their efforts and their courage given the drug gang difficulties.

Wilma interrupted here with a sardonic crack.

"Difficulties? You mean the dead motorcycle gang member we discovered in the temple mound? That difficulty? Boy did he stink. Or maybe you mean the shots fired into Boss Man's truck?"

Shetler looked stunned. He looked at Wilma, then at Boss Man, took a deep breath, and continued. He complemented Denny, Josh, and Cecelia for their hard work and perseverance, but concluded with a real downer pronouncement.

"I'm really relieved that this amazing discovery has been successfully extracted from its exposed position at Hamblin's Fort. Given the late hour, however, it's probably not a good idea to see what's inside this shell right now. There's no time tonight to assess and deal with what's in there. We should wait until tomorrow."

Groans echoed around the kitchen as Denny stepped forward to reply.

"That's your advice, right? Your recommendation?"

Straining to keep the anger from his voice, Shetler smiled weakly and offered an obviously insincere reply. "Of course, Denny. I'm not issuing orders."

Offering Shetler an equally insincere smile of her own, Denny responded. "Great. I agree. But I think we should take a quick peek right now. We can just lift the shell up, see what's underneath, and then set it back down."

As she was speaking, Denny glanced around the room at the crew members as she stepped forward and placed two hands under the rim of the alligator snapper carapace. Josh and Bopper were the first to join her, and the others jostled for a place at the table. Cecelia, Tom, and Paula filled the remaining open places around the shell, and Denny reminded them to lift up in unison, but only maybe an inch, and then pause.

She counted down. They lifted in unison, and the carapace came free with a quiet sigh. A pungent, earthy smell filled the room as the shell was lifted. The carapace seemed solid, and later Bopper would comment that it was a fucking rock. They could have dropped it from an upstairs window, and it wouldn't have developed a crack. On Denny's command, they lifted another few inches, then a full foot. It was difficult to see what was in the shadow under the shell, so they walked the carapace sideways, away from the table, and set it down gently on Bopper's cot.

No one spoke as they all crowded around the kitchen table, trying to make sense of what they were looking at. Expecting a pile of shiny white engraved conch shell cups, they instead saw only a pile of dull blackness.

"Looks like a pile of shite," Dolores offered as she leaned closer to the dull black mound on the kitchen table. Looking closer, she noticed an occasional iridescent quality to the blackness and exclaimed.

"Oh my. It's feathers. It's bird's wings. A bunch of bird wings. Big bird wings. These are from large birds. Must be raptor wings. Eagles maybe. We got a pile of bird wings. Birds. Last time I looked, birds were creatures of the above world, soaring above us. So much for Denny's realm of darkness theory for the Red Mound. Back to the drawing board, bozo." As she delivered the last line, Dolores made the pistol shot gesture with her hand at Denny's head and laughed.

Denny loosely clasped her hands in front of her and looked back at Dolores. She had often amused other grad students by doing impromptu impressions of the various professors in the department, and now, taking on her best professorial posture and mode of speech, she leaned back against the kitchen table and replied.

"First, as the genius over there noticed, we got some bird wings here. Not feathers, complete wings. And they're big. I'm guessing a bird with a five or maybe six-foot wingspan. You might ask why bird wings? Or as Josh might say — 'What the fuck? What are bird wings doing on a temple mound?' My immediate guess would be ceremonial dancers. Ritual performers wore these as part of their paraphernalia. You see a lot of that on conch shell cups. Now, to test my theory, one could look to see if there is any indication of how the wings might have been attached to the performer's arms." Denny turned and pointed in quick succession to two points in the dark pile.

"If I may direct your attention here, and here — notice these braided cords hanging down. They are well placed, I think, for arm attachment at the shoulder and forearm. Pretty good evidence of the attire hypothesis."

Dolores had turned away from Denny's gaze, and Denny surveyed the room as she continued.

"That brings us to the final observation Dolores offered — that bird wings, and birds, belong to the upper world, not the lower world of darkness and death. And for the most part, that is certainly true. But maybe we should consider exactly what species we have here. What are these ritual performers wearing and representing? Whatever bird species it is, it can't possibly be associated with the underworld, with death and decay, with darkness. As Dolores noted — it's a bird, after all, a creature of the sky, the above world."

Denny paused, gazed at Dolores and then Shetler in turn, and reaching over for a fork from the table, she gently lifted several of the black primary feathers in the pile and peeked underneath before continuing.

"But there is in fact a big black bird, with a six-foot wingspan, that is directly and intimately associated with death and especially with decay. And this wing is from one of those. It's a turkey vulture, judging from its distinctive white underwing color."

Beaming at Dolores, Denny went back over to the turtle shell, where she was joined by Josh and Cecelia. The three members of the Red Mound crew then carefully placed the carapace back in its original position, shielding the turkey vulture wing pile from view. Professor Shetler looked on but said nothing.

After the carapace had been put back in position the crew moved out onto the porch, reluctantly leaving the cool sanctuary of the kitchen AC unit. Shetler, Boss Man and Dolores all headed back up to Forrest City but talked a good while down by their vehicles before heading off. Soon after they left the sheriff showed up and joined the group, accepting a beer from Richard and settling in to enjoy the entertainment provided by Bopper and Tom, who were trading theories regarding the turkey vulture wings, seeing who could come up with the most outlandish scenarios.

Denny would often join in the game of spinning ridiculous theories, but not tonight. She stayed quiet, worried about the vulture wings and whatever else the carapace might contain, and struggling to decide what their next step should be. She had seemed confident, even arrogant, in the kitchen earlier as she expounded on the vulture wings, but now she was worried. They still had no idea what lay underneath the wings, but Denny now realized they weren't really set up to take apart this likely complicated pile of ritual paraphernalia. Not here. She had taken a museum techniques course a few years back, and knew they needed a proper lab, not a kitchen table in a crowded living space in the middle of an Arkansas soybean field. The best thing they could do now, she thought, was to pack this amazing discovery carefully into one of the university station wagons and drive it back north to the museum. There they could x-ray it to see what else was hidden under the black feathers. They could also consult with curators and experts around the university about how to properly disentangle and document the wings, and what range of analyses might be carried out. She was damn well not going to fuck this up. Shetler and Dolores and some of the other grad students would be poised to find fault with whatever she did. Denny decided that tomorrow morning she would call the museum director and seek the green light to bring the carapace and wings north.

Cecelia was also quiet, and also thinking about heading back north, but for a quite a different set of reasons. She couldn't stop thinking about Jake, for one thing, and all the nights they had spent together in her tent on the side lawn. There were too many memories of him here. He was pretty much a loser, she acknowledged, but he didn't take himself or life too seriously, and he was fun to be around. Then there was Tom, the gawky stoner who carried a huge torch for her and who was beginning to really grate with his longing looks and ever-present horniness. More than Tom, more than memories of Jake, however, Cecelia wanted to get away from the Red Mound.

Initially mesmerized by its dark red energy vortex, she had become more and more concerned over the last week or so. The vortex seemed to be growing stronger, growing darker and more menacing. It was amazing, she thought to herself, that nobody else seemed to see or feel the vortex, or to be concerned. She felt guilty about leaving Denny and Josh in the lurch but had decided that it was time to embark on the next chapter of her search for meaning in life. Later that night she would call her dad and fill him in on things.

Driving up to his motel room, professor Shetler was also planning to call the university from his motel room that night. He planned on dialing the museum director's work phone after hours and leaving a concise message on the answering machine outlining why he thought Denny should drive the carapace and wings back north in the next day or two. His main point would be the same as Denny's — this amazing discovery needed a proper lab setting for analysis. But he would also add a brief mention of the local drug violence, the body buried in the mound, and the sketchy sheriff showing interest in the materials they were recovering. He had mentioned these plans to Dolores and Boss Man just before leaving the crew house, and they both agreed it was the wise thing to do.

23.
YOU MUST BE GRETA

Denny didn't sleep well that night and the next morning she still wasn't sure that calling the museum director was the right move, even though Josh totally backed her decision. Would she be labeled a quitter, leaving in the middle of the field season? Did she care? Lying next to Josh, who was still asleep and snoring softly, Denny fretted. She dimly heard the phone ring down in the kitchen, and then the Bopper yelled up the stairs.

"Hey vulture lady, the museum's on the phone for you."

Throwing on her pajamas, Denny rushed downstairs and answered the call, expecting it to be the museum secretary. She almost dropped the phone when she realized it was the museum director on the other end of the line. She listened, nodding her head, and said "Yes sir." Continuing to listen, this time for quite a while, she said "Yes sir" again, smiling now, and asked. "All the field notes and grid sheets and photos too?" Denny listened again for a lengthy period before ending the call with a simple. "Thank you sir. This is a big relief. I totally agree. We will be up there with everything by tomorrow night at the latest."

Hanging up the phone, Denny climbed the stairs back to the attic and slid into bed next to Josh, who was awake now and smiling at her. He seemed to be smiling a lot these days. Sliding her hand slowly down across his stomach, feeling it flutter, she told him the news.

"The museum director just called, Josh. He wants us to pack up the turtle shell and vulture wings as well as the bauxite figure and other materials from the enclosure and bring everything up to the museum for proper lab analysis and conservation. All the field notes and everything. We're gonna blow this popsicle stand."

Denny was expecting considerable blow-back from Dolores and Boss Man, as well as from Shetler, when she told them about the director's call, and was surprised when they all seemed to not just accept, but to endorse the decision that came down from on high.

Part of it was likely their shared concern for the proper handling of the material recovered from the Red Mound, she thought, but mostly they probably didn't want to mount any opposition to an edict from the director. Shetler even indicated that he would take charge of backfilling the excavations on the Red Mound for them. Josh and Denny exchanged a concerned glance when they heard his promise, but couldn't really object, and couldn't see how it would disadvantage them and benefit him. He would just be shoveling dirt back into the holes they had dug.

Cecelia also didn't seem surprised, and almost appeared to be taking credit for the change in plans. "That's great news Denny. And if you're leaving, then I'm leaving. Can I hitch a ride north with you?" Tom was standing nearby and overheard their exchange. He looked gobsmacked. Quietly moving away, he dropped his coffee cup on the lawn and drifted off into the bean field.

There were subdued goodbyes before the rest of the crew headed off to Hamblin's Fort, and then Cecelia, Josh, and Denny spent the rest of the day packing stuff up for the trip north. Josh and Denny opted to spend their last night in the crew house sleeping in Denny's room, which freed up Josh's mattress from the attic. It would now provide a cushioned base for the snapper shell and its contents in the back of the station wagon. Their belongings and the enclosure artifacts, along with all the associated field records were then carefully packed around the shell, creating a cushioned cocoon.

It was going to be a long drive — probably a full twelve hours not counting stops, so they were up and out before sunup the next morning. Cecelia almost didn't accompany them because Black Dog was nowhere to be found when they were ready to leave. He had slipped away during the night.

The three took turns driving and monitoring the cushioned cargo, and made good time, arriving back on campus in the late afternoon. Dropping Cecelia off at her dad's place up on Geddes by the Arboretum, Denny and Josh headed for campus. Rather than taking their precious cargo to the archaeology museum, however, Denny had been instructed to proceed to the university's art museum. There they had the x-ray machine, the climate-controlled labs, and conservators ready to advise and lend a hand. Once the snapper shell, bauxite figurine, vulture wings, and other recovered material had been assessed and stabilized they would be moved to the archaeology museum for curation.

The nattily attired staff who greeted them at the loading dock of the art museum were just about to close up for the day and looked rather askance at the two disheveled students who appeared with a giant turtle shell in the back of their station wagon. After somewhat hurriedly helping Denny and Josh to deposit the arriving materials into a secure lab, the staff briskly rushed them back out the door, informing them that they could come back tomorrow morning bright and early. A conservator with experience with delicate materials like feathers would be waiting to consult with them.

Denny then dropped Josh off at the Delt house up on Geddes Ave. The frat house had been kept open for the half dozen or so brothers who were stuck in summer school, and there were plenty of open beds. Josh could crash there for as long as he wanted.

Several of the brothers were hanging out under the broad green awning that extended across the front of the imposing brick structure and watched with silent concern as the university station wagon pulled up. A visit from university officials could mean trouble. They hooted their approval, however, when Josh got out of the car and he and Denny embraced before she drove off. As he walked up the front walk to join his frat brothers, Josh noticed the charred area on the lawn where he had burned all evidence of his Spanish classes back in the spring. It seemed like a long time ago.

A few hours after the Red Mound crew and their special cargo had headed north, Boss Man and Dolores appeared out at Hamblin's Fort, but only for long enough to make sure their reduced crew of six were all in their squares, heads down and digging. Then they drove over to the crew house where they were to spend the morning going over their now somewhat larger assemblages of ceramic sherds that had been recovered from the sampling squares scattered across the site.

Boss Man saw the note Cecelia had left on the kitchen table, asking the crew to call her as soon as anyone saw Black Dog. He had slipped away during the night and wasn't going north with her. Boss Man smiled to himself and hurried back out to his pickup, where he got his pistol out of the glove box and slipped it into his fanny pack.

In the half hour or so they had before Shetler showed up, Boss Man and Dolores laid all their sherds out on the kitchen table, which had so recently held the alligator snapper, and organized them by design motifs. The AC unit purchased for the benefit of the snapper carapace, which was no longer really needed since the snapper had gone north, was running full blast.

Shetler seemed happy with what they were seeing so far — a few distribution patterns for some of the design elements were coming into focus, and things looked promising. Boss Man then pulled out the Hamblin's Fort site map showing the location of all the sampling squares that had been excavated so far, and those still to be done. They adjusted things a bit, adding more sampling squares in parts of the site that had low sherd counts, but the initial sampling strategy appeared to be working.

Shetler and Dolores enjoyed a lengthy back and forth over the possible meaning of several of the designs that showed up on the sherds, showing off their esoteric vocabularies of ceramic style terminology. The mood in the kitchen was definitely upbeat as they sat around the table speculating about what the sherds might eventually reveal and enjoying the air conditioning.

That afternoon Dolores, Boss Man, and Shetler were back out at Hamblin's Fort. Boss Man stroked the pistol in his fanny pack and asked the crew if anyone had seen Black Dog. Now that Cecelia wasn't around to stop him, he was looking forward to taking care of that mongrel once and for all. It looked, however, like he was going to have to wait. Black Dog was nowhere to be found, and he hadn't been seen since night before last when they had opened the carapace.

Boss Man pulled Tom out of his ceramic sampling square and shifted him over to help Shetler backfill the trenches on the Red Mound. It was clear to Tom right off the bat that Shetler had more in mind than just backfilling. The professor assigned Tom to filling in the test pits Josh had dug while he crawled along the base of Denny's south slope trench, peering intently at the side walls. Tom realized that Shetler was looking for more of the black and red speckling that had indicated the presence of the snapper shell. The professor clearly was hoping for a reason to do more digging in the Red Mound. After a half hour of squirming along the bottom of the trench Shetler gave up and climbed out of the trench to stand guzzling from a water bottle.

His shirt was soaked with sweat and Tom was worried he might be about to pass out from the heat. It also looked like Shetler was swaying slightly, Tom thought, or maybe it was the ground moving. He started over to suggest to Shetler that he move into the shade when the professor turned, frowned at him, and barked further directions.

"When you're done filling in Josh's holes you can extend their trench down the mound slope on the north side. The trench really should be completed before we finish backfilling. That ought to keep you busy till I get back."

Shetler then turned and walked down the side of the mound and over to his car and drove off. Tom watched Shetler drive off, then summed up his opinion of the man. "That guy's a douchebag."

Josh was standing in the shade under the awning in front of the Delt house when Denny pulled up the next morning. Emerging into the bright morning sun, he shielded his eyes and squinted in obvious discomfort. A few of his frat brothers had cajoled him into a beer pong game the previous evening and it had gone on for far longer than he realized. Denny laughed as Josh got in the car, seeing the signs of a solid hangover. She thought about teasing him by turning the radio up really loud but decided instead to offer a smile and a gentle pat on his thigh. Denny was still driving the university car, so they had no problem finding a parking place in the art museum parking lot.

Entering the museum through the loading dock doors, they retraced their steps to the lab where they had left the turtle shell the previous evening. The doors to the lab containing the carapace were locked, but hearing voices from down the hall, they continued walking. Turning a corner, they almost bumped into two women having an animated conversation.

"I don't give a flying fuck, Natalie." A white-coated woman with short brown hair was telling the other woman. "We have our own work to do. I don't see why we have to deal with people from other museums that need advice. Why don't they hire their own fucking conservators?" Noticing Denny and Josh as they turned the corner, the woman stopped speaking and gazed at them with a sour expression. Without missing a beat, Denny stepped up to the sourpuss and extended her hand.

"Hi, you must be Greta. I'm Denny and this is Josh. We're from one of those other museums and we need your advice."

Natalie tried to hide a smirk as Greta shook Denny's outstretched hand and replied. "So let's see what you have for us to look at this time. Is it a bit of tattered Inca textile, or maybe another ratty grass sandal?"

"No, nothing like that," Denny answered. "I guarantee you've never seen anything like this. It's in a lab just down the hall." Denny turned, her shoes squeaking on the burnished linoleum floor, and walked back to the locked lab doors. Greta caught up to her and reaching for her keys, opened the doors.

Seeing the snapper shell, Greta walked toward it and called back over her shoulder. "What is it, a million-year-old fossil turtle? Fossilized material doesn't need much conservation, you know."

"No, it's not a fossil, and it's about 700 years old," Denny replied. "It's from a Native American temple mound in Arkansas. And it's not the turtle shell we need advice on, it's what's inside."

"Inside?" Greta asked. "Inside? There's material inside?"

"Yes," Denny replied in a level voice, leaning into the ensuing silence for a few beats before continuing. "It looks like ritual paraphernalia worn by Native American ceremonial dancers 700 years ago. Turkey vulture wings is all we can identify so far, but there's more there."

"Inside? Vulture wings?" Greta repeated, not quite believing it.

Denny stepped over to the shell and bending over in preparation to lifting it, looked over at Greta. "Shall We?" She asked.

Greta reacted immediately, waving both arms excitedly in front of her face and vocalizing a long string of rapid objection. "No, no, no, no, no, stop." Pulling Denny back from the shell, Greta continued. "Not yet. We have to get set up first. And I need more information before we do anything."

Leading Denny and Josh down the hall to her office, Greta asked a number of questions about the shell's history. How long had it been out of the ground? What kind of soil and how deep had it been buried? How tight did they think the seal was between the shell and the underlying soil? Had they opened it, and if so for how long? What had they seen inside?

When she had run out of questions Greta seemed satisfied and led them back to the lab, where they rolled the table holding the snapper shell over to the center of the room, positioning it under a large light. Another similar sized lab table with a firm inch-thick foam pad on top was rolled over next to it, along with a stand crowded with a variety of different items, including spatulas, scalpels, tweezers, tissues, dissecting needles, Q-tips, cotton balls, and several bottles of solvents.

Greta and Natalie then joined Denny and Josh in lifting the shell up and off the vulture wings, moving it over and setting it down gently on the adjacent padded table. Before turning back to the table holding the vulture wings Greta raised the padded table higher so she wouldn't have to bend over to examine the carapace. Reaching over to the tool stand she picked up a visor-headband with magnifying lenses and a light, which she turned on before donning the headgear. She then slipped on a pair of white cotton gloves and slowly circled the turtle. Her lips were moving, and Josh and Denny could hear Greta softly talking to herself as she examined the carapace from about 8 inches away, occasionally reaching out to tap the shell lightly. She seemed oblivious to the presence of anyone else in the room. Completing a circuit of the shell, Greta pronounced it in stable condition and stroked it gently, almost sensually.

Turning to the other table with the stack of vulture wings, Greta pulled up a lab stool to sit on and went back into total focus mode. Circling the table on her rolling lab stool, once again murmuring softly to herself, she lifted feathers here and there, slipping what looked like a long wooden chopstick into the stacked wings and probing around, sometimes deep into the pile. Denny and Josh found places to sit and watch Greta work. Natalie had gone in search of the museum's portable x-ray machine and returned with it just as Greta was ready with her initial assessment.

"You've got four vulture wings stacked up here. They all seem to still be articulated, and some of the cords used to attach them to the performer's arms are visible. The seal between the turtle shell and underlying clay must have been tight, providing remarkable protection from moisture and insects. The wings look to be in a very good state of preservation. Given the amount of fluctuation in temperature they have experienced over the past seven hundred years, and their current stable condition, I think the only thing we need to monitor is relative humidity, which should be fine here in the lab."

Pausing to take off her magnifying goggles and setting down her giant chopstick, Greta continued. "That's the good news. The not-so-good news is that some of the feathers of the different wings have become stuck together, which means they will have to be slowly, ever so carefully, teased apart, starting, obviously, from the top and working down. The top wing should be pretty easy to detach from the one under it, but it will get harder as you work your way down through the lower wings."

Smiling now, Greta held out two of the illuminating magnification visors and two of the giant wooden chopsticks to Denny and Josh.

"Here's your de-sticking tools. Just slide them in, find where feathers from the top wing are sticking to feathers underneath, and carefully tease them apart. Slow and gentle is the secret. We have all the time in the world."

Pulling over a second lab stool for Josh, Greta pushed the one she had been using toward Denny and offered a final admonition before leaving them to their task. "You are going to be here all day teasing those feathers apart, so don't try to power through this. It's not rocket science, but you can definitely do some damage if you rush things."

Natalie and Greta then positioned the x-ray machine over the pile of vulture wings and powered it up. Looking at the x-ray image appearing on the screen, Greta used her giant chopstick as a pointer. "It's a cluttered image, with the wings piled on top of each other, but here are the bones of the top wing. It looks like this bone here…"

Denny interrupted. "Carpometacarpus."

"…is broken." Greta concluded. Leaning closer and searching the image, Greta continued.

"And you can see here, here, and here, the other wings have broken bones in the same location. Must have been deliberate."

Josh leaned closer to the image and pointed.

"I see two big dark shapes. Those must be the conch shell cups we were expecting. But what's all the other blurry imagery?"

Greta responded. "I think it's several layers of feathers separating the four wings on top from the dark objects below — what you think might be shell cups. We won't know for sure until we get the wings out." Greta left them then to their task of feather separation, telling them that she would be in the next lab and to come and get her when the first wing was free of the pile and ready to be extracted.

24.

THE PRODDING PROFESSOR

As Josh and Denny peered into opposite sides of the wing pile with their lighted visors and worked through the morning to separate the wings from each other, back down at Hamblin's Fort, Zack had taken Tom's place working on the Red Mound with Shetler. Boss Man had made the switch after Tom's outburst that morning shortly after the crew arrived at the site. Usually laid-back, Tom had announced that he refused to work with "Dr. Douchebag" anymore. When pressed for specifics, Tom explained.

"So, I'm up there on the mound yesterday. Workin my ass off. Backfilling frat boy's holes for the professor. Sweatin like a pig. And I look over and see the professor sliding along the bottom of Denny's trench. I think 'What the fuck?' He's lookin for more black and red speckles in the wall, lookin for more goodies. He wants to dig the mound. I'm thinkin he was behind sending the Red Mound crew back north. Got em out of the way so he could do some diggin on his own. Cecelia would still be here except for him. He's a douchebag."

Bopper was skeptical, and shook his head when Tom finished.

"Naw, I doubt that." He knew that Tom could often draw strange conclusions from a set of facts. Boss Man and Dolores stayed quiet and the rest of the crew seemed to believe Tom, who offered a final observation.

"But the joke's on him. There's nothing left in the Red Mound except some looter's potholes or maybe another gang member's corpse."

Shetler arrived at Hamblin's Fort a half hour after the crew, and Tom's suspicions were quickly confirmed. Reaching into the back seat of his car, the professor pulled out a steel rod that was maybe three eights of an inch in diameter and five feet or so in length. A piece of metal pipe had been welded onto one end of the rod, forming a T-shaped handle. It was a probe, or what the pot hunters who looted Indian mounds called a 'prod.' The prod was the pot-hunter's tool of choice. Walking across a mound summit or a Native American cemetery and stopping every yard or so to thrust the prod deep into the sandy soil, they could search for burials and associated grave goods without having to dig. Their efforts were usually focused on locating decorated ceramic vessels that would bring a high price on the antiquities market.

Zack had been unusually quiet the last few days, his throat brain seemingly shut down. But he stopped his shoveling and confronted Shetler as the professor reached the summit of the Red Mound with his probe. "Hey prof, what are you gonna do with that probe? That's a pot-hunters crutch, not something that's used on a legit excavation."

Shetler condescendingly replied. "It's a tool Zack, just like a shovel or a trowel. And it's going to help me locate the high-status individual I believe to be interred in this mound. Denny missed the main prize with their misguided search for trash on the mound slope." Waving the probe in a horizontal arc that encompassed the mound summit, Shetler continued. "Cahokia sent a delegation down here for a reason, and there's a high probability it was for the interment of a very important, high-status individual. Why here at Hamblin's Fort? I don't know yet, but when I find the burial, there will be answers for sure."

Unconsciously Zack nodded and quickly replied as he unconsciously touched his still tender head. "Sounds like a plan, professor. And you won't need this trench dug out anymore, with you deploying your probe and all. So if it's alright with you I'll be headin back over to finish the square I was digging for Boss Man."

Zack turned and hurried down the side of the mound before Shetler could say anything. Striding over to Boss Man in a huff, Zack told him what Shetler was up to, and was surprised, then confused, when Boss Man seemed undisturbed.

"It's okay Zack. I guess probes are more accepted down where Shetler works. Let's just keep our heads down and dig these ceramic sampling squares and let the professor do his thing."

Starting in the southwest corner of the Red Mound summit, Shetler pushed his probe down into the soil every yard or so, paralleling the west edge of the mound until he reached the northwest corner. Then he moved a yard east and walked back, again probing every yard or so, in a parallel line to his first pass. He only had to push the probe in two feet or so, through the white sand layer and into the underlying mound, in order to feel if there was anything solid — like stone, ceramics, or human bone, hidden below.

The professor could understand the crew's attitude of distain toward him. They probably wouldn't understand even if he explained it to them. He wasn't out to steal the Red Mound research and results from Denny. He honestly thought it possible, even likely, that she had missed a central burial feature on the mound. If so, he needed to find it and rescue it from the looting that was sure to come in the fall, after they left. And if his search didn't turn up anything, that would also be good news since they could be confident a thorough search had been conducted and nothing had been overlooked.

On the other hand, if he found something, then it might provide the final, and central, piece of the Cahokia visitation puzzle. The first two pieces of the puzzle were less important than the one Shetler was searching for. Denny had found mound summit ceremonial paraphernalia. Boss Man and Dolores had discovered a rare bauxite figure in an adjacent enclosure, along with shell cup debris linking it to the mound. Now Shetler hoped he would discover the central personage for whom all the different ceremonies had been conducted. Once the central burial was located, if it was here, there would likely be good indications of the role the deceased played in life. And of course, since the central burial, when he found it, would be, well, central, he obviously would have to be first author on the resultant research monograph that he, Denny, Boss Man and Dolores would be writing.

Repeatedly pushing the probe into the summit of the Red Mound did not turn out to be as easy as Shetler had anticipated. He had just bought the probe the previous afternoon, after asking at the hardware stores in Forrest City. He had never actually used one before, and his right arm was aching after the first twenty minutes. He seemed to be hitting a lot of small objects, slowing down his progress. He would hit something solid, then move the probe another few inches, and hit nothing. He switched to his left hand, but after another quarter hour needed to take a water break in the shade before continuing. By lunchtime Shetler had covered almost half of the summit with his probe, with no substantial hits except for the murdered motorcycle gang member's burial, where he hit a Dr. Pepper can maybe six inches down. His arms were like lead.

Shetler hadn't mentioned the probe, or his plans to look for a central burial, to anyone other than Boss Man and Dolores. The museum director had no idea what he was up to. Neither did Denny. He figured that none of them would like his use of the probe as long as he hadn't located the big-shot burial he was sure must be there. But everyone quickly would forget all about how he had found the high-status grave once it had been discovered.

After lunch Shetler was back on the Red Mound summit, probing in search of the elusive interment he knew must be there. He had started to tire again from pumping the prod when the sheriff's truck pulled up and Sheriff Hogg climbed the mound to see what he was up to.

"Where's Denny and her crew?" The sheriff asked, concern in his voice.

"They left yesterday, early in the morning," Shetler replied. "Drove the turtle shell north so it can be analyzed in a proper laboratory."

"Fuck" whispered the sheriff under his breath. He fell silent for a moment, coming to terms with the loss of the anticipated conch shell cups he had been counting on. He was pissed. Then he noticed what Shetler was doing and broke into a nasty smile. "Well, lookie here now. We got us a university professor, a pipe smokin pointy head, up here prodin away on an Indian mound. Just like the pot hunters I put in jail now and then." Crossing his arms on his chest, the sheriff warmed to his subject. "Yes sir, a pointy-head professor, prodin away on an Indian mound."

Turning and forming a megaphone with his hands, the sheriff called down to Boss Man and the crew. "Hey, did ya'll know the professor is prodin up here on the mound? He's the proddin professor."

Turning back to Shetler, the sheriff put his hand out palm up and wiggled his fingers. "Lemme see that probe, will ya. I can show you how it's done."

Realizing that the sheriff was half-drunk and sensing that he could turn mean in a heartbeat, Shetler handed over the probe and stepped back as the sheriff proceeded to move quickly across the mound summit. Continuing the professor's line of probing, he snaked the rod down into the mound and withdrew it, then moved forward again at a surprising pace, much faster than Shetler had managed.

The sheriff ran out of steam after a few dozen thrusts of the probe and handed it back to Shetler just as Boss Man appeared, having walked over in case he needed to head off a dust-up between the sheriff and Shetler. He'd seen the sheriff drunk before and knew it could get ugly without much warning.

Turning to Boss Man, Sheriff Hogg staggered a bit sideways. "It looks like the professor thinks Denny and her crew missed something, and it's still down there. What ya'll lookin for?"

Squaring his shoulders and facing up to the sheriff, Shetler attempted to regain face by repeating, in his best professorial manner, what he had told Zack earlier. "This probe is a just a tool, like a shovel or trowel, sheriff. It's sometime used by looters looking for grave goods, but that doesn't make the probe itself bad. And you're right, Sheriff Hogg. I suspect Denny missed a burial chamber and its high-status interment. Since there's a good chance pot hunters are going to be ripping this mound apart after we leave, once they learn we've found something, I think it's imperative to locate and recover the contents of the burial chamber before they do."

Boss Man asked how much of the mound had been probed, and Shetler walked it off for him as the sheriff watched. Boss Man scratched his head, reaching for a fleeting memory that seemed just out of reach, and then turned to Shetler. "You haven't hit anything yet?

Shetler shook his head, frowning, and Boss Man followed up with another question. "What about that burned clay area Denny and Josh found, early on, right when they were cleaning out that pothole. I don't think they ever got around to investigating it."

The sheriff visibly perked up as Shetler replied. "What burned clay area?"

Taking the probe from Shetler, Boss Man walked over to the now partially backfilled trench that Denny, Josh, and Cecelia had dug and walked slowly along it. He pushed the probe down into the loose soil of the backfilled trench several times, feeling it slip easily through the trench fill and into the underlying mound soil. On his third try the probe easily went through the loose trench fill again before making a muffled "thunk" sound as it hit the hard surface of Denny and Josh's burned clay feature.

Pleased with himself, Boss Man handed the probe back to Shetler and without a word walked back down the side of the mound and returned to the ceramic square he had been digging, leaving the sheriff and Shetler alone on the mound summit. The sheriff, his eyes narrowing and a cunning expression creeping across his face, departed soon after with a cheery goodbye for the professor. "Looks like you got some serious digging in front of you professor — and I'm not sure you're gonna get much help outa that bunch."

Shetler followed the sheriff's gaze over toward the crew working away in their scattered squares. They all had their heads down and were very clearly avoiding any sort of eye contact with him. No volunteers from the crew were going to join him in uncovering the burned clay area for a second time. That was clear.

Undeterred by the absence of anyone eager to join him in re-excavating the trench backfill to uncover the burned clay feature, Shetler started digging. After a half hour of solitary shoveling, Shetler was joined by Richard, who came over to lend a hand, telling Shetler he had always thought it stupid for Denny to dig the mound slope. By quittin time Shetler and Richard had shoveled out the backfill from on top of the red clay platform, and Shetler was elated by what he saw — a sharply defined 3x5 rectangular mass of burned red clay, waiting to be investigated.

25.

UKTENA

The morning seemed to pass quickly for Denny and Josh, sitting on either side of the pile of vulture wings, peering into it with their visor headlamps and carefully disentangling the feathers of the top wing from the one underneath it. There was a certain intimacy to it, alone in the quiet lab, not being able to see each other, but talking through the pile about lots of random everyday stuff. Natalie stopped in every half hour or so to check on how they were doing and to make a photographic record of their progress.

The top wing was freed from the next one down by mid-morning. Denny and Josh used their long chopsticks to lift it slightly and Greta slid a large piece of acid-free foam board under it. They then shifted the wing into a large shallow cardboard box that was waiting to receive it. It was a right wing, and the second wing down was a left wing. When compared in terms of size, they looked to be a matched pair from a single vulture.

The museum director stopped by soon after the removal of the first wing. Admiring the glossy black iridescent pile, he said it was a stunning discovery and compared them to the remarkably preserved feathered textiles recovered from the famous Craig Mound at the Spiro site in Oklahoma. He asked

Denny if it would be OK to let people around the university know that the carapace and wings were here in the lab in case someone might have potential research questions that could be addressed with them. Excellently preserved seven-hundred-year-old vulture wings appeared to be a hot commodity in some circles. Josh hid a smile at that, thinking to himself "calling all nerds, calling all nerds." The director caught the smirk, and ignoring Josh, let Denny know that several vulture experts from the National Museum of Natural History in Washington had already somehow heard about the wings and would like to come to see them. They were apparently quite excited about what they might learn about vulture lifeways and diet in the ancient past through isotope analysis of the feathers. As he was leaving, the director asked Denny to call him as soon as they had gotten to the bottom of the feather pile and hopefully uncovered some conch shell cups.

The second wing down took longer to disentangle from the one under it, perhaps because of the weight of the top wing pressing down on the ones below. Once freed from the pile, just before noon, it was also moved over to a waiting cardboard storage box. Shining a bright light on the top surface of the second wing to see if any loose feathers from the top wing were still stuck to it, Greta noticed a light dusting of red ocher on its shoulder area. Looking back at the top wing from the pile, and then at the third wing down, still attached to the bottom wing, she saw a similar dusting of red. She took photos of the ocher dusting on all three wings.

After lunch they started to tease the third wing away from the bottom wing. It took a little more time than they expected, but they had freed it by mid-afternoon and moved it over to its waiting storage box. It too was a right wing, and the one under it — the bottom wing in the pile, was a left wing and looked to belong to the same bird as the right wing laying on top of it. The bottom wing, now exposed, also had a noticeable dusting of red ocher scattered on its shoulder area.

It took another hour to separate the bottom vulture wing from what lay beneath, which at first glance looked to be a thick layer of smaller black feathers. Once the final vulture wing was lifted free, however, this underlying layer of smaller feathers was revealed to be a folded feather garment — thousands of small vulture feathers woven into a flat poncho-like cloak. When Josh and Denny tentatively explored the feather cloak with their chopsticks they were surprised when it easily separated from a second folded cloak that was stacked underneath.

Greta immediately moved in and spent quite a bit of time poking and lifting and slightly bending the top poncho before declaring that it could be moved over to another large well illuminated table across the lab and placed on a rolled-out sheet of acid-free paper. They definitely had Greta's full attention now. Pulling her stool over to the table holding the feather poncho, and talking to herself under her breath once again, Greta slowly unfolded the garment, bit by bit, checking to make sure that the woven latticework of string that held the feathers in place retained enough flexibility to remain intact during the unfolding process.

After twenty minutes Greta had successfully unfolded the poncho, which formed a narrow rectangle maybe six feet long by two and a half feet wide, with a circular opening in the center for the wearer's head. Cords attached on the side of the poncho served as ties at the wearer's waist, and it would have been worn tight to the performer's torso.

The second poncho was then lifted, moved to the lab table holding the first poncho, and unfolded in the same manner. Side by side, the two ponchos were nearly identical in appearance, and both had a heavy dusting of red ocher all around the central openings for the wearer's heads.

Denny had a crazy idea to explain the ocher stains but was hesitant to share it yet with the museum director or any other faculty members or even grad students. It had to do with turkey vulture heads, which were bald and bright red. Maybe the turkey vulture ritual performers also had bald heads that were brightly coated with red ocher, which would explain the red ocher deposits on the ponchos and wings. She decided to try out her speculation on Josh later, over a beer at the Brown Jug.

With the second feather poncho removed, the objects that were nestled deep under the turtle carapace, vulture wings and feather cloaks for more than seven hundred years were revealed. Two engraved conch shell cups rested on a woven grass mat having a design of thick sinuous parallel lines - snake imagery perhaps, or a water symbol. Both cups appeared to have been deliberately broken or 'killed' as they lay on the grass mat. A single fragment of one of the cups was missing, and Denny was confident that it was the fragment found earlier by Shetler in the mound slope trench. Aside from being broken into large fragments, the shell cups were in an excellent state of preservation, and the designs engraved into them could be clearly seen.

"What in the world is that?" asked Natalie as she started taking pictures of the cups from different angles.

Denny stepped closer for a better look at the designs on the cups before answering. "It's certainly an unusual composition of design elements. There are a number of smaller designs around the edge — entwined snakes and water spiders. The central element on both cups — the big creature in the middle, that's a depiction of an *Uktena*. They are mythical, spiritual denizens of the watery underworld. They take a variety of different composite forms, but usually combine the thick body of a snake, often spotted, with elements of other creatures, sometimes including bird's wings, a puma tail, deer antlers, or a raptor's beak or talons. The Uktena also has a blazing crest on its forehead and bright flashing scales, and breath that can kill, literally."

Josh smiled. "I knew someone like that in high school. She could take the varnish off a coffee table with single breath." Leaning in next to Denny, he compared the Uktenas on the two cups. "They aren't exactly the same. This one has bird's wings and the head and tail of a puma, and the other one has a bird's head and a rattlesnake tail."

"Yeah, the Uktena seems to take a range of different forms in Mississippian cosmology," Denny replied. "But whatever specific form it takes, it's the big kahuna of the dark underworld of death and decay. Uktenas can wreak havoc in the environment when angered — violent thunderstorms, floods, crop failures, earthquakes, blizzards, raging forest fires, you name it. Not something you would ever want to encounter. And they never die, Josh, unless struck at the seventh spot on its body. That's where its heart is."

Denny and Josh were pretty much done in after a day of focused effort, and with Greta's assurances that the lab would be locked up tight until they returned the next day, they headed off to the Brown Jug for something to eat and maybe a few beers to celebrate. They stopped by the archaeology Museum on the way to the restaurant to let the director know that the cups were now available for inspection. His secretary told them the director had left for the day, but that she would leave him a message about the cups. She also passed on stunning news from Arkansas. Professor Shetler had called and left a message for the director a short while ago to alert him that what appeared to be a central burial chamber had been discovered on the temple mound, and that they planned on opening it in the next day or two.

Struggling to show no reaction, Denny hurried down the hall and called the Hamblin Mansion from one of the lab phones. Tom picked up on the first ring and filled her in on Shetler's machinations since she had headed north. He recounted how

Shetler had probed the mound, eventually finding and re-exposing their red clay feature, and had declared it a high-status burial chamber. Tom laughed then. "He ain't got shit unless the big shot here was a midget. What professor douchebag's calling a burial chamber is only three feet by five feet."

Tom then asked them to pass on two more news items to Cecelia. He hadn't talked to her yet, and knew she would want to know. From the excitement in Tom's voice, Denny could tell he thought both items were good news.

"First, Black Dog is OK." Tom said. "We spotted him at Hamblin's Fort a few times, but he was keeping his distance — probably sensed that Boss Man was lookin to drill him. Second, the sheriff stopped by to pass on some news. Jake and his sister and mother were stopped in Texarkana a few days ago by the Arkansas State Police. Somebody musta fingered them. Anyway, when the troopers popped the trunk they found drugs — weed and crank. Lots of both. Looks like he took on a mule job to fund their getaway. The fool didn't even make it out of state." Before hanging up, Tom promised to let her know what they found, if anything, in Shetler's newly discovered tomb.

Lying in bed that night, hearing the murmur of the Jonny Carson show from the TV in the living room and her dad's occasional laughter drifting up the stairs, Denny was in a liminal state, on the glide path to sleep. Her mind skittered from topic to topic, seemingly randomly, then her eyes opened suddenly, and she was wide awake. She understood now what had been nagging at the corners of her consciousness since she had seen the Uktena cups that afternoon.

Shetler was convinced that he had found a big shot's burial chamber, and that the funeral ceremony had included the preparation of black drink in an alligator snapper carapace and its subsequent consumption from engraved shell cups, as well as a ritual performance of some sort by a pair of vulture dancers. After the interment, a red wolf — a mystical canine guardian, was buried nearby the high-status burial to protect it from disturbance until the end of time.

But Denny viewed the Red Mound in a different light now, from a different angle — her new perspective seemed to come together out of nowhere, out of her liminal state of consciousness. What if Shetler had it all backwards? The Red Mound was not a place of interment, not the resting place of an important personage — a chief or spiritual leader, midget or otherwise.

It was instead a place of containment, of confinement. The cups for the black drink ceremony, the snapper carapace, the vulture dancers, the bauxite earth mother figure — none of these were what would be expected of a departure ceremony for someone on their way to the stars, to the upper world. The symbolism, the animal entities present in the Red Mound — snake, alligator snapper, vulture, Uktena — they all pointed to the watery underworld, to death and decay, not the stars. All of the extensive efforts by a highly specialized delegation from Cahokia were designed and intended not to celebrate and say goodbye to someone who had recently passed away, but instead were part of an effort to seal up and confine something dark and evil for all time. Maybe Cecelia's warnings about the dark red vortex coming out of the mound should be heeded.

Getting up and heading to the bathroom, Denny laughed out loud. "Jesus Denny," she thought to herself. "You're goin right off the deep end with this weird shit you're thinkin'. You better keep that scenario to yourself."

26.

A DEAFENING HIGH-PITCHED CRY

Shetler arrived at Hamblin's Fort the next morning about twenty minutes before the crew arrived. They found him up on the Red Mound cleaning off the surface of the clay feature with the blade of his shovel. The sky was again a deep red all along the eastern horizon. The air felt heavy, oppressive, and there was no breeze. It was going to be another brutally hot and humid day.

As soon as Boss Man saw what Shetler was doing he hurried over and grabbed his arm.

"Not the shovel, boss. Any feature like this on a mound we switch to a brush and proceed carefully." Squatting and taking a two-inch brush from his back pocket, Boss Man started gently sweeping across the clay platform. He stopped several times and squinted at the surface from a low angle. Soon Shetler grabbed another brush and joined in cleaning off the top of the three by five slab of burned clay. After a few minutes a quite bizarre tableau came into view — a number of snake skeletons had been imbedded into the clay when it was still wet, and now formed a sinuous pattern on its surface of long parallel vertebral columns and the distinctive triangular skulls of pit vipers. A close examination of their skulls would be required to identify the species, but Shetler was guessing that they were water moccasins.

All around the edge of the top of the clay slab, forming a six-inch-wide border around the pit viper skeletons was a solid layer of thousands of carefully placed diamond shaped fish scales that resembled a completed jigsaw puzzle. Boss Man easily identified them as belonging to alligator gar — a top predator in the river system that had scales thick enough and hard enough that they were used as arrow points by ancient Native American hunters. Boss Man and Shetler spent the next several hours cleaning off and photographing the snake skeleton and gar scale surface before covering it with a tarp. Shetler thought it would make a great display piece in the archaeology museum and was intending to remove it intact.

The next step in documenting the Red Mound's central chamber would be to excavate soil away from its vertical sidewalls and establish how far they extended down into the mound. By lunchtime they had cleared the soil away from around the chamber's sidewalls to a depth of a foot or so and had exposed yet another snake. This one resembled a fire hose and was molded out of clay and wound its way completely around the chamber, just below its top edge. It was a strange, anomalous snake, more mythical than real. It had a raptor's head, a thick snake's body with circles along its length, and a rattlesnake's distinctive tail.

Boss Man suspected that this molded clay snake and its continually undulating body served to symbolically seal the slab that formed the top of the chamber to its side walls. Brushing vigorously down the side of the chamber he quickly exposed a portion of the horizontal line that marked the juncture between the massive lid and the sides of the burial chamber.

It looked like removing the decorated lid would be easy to do, once they had figured out how to deal with the molded clay snake that undulated back and forth across the juncture between the lid and the side walls of the chamber. They broke for lunch and Boss man sent Tom back to the crew house for a fine-toothed saw they used to cross-section pottery sherds. With it they could make clean cuts through the clay snake along the juncture line between the lid and sides, breaking the chamber's outer seal. Then it would be a delicate maneuver to slide shovels into the juncture line at two corners and, with luck, gently pry the lid off without damaging it.

Shetler and Boss Man groaned in unison when the sheriff showed up in the middle of lunch, eager to learn what the professor had managed to find with all of his probing of the Red Mound. Shetler and Boss Man had been hoping to keep the discovery of the high-status burial chamber under wraps, and to have it safely on its way north before any word got out locally. Now that Hogg had arrived, there was no chance of that. Shetler also worried, with good reason, that Sheriff Hogg would be thinking of ways he might get his hands on whatever they found.

After lunch Shetler personally took charge in cutting through the clay snake where it crossed the juncture line around the circumference of the chamber. He was soaked with sweat by the time he finished. Boss Man, Hogg, and the rest of the crew were crowded around, lounging on the back dirt piles under a brutal sun, waiting for the big moment — the opening of the tomb. After Shetler finished cutting through the snake Boss Man and Richard then used their trowels to scrape a few inches into the juncture line at two corners — far enough to insert a couple of shovels and gently lift the lid.

The moment had finally arrived. With this discovery, Shetler was convinced that getting tenure and promotion was assured, and a place among the pantheon of the "New Archaeology" would be within his grasp. Professor Shetler, Boss Man, and Sheriff Hogg took the front row, primo positions to watch the lid being lifted, while the rest of the crew crowded behind them.

Richard and Zack grabbed shovels, slid the blades into the creases that had been troweled out, and slowly began pulling down on their shovel handles, leveraging the lid upward.

Lounging on the backdirt pile, Bopper felt the Red Mound shudder under him. No one else seemed to notice. Standing up in alarm, he saw what seemed like hundreds of birds silently rising up from the nearby woods. Bopper felt the Red Mound shift a second time, and still no one but him seemed to notice. They were all intently watching Zack and Richard trying to leverage the lid up. So far, it had not budged.

With everyone watching Zack and Richard, Bopper's rapid descent down the west side of the mound at first went unnoticed. Bopper rarely exerted himself unnecessarily, so Tom was surprised to suddenly notice him sprinting across the plaza, heading for one of the ceramic sampling squares. Bopper barely broke stride as he grabbed the square's two-legged sifter screen along with its shade tarp and attached ropes. Scurrying around in a frenzy, he grabbed three more sifters and shade tarps and, using the ropes he had collected, tied the sifters together into a crude pile.

At lunch, Tom had snuck off into the woods for a quick fatty. He figured he had to have a buzz on for the big reveal. Now as he watched Bopper's antics with the sifters, he was giggling and wondering 'WTF?' But then Bopper did something that totally freaked Tom out. The hair on the back of his neck rose as he watched Bopper wrap a rope around his waist and sitting down, tie himself securely to the sifters.

A sudden strong burst of air, a loud roaring noise, and a horrible stench drew Tom's attention back to the burial chamber. The clay lid had blown straight up into the air, like a cork from a champagne bottle, and it was now arching west over the plaza, twisting slowly, and beginning its fall back to earth. The stench was coming from a dark red column of vapor now welling up out of the Red Mound's central chamber.

Several of the crew started vomiting from the foul smell as they all stumbled backward and scrambled down the west side of the mound in an effort to escape the energy vortex and the stench. The air was not as bad at the base of the mound and the crew, now huddled together on the edge of the plaza, watched the vortex swirl and climb upward to the heavens. From their position on the mound's west side, the crew could not see that Black Dog had approached, unnoticed, from the woods, where he had been lurking for days, and now crouched silently, tense and waiting, at the eastern base of the Red Mound.

Sheriff Hogg and Boss Man cautiously crawled back up the west slope of the mound from the plaza, and watched from the edge of the summit as the upwelling from the central chamber grew suddenly darker, and other sounds joined the deep background rumble of the vortex. A hollow-sounding rattling noise had begun deep in the central chamber, and its source slowly drifted up into view, floating on the vortex and pausing in place maybe eight feet above the summit of the Red Mound.

It was an Uktena. Known only from Cherokee myths and from engraved depictions on ancient shell cups, it was the great destroyer, calling forth death and destruction when angered. It was a mythical monster, but here it was in the flesh. Surprisingly small, it had a body maybe four feet long, with a thick body and a jerky, writhing tail. Its head resembled a mountain lion, but with the addition of short four-point deer antlers. In the center of its forehead a brightly blazing diamond shaped third eye flashed a painful light wherever it directed its gaze. The Uktena's body was covered with glowing iridescent snake scales, and its long, constantly flailing tail ended in a rattlesnake's rattle. It had the wings of a raptor, which were furled close to its body, as well as a raptor's sharply taloned feet, which were opening and closing in a leisurely fashion. A line of spots or circles ran down the length of the Uktena's body, with the seventh one pulsing every few seconds, indicating the location of the mythical beast's heart and life.

Sheriff Hogg, emboldened by the Uktena's small size, drew his pistol and pumped three quick rounds into the beast. The shots did not seem to have any effect on the Uktena. Either the sheriff had missed or they had passed through the creature without causing any damage. But the shots did draw the Uktena's attention to the sheriff.

Its body continued floating in the same position, buoyed by the upwelling vortex, but it slowly turned its head in the sheriff's direction. Once the Uktena located the sheriff, it shot a short burst of something from its mouth toward him with a loud hissing sound. This was the breath of the Uktena, often described as so pestilential, so foul, that even a small amount was lethal. The burst of foul breath didn't look like much — a fast-moving yellow mist. But when it reached Sheriff Hogg, it peeled the flesh from his face and exploded his skull. His body collapsed and rolled down the side of the mound, coming to rest not too far from where the crew stood, slack jawed.

Boss Man still stood next to where the sheriff had been standing on the Red Mound summit. He had drawn his own pistol as soon as the sheriff started shooting, but now dropped it and wiped at his face in confusion at the bits of flesh and skull that had spattered him when the sheriff's head exploded. He turned and stumbled down to join the crew on the plaza.

Frozen in place now, afraid to move, to draw attention to themselves, the crew watched as the Uktena slowly unfurled its wings and rose a little higher in the vortex. Suddenly, unexpectedly, the Uktena grew to three times its original size, and shot several more bursts of lethal vapors in the crew's direction. Not needing any more encouragement, the crew members scattered in different directions. Dolores and Boss Man scurried toward Bopper and his pile of sifters. Paula and Wilma made a beeline for the promising shelter of the nearby woods. Richard circled south around the base of the Red Mound and hid behind a brush pile. Zack and Tom ran for the conical mound. Zack circled behind it and Tom climbed to the top and sat down.

He figured he was at a safe distance from the Red Mound and had a great view of the Uktena.

Professor Shetler, still quite disoriented, slowly wandered in the plaza, walking unsteadily in small looping circles and mewing like a lost kitten. Behind the fleeing crew members, the Uktena grew in size again, and then spreading its wings, it began to gradually ascend.

A reddish blur raced up the east slope of the mound. It was Black Dog, but he had doubled in size and was now more red than black, with huge canines and empty eyes. The ancient protector spirit within Black Dog — what the Cherokee called "Weya," had now awoken and was intent on fulfilling its destiny. Black Dog and his ancestors had guarded the Uktena's containment chamber through many generations, across seven centuries, scaring off casual snoopers and even more determined pot hunters. But he had failed in stopping the excavation efforts of Professor Shetler. The containment chamber had been breached and the Uktena was released upon the world. His duty now was to stop it before it could call forth the forces of the underworld.

As Weya hurled through the air on a trajectory to intercept the Uktena, it turned and saw the approaching enemy. Beating its wings furiously and accelerating upward, the Uktena emitted a deafening high-pitched cry that quickly moved out of the range of human hearing. It was the cry that would summon the forces of the underworld.

The cry was cut short, however, as Weya reached the ascending Uktena and its jaws locked on the mythical snake's seventh spot, the location of its heart and its life. With the exception of Tom, who was sitting in Cecelia's spot on the top of the conical mound, none of the fleeing crew were watching this unfolding cosmic struggle above the summit of the Red Mound. But they all stopped and looked back when the roar of the Red Mound vortex and the cries of the Uktena abruptly stopped.

The air space above the Red Mound was now empty. The Uktena and the Weya had vanished. A slight wisp of vapor drifted up from the central chamber, but the stench was gone, and the danger seemed to have passed. Paula and Wilma cautiously emerged from the protection of the woods, Richard stepped out from behind the brush pile he was using as cover, and Boss Man and Dolores joined Bopper, who was untying himself from his makeshift raft. Zack had emerged from behind the conical mound and was trying to comfort Professor Shetler, who had collapsed on the ground and seemed unresponsive.

The first indication that the Uktena had been successful in summoning the dark forces of the underworld came about three minutes after the collision and vanishing of the two mythical creatures in the air above the Red Mound. The silence that had descended on Hamblin's Fort was suddenly broken by the distant sound of falling trees. And then the ground beneath Hamblin's Fort began to move again. The plaza began to undulate in waves that quickly grew to more than ten feet in height, and both the Red Mound and conical mound slowly began to collapse, to melt and merge with the undulating plaza.

Tom started running down the side of the conical mound, awkwardly trying to navigate across the softening ground surface. But there was nowhere to run. No safe harbor. He was heading toward Bopper, Dolores, and Boss Man, waving his arms and crying out, when the ground beneath him turned suddenly liquid, and he slipped out of sight.

Bopper had already tied himself to his sifter raft again by the time Tom vanished into the alluvium and was fiercely fighting with Boss Man and Dolores, trying to keep them from climbing onto his sifters. He was helped in his struggle when a sand blow lifted both him and his raft a good twenty feet in the air before dropping him on undulating ground a good distance away.

He turned to look for Boss Man and Dolores but could see nothing through the curtain of sand and dark clouds that were sweeping across the site. The sand blow that had lifted Bopper from the clutches of Boss Man and Dolores had also swallowed them deep into the now liquid alluvium that lay beneath Hamblin's Fort.

Out in the middle of the plaza Zack and Professor Shetler were now lying face down on the rolling ground surface and waiting helplessly for what would come next. Slowly at first, the plaza began to fill with water. Then a wall of water maybe ten feet high abruptly rushed in from the east, taking the professor and Zack with it.

Bopper braced himself as the dark mass of water, teaming with entire uprooted trees and branches, swept toward him. He and his raft were submerged in the wave for a long ten seconds or so before popping up, already a hundred yards west of Hamblin's Fort.

Paula and Wilma watched the approaching wall of water from their perch halfway up a sturdy looking tree. As the wave hit, the entire woods collapsed, and the two women were swept away.

EPILOGUE
VALLEY OF THE WHALES

Two months had passed since the earthquake. It was a pleasant sunny afternoon on campus, and a memorial service at the archaeology museum for the Hamblin's Fort crew was well attended. Except for the Bopper, nobody that was at Hamblin's Fort that day appeared to have survived. Paula's body had been recovered from a tangled pile of dead trees twenty miles west of the site, but all of the other crew members were still missing. They were assumed to be entombed somewhere in the alluvial depths of the Mississippi River Valley.

Bopper was the headliner at the memorial service. Dressed in a somber suit and sporting a short haircut, he gave an uplifting account of his harrowing ordeal — thirty hours on his makeshift raft before he was finally plucked from the muddy water by a U.S. Coast Guard chopper. But it was his description of the events at Hamblin's Fort when the earthquake struck that held the memorial service audience spellbound.

The Bopper's account deviated in a number of key respects from what had actually happened that afternoon. Not surprisingly, he left out any mention of the Uktena and the crew's possible complicity in releasing the monster that summoned forth the earthquake. He figured nobody would believe such a fairy tale anyway, and it would undercut the significance of their scholarly pursuits and the sacrifice the crew had made in the name of science. He also steadfastly insisted that there had been no burial chamber, no burial, no chamber at all. When they finally exposed the red clay platform, according to Bopper's account, it turned out to be just that - a red clay platform. He described the imbedded snake skeletons and alligator gar scale design of the three by five platform but insisted there was nothing else under it.

Bopper also cast Shetler as the brave leader, since he was the professor, and naturally should be given the lead role in the disaster story. He didn't mention Shetler crumpled on the ground sniveling just before he and the students around him disappeared down into the alluvium.

And rather than describing how he had viciously kicked at Boss Man and Dolores to keep them off his raft, Bopper told the memorial audience how he had risked his own life by trying to pull them to safety on his little craft, but they had been swept away. With those exceptions, Bopper spun a mostly accurate, and certainly terrifying, narrative of turbulent waters, crashing trees, sand boils and foul smells.

After the service, as Denny and Josh left the museums building, Josh wondered how long before the memory of the lost crew would fade away. It hadn't surprised him that the demise of an archaeological field crew, fewer than a dozen people, ended up being a just a minor footnote in the subsequent news coverage of what was called "The Forrest City Earthquake." More than five thousand people had lost their lives, after all, and thousands of communities, from small towns to major cities, including Memphis and St. Louis, had been impacted by the temblor. Memphis was hardest hit, with widespread building collapse and infrastructure damage. Bridges across the Mississippi had been downed from St Louis south to Greenville, Mississippi, and the highway system over large areas of the Mississippi Valley were no longer usable. There would be no fall harvest of thousands of acres of soybeans and rice this year, and it would take a long time to rebuild.

Denny had met with the museum director a few days ago to discuss her research plans. He had agreed to serve as her dissertation advisor and to head her committee. Her dissertation would encompass all aspects of the Cahokian visitation at Hamblin's Fort, including the red cedar enclosure and its shrine, statue, and conch shell workshop, as well as the turtle carapace caldron, vulture wings, and ritual garments.

The dissertation would include detailed descriptions of all the excavation carried out on the Red Mound and the enclosure, and all the artifacts recovered, as well as what Denny thought the artifacts said about what the Cahokians were doing at Hamblin's Fort. Beyond this basic story of what appeared to have transpired when a Cahokian delegation visited this provincial mound center, there would be ample opportunities for Denny to demonstrate her scholarly chops by situating this short duration and isolated event within the broader conceptual framework of ancient Mississippian cosmology.

It wasn't clear yet if Denny could pull this dissertation off, but the director was very solidly behind her work, and upbeat about getting her a graduate fellowship to support her research. She was on the scholarly launch pad now and facing several years, at least, of glorious self-indulgent research. Her personal life was also looking up. She and Josh were still trying the couple thing, and she thought it continued to be working out pretty well,

Josh had been to dinner a few times at Denny's and immediately hit it off with her parents. Her mom was a research librarian at the grad library, and her dad was a tenured prof in the Paleontology department who studied, of all things, ancient whales. Denny's dad had already invited Josh to tag along on his next field season to the "Valley of the Whales" deep in the desert southwest of Cairo. Sure, it would be hot. But Josh figured it was a dry heat, not like the Mississippi Valley. And unlike Denny, Josh was not locked into archaeology as a life choice. He was interested in lots of things and digging up whales sounded cool.

Maybe he'd try the whale thing but had a number of interesting classes lined up for the fall, including Pleistocene Geology, another East Asian History course, and an art history course. Josh also thought it was a good idea to look for something distinct from what Denny was doing. He had no interest in struggling to find his way in the same field as Denny, where he thought he would always be in her shadow. Who knows, maybe pre-law or pre-med might be right for him. There were still lots of directions his life could go.

ABOUT THE AUTHOR

B.D. Smith is a retired archaeologist and the author of numerous scholarly books and articles on a range of topics, including the origins of agriculture. After having to pay attention to facts and empirical reality for many years in his non-fiction writing, he now enjoys making things up. His favorite place to write is on the screen porch of a lakeside cabin in Bowerbank, Maine, where he spends summers with his wife Melinda and their dog Fred. In the winter months they live in Frederick, Maryland.

OTHER TITLES BY B.D. SMITH

NOTE FROM B.D. SMITH

Word-of-mouth is crucial for any author to succeed. If you enjoyed *Red Mound*, please leave a review online—anywhere you are able. Even if it's just a sentence or two. It would make all the difference and would be very much appreciated.

Thanks!
B.D. Smith

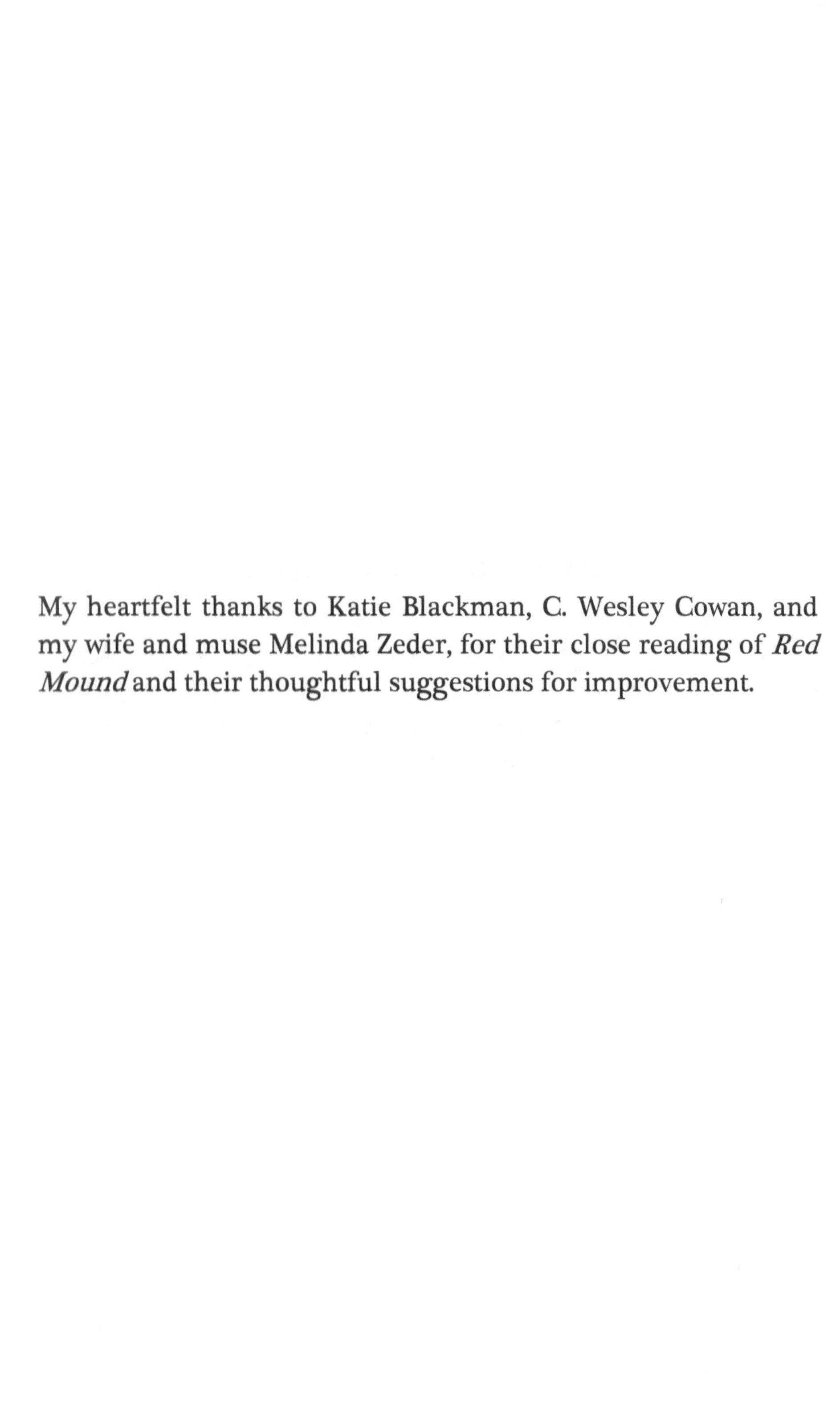My heartfelt thanks to Katie Blackman, C. Wesley Cowan, and my wife and muse Melinda Zeder, for their close reading of *Red Mound* and their thoughtful suggestions for improvement.

We hope you enjoyed reading this title from:

www.blackrosewriting.com

Subscribe to our mailing list – *The Rosevine* – and receive **FREE** books, daily deals, and stay current with news about
upcoming releases and our hottest authors.
Scan the QR code below to sign up.

Already a subscriber? Please accept a sincere thank you for being a fan of
Black Rose Writing authors.

View other Black Rose Writing titles at
www.blackrosewriting.com/books and use promo code
PRINT to receive a **20% discount** when purchasing.